ALSO BY STEPHEN GREENLEAF

FLESH WOUNDS

STEPHEN GREENLEAF

SCRIBNER

New York London Toronto Sydney Tokyo Singapore

SCRIBNER
1230 Avenue of the Americas
New York, NY 10020

SCRIBNER and design are trademarks of Simon & Schuster Inc.

DESIGNED BY ERICH HOBBING

Manufactured in the United States of America

10   9   8   7   6   5   4   3   2   1

Library of Congress Cataloging-in-Publication Data
Greenleaf, Stephen.
Flesh wounds: the daring new John Marshall Tanner novel/Stephen Greenleaf.
p. cm.
I. Title.
PS3557.R3957E44   1996
813'.54—dc20   95–24412   CIP

ISBN 0-684-81583-4

To Sara and Jim McManis

FLESH WOUNDS

The routine is so familiar she completes it without thinking: the crusty stick of pancake dabbed onto the offending bruise, then powder brushed across the base to meld with the pink of her depilated flesh. Four moles and one scar are similarly obliterated—shoulder, chest, knee, and forearm—plus two minor bulbs of acne dispensed with in the way she dispensed with them in junior high school. For the physiography below her neck, the process takes five minutes. It is one of the reasons he uses her, she knows, the comparatively unflecked ocean of her skin. It is as though God had foreseen her calling and airbrushed her out of the box.

The only mirror leans against the wall of the closet that serves as a dressing, or rather undressing, room; the only light is a naked bulb activated by a dingy pull cord. Ten years from now such an environment will produce a jarring reflection that will confirm her mortality by highlighting her erosions, but for now the pitiless glare reveals no hint of the withering that lies in store. She has, she concludes for the hundredth time because it is crucial for her to do so, the best body she has ever seen. It is her triumph that she is at long last using it for a worthy purpose.

To make certain her lips and hair and eyes are edged and curled and greased the way he likes them, she must get on her knees like a charwoman for inspection in the makeshift mirror. A month ago, she submitted to such indignities without objection, as a necessary prelude to her art. Now she is as insulted by them as she is by the ego and ethics of the man whose personal and professional impulses she is about to indulge for the last time, unbeknownst to him.

She adds one last smear of gloss to her lips, makes a final shove at her hair, runs a comb through the wiry tuft at her pubis, blots away the drop of sweat that tarries between her breasts, and walks into the studio, which is in reality the dreary apartment of the photographer. More confident now that she is out of her clothes than when in them, she takes her place in front of the gray sheet he has tacked to a hideously paneled wall to form the proverbial neutral backdrop and waits for him to finish with the floodlights. Her feet hurt already, and she is cold enough to shiver, but only the latter sensation will be of interest to him, since it causes her nipples to elongate and that might not be what he has in mind this afternoon although he has certainly had it in mind before, to the point of applying ice.

Finally, he looks up. His appraisal is quick and clinical and suddenly mean. "You've gained weight."

"No, I haven't."

"If your belly gets any bigger, I can't use you."

She resists the urge to tell him, then and there, that she is finished with both his ego and his talent, that tomorrow she will resume her search for someone who can more fully realize what has become her only dream. But she promised him another shoot after he begged forgiveness for the last one, and his gear is set up and her afternoon is free, so she stays because she owes him, both for introducing her to the ecstasy of figure modeling and for buying her a new CD player when her old one got ripped off.

It seems impossible that it was a whole year ago that Gary made his move. It had taken weeks of pleading and begging and bribing, plus a lecture on the history of artists and models and the symbiosis implicit in such relationships, before he persuaded her to pose for him, first for a series of sullen head shots for use on alternative rock posters, then in some low-end fashion layouts featuring leather mini-dresses and studded bustiers. Only then did they move to figure work.

She can still marvel at the moment she slipped out of her robe as he bent over his viewfinder, and there was no obstruction between her and the omnivorous lens that inspected her so piteously. She was nervous, and scared, and ashamed, and on the brink of flight until she realized that the one-eyed God perched atop its tripod passed no judgment on what it saw, offered no warnings, issued no advice. With realization came transformation: her mind encompassed only her topology; the experience of oneness with her flesh was a revelation as intoxicating as her first forays into sex. When she is naked, and the shutter lurks in readiness to suck her image off her self and onto the emulsion to its rear, she is empty of all but the desire to let the camera have its way with her, the desire to inform and impress and astound, the desire to make what the world will ultimately acknowledge as the truth and magic of pure art.

¤　　¤　　¤

LONELINESS.

I don't know anyone who isn't lonely. Charley Sleet, my cop friend, has been lonely in every hour of his life since his wife died ten years ago; ditto Ruthie Spring, the detective, since her husband Harry was found murdered out in the valley. Clay Oerter, my stockbroker buddy, has a wife and two kids, but he seems eager nonetheless, and on occasion even desperate, to join our poker group on Friday nights and urges us to convene on Sunday afternoons as well. My former girlfriend, Betty Fontaine, is both pregnant and newly married, but she calls me twice a month at midnight to talk about Barbara Kingsolver or Jane Campion or Hillary Clinton or whatever else is on her mind because her husband doesn't read novels or like movies or find humor in the nation's madcap political machinery. Before he was killed, my friend Tom Crandall read history at Guido's bar six nights a week while his wife did her turn as a big band chanteuse so he could keep loneliness from fostering an addiction to TV.

And me. Whenever I stop to think about it, I conclude that loneliness is to blame for most of my afflictions. I eat out a lot, because a waitress at Zorba's is often the only being I converse with in the course of a day, and as a result I'm twenty pounds overweight. I end far too many evenings at Guido's, because the chilly cheerlessness of my apartment is a destination I increasingly defer, and as a result I spend too many mornings sparring with a hangover. I date too many women who neither interest nor excite me while allowing them to believe otherwise, just to have something to do and someone to touch. As a result, I cause too much pain to too many good people.

Paradoxically, I'm often loneliest when I'm with someone: a colleague who reminds me how much I miss Harry Spring; a woman who reminds me how much I miss Peggy, my former secretary; a new client who reminds me how many former clients are long dead. I shed a tear for them, sometimes, the real people who are no longer around and the fantasy people who have never been other than yearned for, and on such occasions I'm overcome by the thought that my life is as empty as space and has brought me little I treasure. I think such things, then hurry to employ an antidote. Luckily, one was close at hand.

It was Thursday night. My shoes were off and my feet were up and I had a bag of Oreos and a bottle of Ballantine's within arm's reach, all in prelude to a ninety-minute lifting of the load, courtesy of NBC. Eighteen minutes later, as I was imagining what an affair with a woman like Helen Hunt could do for my state of mind, I realized I'd omitted an essential element of my preparations—I'd forgotten to turn off the phone.

I could have ignored it, of course, but that's a pledge I made when I first took up detecting—when the phone rings, I answer it. So I pressed a button to silence the set, then picked up the receiver and uttered my name with such peevishness as the intrusion warranted.

"Marsh?"

"Yes?"

"It's Peggy."

The name alone was enough to erase all thought of cookies or booze or even Helen Hunt. It was, to synthesize a bit, the voice I had hoped to hear every time I'd answered the phone over the past six years.

"Peggy?" I repeated dumbly. "Peggy *Nettleton*?"

Her laugh was quick and constricted. "You remember. I was afraid maybe you wouldn't."

"No, you weren't."

"Well, I *was* afraid you'd hang up. And I wouldn't blame you if you did."

I considered it for a nanosecond. "Then I'd wonder why you called and it would be another six years before I got an answer."

"Yes, well, I'm sorry for that. And for everything else, as far as that goes." Her tone tried to make it as light as a Thursday sitcom, a one-size-fits-all apology, but beneath the banter was a ledge of purpose and a plea for understanding.

"There's no need to apologize," I said, even though I didn't mean it. Even though I meant an apology wasn't nearly an adequate eraser.

"Yes there is. There was no reason for me to stay out of touch for so long. I should have done this years ago."

"Well, I'm glad you did it now."

"So am I. You sound good, Marsh."

I put the phone in the other hand and sneaked a sip of Ballantine's. "Thanks. So do you."

It wasn't true, quite. She sounded pressed and edgy and uncertain of her objectives, much the way she had sounded when she was under the spell of the predator in the office down the hall from mine, the man who had turned her life inside out and made everything she did and was seem seamy.

I struggled to mount a strategy that would both prolong the conversation and intensify it. "Where are you? Here in the city?"

"No. I'm home."

"Where's home?"

"Seattle." She paused. "I thought you knew."

"I don't know anything. I haven't known a single thing about you since the day you left town."

"How odd. I just assumed you've been out of touch on purpose."

"I was out of touch because there was no other place to be."

She paused again. "I'm sorry. I assumed Ruthie told you where I—"

Sweat traveled my brow like a spider. "Ruthie Spring knows where you are?"

"Yes."

"For how long?"

"I don't . . . several years. I called her to . . . She didn't tell you, I take it."

"No. She didn't."

Peggy chuckled with a bitter curl. "Well, I'm sure she had her reasons. Figured it was for your own good, I expect. And who knows? Maybe it was."

"She didn't have the right to make that decision."

Her ire leached toward compassion. "Don't be hard on her, Marsh. She loves you like a mother and a sister and a lover all in one. It would crush her if you got mad at her."

I didn't say anything because I couldn't think of anything except the thousand nights I'd sat brooding in a dark apartment, wondering where Peggy was, wondering if she regretted leaving me, wondering if she would ever ask to reenter my life and what I would do if she did, wondering why I still seemed to be in love with her even after so many vacant years.

"This must be quite a shock to you, then, me calling out of the blue like this," Peggy was saying with forced levity. "Do you want me to hang up and try again later?"

"Of course not."

"Good."

The ensuing silence was both comforting and terrifying. Comforting because she had returned to me in one sense; terrifying because it wasn't anything like I had dreamed it would be.

"I take it you're not calling to get your old job back," I said with as much savoir faire as I could muster. All of a sudden it seemed important to define our terms and keep most of my emotions out of earshot.

"Sorry, I'm not in the job market at the moment. I've got a pretty good one, as a matter of fact."

"Doing what?"

"I'm the executive assistant to the Dean of Students at the law school."

"What law school?"

"University of Washington."

"Do you like your work?"

"Most of the time. The dean is nice and he delegates a lot of responsibility so I feel like I'm contributing. The building is a nightmare, but you can't have everything, I guess."

"That's certainly been my experience."

Peggy forced a laugh that sounded like the one that had issued from the woman I'd hired some fifteen years before when I'd made a similarly inane observation in response to a question about the ethical predelictions of my clientele.

"So how's Seattle?" I asked lamely, now that the stakes were less immediate, now that a major portion of my hopes seemed doomed to lapse unnourished.

"Seattle's nice. It reminds me of San Francisco in the seventies—lots of music; lots of coffeehouse philosophizing; lots of smirky talk about the quality of life. And lots of traffic," she added with a burst of balance.

"So you're staying put."

"For now, at least. How about you? Still in the same apartment?"

"Yep."

"Same office?"

"Yep."

"Still eating Oreos for dinner?"

I glanced to my left. "Yep."

"You've got some right beside you, am I right?"

"Yep."

"You need a personal chef, you know that? I'll bet your cholesterol count is a thousand."

"Two-fifteen, as a matter of fact."

"At least you got it checked. Congratulations. Is Charley still working eighteen-hour shifts?"

"On his light days."

"Are Ruthie and Caldwell still happy?"

"Except when Ruthie quits drinking."

"So not much has changed is what you're telling me."

"Not for the better, at least. How about with you?"

She countered my question with a question. "Are you getting gray yet, Marsh? I am."

"I'm speckled on top but my beard would be white if I let it sprout."

"Maybe you should. You'd look formidable in a beard."

"I think you mean venerable."

Peggy laughed and then fell silent, as though she'd breached some sort of promise to herself. I didn't want the conversation to end, but I didn't want her to know how disappointed I was, either. She was keeping us at arm's length, when what I wanted was a warm embrace.

It was a while before she spoke. When she did, her voice

dropped to a cautious buzz. "The reason I called is, I think I need your help."

"What kind of help?"

"The kind you get paid for."

My stomach knotted and my tongue thickened. "What's wrong? Are you all right? What's happened?"

"I'm fine," she assured me quickly. "And it's not me who needs the help, actually, it's someone close to me. I'm not sure you can improve the situation, but I didn't know what else to do so I thought . . . anyway, I was hoping maybe you could come up here, so we could talk about it."

"When?"

"As soon as you can. There's no rush, I don't think; another week or two won't matter. Probably."

"You sound upset."

"I am upset."

"Then maybe we should discuss it now. It's cheaper than a plane ticket if I decide there's nothing I can—"

"But I'd like to see you, regardless. I'd like us to have time to catch up. I've missed you, Marsh; I really have."

"I've missed you, too."

Soaring on lust and implication, my mind took a tour of my calendar. "I could fly up the end of next week, I think. I'll have to double-check at the office, but I think that's clear for me."

"That would be great."

"Is there a hotel that's convenient?" I asked, expecting she would ask me to stay with her.

"There's a bed-and-breakfast that—"

"No bed-and-breakfast."

"Oh. Right. Well, there's a motel not too far away. It's centrally located, but I don't know how plush it is."

"I don't do plush. Book me for a week from Sunday."

"Great."

I mustered some good cheer. "This will be fun. I've never been to Seattle before."

"I'll be interested to hear what you think. After we go over our business, I'll give you the grand tour."

"Great."

"And Marsh?" Her voice dropped an octave and doubled in density.

"What?"

"There's something you need to know before you get here."

My stomach churned again and the phone became hot and wet and evil. "What's that?"

She waited so long I thought she'd forgotten the point. "I don't know how to . . . oh hell, I might as well just say it. I'm getting married."

"What?"

"I'm getting married. In three weeks if our plans work out. To a man named Ted."

I should have expected it, of course, should have steeled myself appropriately, should have accepted the fact that my time with Peggy had fallen into history and that it didn't matter what she was doing now or who she was doing it with. But I hadn't done any of those things because I couldn't.

I grasped for a word and a posture. "Congratulations."

"Thank you. He's a great guy."

"Good. Great. I'm happy for you."

"Really?"

"Really."

"Thank you."

"You're welcome."

"I . . . it's relevant, sort of, me getting married, I mean. Because of the person in trouble."

"Why? What about him?"

"Her. She's my stepdaughter. Or will be. Ted's daughter by a former marriage."

"What kind of trouble is she in?"

"I'm not sure. That's one of the things I want you to find out."
She paused. "Does my engagement change things, Marsh? Be
honest. You can back out, if you want. You certainly have no obligation to me; I just thought you'd understand more than anyone
why I need to help Ted with whatever he . . . but if you don't want
to get involved, I'll certainly—"

"It's not that. I just . . . it will be hard seeing you with another
man, Peggy."

"I know it will be. But you won't actually be seeing us, I don't
think."

"What do you mean?"

"I don't want Ted to know you're here."

"Why not?"

"Because he wouldn't want me getting involved in this. He
thinks he can handle it himself. But he's a simple man, he's lived
a charmed life, he doesn't have a clue to what's out there, to what
kind of trouble Nina might . . . This is difficult over the phone,"
Peggy concluded lamely.

She wanted me to say something supportive but I didn't trust
myself to try it.

"Will you let me know by Wednesday?" she asked. "If you're
coming up?"

"Sure."

She gave me her number at the office. "I'll understand if you
don't want to get involved. I really will. Well, I guess I should go.
You're probably off to Guido's, or something."

"Not tonight."

She inhaled sharply. "I hope you don't have company. I didn't
think to ask, I just assumed—"

"It's not a problem." I'd never wanted a woman at my side
more avidly in my life, not even when I was in the Army and the
nearest woman was a prostitute.

"Well, anyway, it's been great talking to you, Marsh."

"You, too, Peggy."

"I always loved the sound of your voice, you know. It's very comforting. I don't know if I ever mentioned it."

"No, I don't think you ever did."

CHAPTER 2

"More chin. That's right. Raise the arm. More. Good. Now the leg. I want the tit—"

"I told you not to—"

"Okay, okay—breast. I want the breast to brush the thigh. Just touch; no compression. Good. Now lean back. Back farther. Rotate the shoulder toward me. Leg up. Right leg, idiot. Sorry, sorry. Good. Now scrunch together. Make yourself as small as you can— a popcorn ball. Right. Smaller. Smaller. Good. Take five.

"Want some weed?" he asks casually as he adjusts the barn doors on a flood then tilts a reflecting screen to provide for more backlight.

"Not after last time, I don't."

He shrugs. "Whatever."

That he doesn't reprise his apology, or offer another reassurance, infuriates her. "Speaking of which, where are they?" she demands.

"What?"

"You know what—the negatives."

"You don't trust me. Is that it?"

"Bingo."

"Come on, Nina. It wasn't that bad."

"The. Fuck. It. Wasn't."

"Hey. No one locked the door. No one held a gun to your head."

"I was doped and drunk; I could barely sit up. Not that it was a requirement."

"*You make it sound pornographic.*"

"*It was pornographic.*"

"*You've been reading that MacKinnon bitch again. She'd say* Mapplethorpe *was pornographic.*"

"*So you're equating yourself with him now. Last week it was Weston. Time before that it was Friedlander. Next I suppose you'll be Diane Arbus and I'll have to put a lampshade on my head and a cigar in my ear.*"

"*We're photographers, Nina. We make statements with our work. It's what we do.*"

"*What statement was it when I was crawling around on all fours with my ass in the breeze and my nose in the rug?*"

"*I'm trying to say something about censorship. About the untenable line between art and obscenity.*"

"*Yeah, well, you're not trying hard enough.*"

"*What's that supposed to mean?*"

"*It means you're not saying anything that hasn't been said a hundred times before. I get the negatives or I'm out of here, Gary. I mean it.*"

He shrugs and yields. "*They're in my bag. You'll get them when we finish.*"

"*Promise?*"

"*Promise. But you're wrong about the session. The images are intense. They leap off that paper like you're in a third dimension. It's all there, babe, the whole eroto-fascist trip: the circle jerk of sex and power.*"

She closes her eyes and sighs. This isn't the way it was supposed to be. They were supposed to make art together, probe deep into the miracle of flesh and form, but all of a sudden he seems to be going for shock and schlock, playing to the press and the perverts, pressing her toward the slime instead of letting her soar free of small minds and base urges, making her ever dirtier instead of helping her to cleanse herself.

She will leave him, certainly. That much is decided. But then what? What will she do for money? Who will protect her from the creep who's been stalking her? And who will make her happy besides Ted?

¤　　　¤　　　¤

WEDNESDAY WAS A DAY AWAY.

I'd promised Peggy an answer by then, but I still didn't know what that answer should be. It would have been simple if the jeopardy were hers—in that case, I'd have been in Seattle already. It would also have been different if she were unattached—the romantic potential of a reunion would have overridden the risk of a crash if the potential went unrealized. But as things stood, a trip to Seattle would be analogous to an alcoholic going to work for Jack Daniel's while forbidden a sip of the inventory.

I'd spent the week reminiscing—part of it pleasant; part still painful. I could remember the day she'd applied for a job as though the ink were still wet on the résumé. She'd worn a brown wool suit with yellow buttons up the front and shoes with heels high enough to make her calves and thighs puff nicely, which I hear is the point of the exercise. Her hair was short and unprepossessing; her fingers and wrists and neck were free of jewelry but not of sun. Her gaze was frank and unabashed and maybe a little hostile; her answers to my questions were so brisk and to the point that I suspected she was late for a more promising interview.

She'd allowed herself to smile at my opening jokes but at the first opportunity she made it clear that she wouldn't fetch my laundry or order my groceries or phone for Giants tickets or similar chores that too many secretaries are saddled with. She eventually did all those things and more for me, of course, but never because I asked her to.

At one point she'd interrupted the narration of her previous experience to turn the tables. "You used to be a lawyer," she declared out of the blue.

"I still am a lawyer," I corrected.

"But you're not practicing."

"No."

"Why not?"

"I can't afford the neckties."

Her lips wrinkled. "You're kidding, right?"

"Have you priced one, lately? Twenty-five bucks, and by the time you get it home it's already too wide or too skinny or too plain or too something."

Her focus wasn't fashion. "I heard you got disbarred."

"Not disbarred; suspended."

"Was it for anything illegal or immoral?"

"Not on my part."

She cocked her head. "How can I know whether to believe you?"

"Do you want to believe me?"

She indulged my inspection for the first time. "I'm beginning to think so."

"Then come to work and find out. You can quit on ten minutes' notice."

So that's what she did, and the notice didn't come for nine years.

Peggy Nettleton is five years younger than I am, which puts her a step away from forty-five. Over time, I learned that she had been raised in the East, been married and divorced, and had a daughter named Allison, who was struggling to make a living as a dancer. But when she left, there were corners of Peggy's life that remained in deep shadow, lines of autobiography that were firmly forbidden, parts of her past that she refused to discuss for reasons that had left town with her.

But our affinities more than compensated for her reticence. We had similar tastes in books and movies, found pathos and humor in like phenomena, had more or less the same worldview, and gave our individual contributions to that selfsame planet

equal degrees of weight, which was somewhere south of stupen-
dous. What differences we had were minor—she hated football
and loved sushi; I loved Raymond Chandler and hated Diane
Sawyer; I hated Reagan and she hated Jerry Brown. But where it
counted most we were simpatico—on points of professional ethics
and personal morality we invariably occupied the same vicinity—and our relationship was soon symbiotic and indispensable.

Years went by. We shared professional ups and downs and personal vagaries as well. We moved in and out of relationships with
other people, compared notes, offered tips and then condolences,
and became each other's psychotherapist when we weren't each
other's best friend. We'd share a drink at the end of most work-
days and call each other at least once on weekends to make sure
solitude wasn't taking its toll. Talking with Peggy about whatever
came up and following wherever it led us became my favorite
pastime, the part of the day I most looked forward to, the only
hobby I had outside baseball and poker and teasing Charley
Sleet. Then she got in trouble.

A guy started calling her on the phone, getting more and more
intrusive, his demands increasingly sick and salacious, his probe
of her psyche ever deeper and more perverted. For reasons origi-
nating in past trauma and present frailty, Peggy had done less
than she might have to dissuade him. I reacted less than majesti-
cally to the situation, both physically and psychologically: in the
course of ferreting out her tormentor, I put Peggy's life in jeopardy and, even less commendably, took advantage of her vulnera-
bility to advance our relationship to a plateau that included sex. I
hadn't forced her to sleep with me, of course, but neither had I
realized that she was in no shape to make that decision at that
particular point in time. The harassment had, among other
things, deprived her of free will while making her desperate for a
champion; wittingly or not, I had taken advantage of her plight.

Eventually I'd caught the guy, thanks to a lot of help from

Peggy and some from Ruthie Spring and Charley Sleet. Peggy hadn't been harmed, on the surface at least, though her psyche had been scarred by both the problem and the fix, which had ended in the narrative sense when Peggy stabbed a man through the throat with a screwdriver. In the psychological sense, the incident probably wasn't over yet. Anyhow, when things were back to normal, or so I thought, Peggy decided to leave town, as an aid to putting her problems behind her. I was cut to the quick when I realized that at the top of the list of problems was my name.

I'd begged her not to go in as many ways as I could think of. Or almost as many—men's pride seems to keep them from taking that one last step of apology and supplication, which is often the only step that women need them to take. I've often wondered what Peggy would have done if, on the day she left town, I'd dropped to one knee and proposed. Usually I decide that it wouldn't have slowed her down.

We'd had our last conversation six years ago and I hadn't seen or heard from her since. It had been like divorce, at least for me—my life seemed cored and incomplete and I seemed incapable of attaching emotionally to anyone else because my heart still reached for a woman who was no longer there.

Now she was back. Just when I thought the storm had passed, here she came and the allure was as potent as ever. That same throaty voice, that same endemic melancholy, that same store of inner strength, that same suggestion of real yet calibrated affection, all and more combined to place her back at the base of my existence after a ten-minute telephone conversation.

When I'd acknowledged the inevitable, I called Charley Sleet, Detective Lieutenant, S.F.P.D., to tell him I was leaving town. When he asked where I was going and why, I told him.

"Good," he said. "It's about time you worked that out."

"What out?"

"You and her. You haven't been the same since she left."

I was irritated that I'd been that obvious. "I don't think there's much left to work out, Charley—she's getting married."

"Good," he said again.

"What's good about it?"

"If she's married, you'll leave her alone. Even you aren't low enough to hustle a married woman."

"I thought you liked her."

"I do like her. But she took a walk. When they walk, you don't get over it. You think you will, but you don't, so since it can't be the way you think it will, it's good you won't even try."

I laughed at the end of his essay. "Jesus, Charley. Where'd that come from?"

"I get around. I seen lots of people think they'd be happier apart, then try it and decide they wouldn't, then try to patch it up and make it like it was. It never works, is the problem—the cracks are still cracks, which means the next time it hits a bump it breaks apart real easy."

"I appreciate the lesson in love, Charley. Maybe you should write a book."

"And maybe you should call me when you know what her situation is so I can keep you from being a hero."

"What's wrong with being a hero?"

"She don't need a hero, she just needs a PI. She tell you anything about it?"

"Not much."

"When she does, call me."

A minute later, I was on the phone to Ruthie Spring. "Why?" I asked when she came on the line.

"Why what, sugar bear?"

"Why didn't you tell me Peggy was in Seattle?"

The hesitation suggested the answer was amorphous. "I didn't think it was something you needed to know," she offered finally, her usual brass muted to a rasping whisper.

"That wasn't your decision to make."

"If she wanted you to know where she was, she could have told you herself. I wasn't brought up to be a goddamned messenger."

Ruthie had been brought up to be a combat nurse and a sheriff's deputy and a good wife and friend and a dozen other things, all of which were exemplary except for the fact that she had never, in the vernacular of her native Texas, taken a liking to Peggy Nettleton.

"It would have helped to know that she was okay, Ruthie. It would have helped a lot."

"How? By driving you crazy over what to do about it?"

"I was crazy anyway."

"So I noticed. But you were coming out of it. Now you're back in the shit soup. When are you leaving?"

"For where?"

"Seattle."

"How do you know I'm going to Seattle?"

"How do I know you're pissed off?"

I spent the rest of the evening wondering how I'd become so predictable.

When I telephoned Peggy the next day I didn't beat around the bush—I told her I could clear the decks at the office and be in Seattle on Sunday. I said I could stay for a week, if need be, and asked how difficult her problem was likely to get—in other words, I asked if I should bring my gun.

She suggested that maybe I should.

CHAPTER 3

When she is dressed, Gary is waiting at the door. "Next week?"
He's as casual as a hairdresser filling his book.

"Nope."

"What's that mean?"

"It means I'm not going to work with you anymore."

He scowls and turns scarlet. "If this is about last time, I told you
I was sorry. It got a little lurid. So what?"

"This isn't about that. This is about us."

"What about us?"

"It's over, Gary. The relationship hasn't worked for a long time."

"Worked? What do you mean worked? It worked well enough
when I got your face plastered all over town in promos for the
Salmon. It worked when I got you that lingerie shoot for
Intimates."

"I'm talking about love, not layouts, Gary. But if you think
you're entitled to a commission, I'll try to come up with some
cash." She leaves no doubt that she regards the claim as pimpish.

He grasps her shoulders with icy hands. With another man, she
might be scared, but Gary quails at the slightest sign of strength in
the opposition. With him, she is only contemptuous.

"Look, babe," he says with the phony hipness she abhors. "We
sleep together and we work together. Too much face time is the
problem. So what we do is back off. Give each other some space.
Keep it where it is till we get straight with each other again, then

pick up where we left off. I got some other chicks I want to work with, anyway."

"I'll bet you do."

Her derision doesn't penetrate. "So we're cool, right? Come by tonight about eight. I'll do that pesto thing you like."

"No, Gary. It's over. What we had is history. I'm not going to end up like Mandy."

"Fuck Mandy. I didn't have anything to do with what happened to her."

"The pathetic thing is that I used to believe that."

He squeezes her delts and she twists out of his grasp. For a moment she thinks he might strike her. She wonders if she could beat him up if it came to that, and thinks maybe she could. From the cast to his eye, so does Gary.

"You'll change your mind," he says haughtily. "A month from now you'll be begging me to take you back. But you know what? I won't take you on, even for a spread in Penthouse."

"You're just another pervert, Gary. The sad part is you've got talent. I don't know why you don't use it."

"Talent? Talent don't cover the nut, babe. To live on talent, you need a government grant and Jesse Helms flushed the NEA down the toilet."

¤   ¤   ¤

AS PER THE PLAN I'd discussed with Peggy, I landed at Sea-Tac airport on Sunday afternoon, splurged on a rental car that turned out to be a Camry, drove north on I-5 to the Madison Street exit, then took Sixth Avenue north to the aptly named Sixth Avenue Inn, where I asked for the room reserved in my name. The desk clerk told me I was paid for five days. I told her I thought that would be sufficient. I grabbed a dozen business cards off the rack in case I ran into someone who wanted to know how to reach me, and ambled off to my room. After I unpacked my bag and washed my face and tore the sanitary tape off the john, I went out to inspect Seattle.

I had two hours until my dinner date with Peggy, so I wandered the neighborhood in search of some scenery that came complete with a saloon. The neighborhood turned out to be on the north edge of downtown and the bar occupied the corner of Virginia and Second Avenue. The clientele was youngish and toughish and boisterous, but they seemed friendly nonetheless so I grabbed a seat at the dark side of the room and ordered a beer. The barmaid asked me what kind. I asked her what she had. She pointed to a chalkboard that contained a list of beers and ales and bocks and pilsners, most of which I'd never heard of—Guido thinks Michelob is uppity. I opted for something called a Ballard Bitter.

The bitter beer was good, the bar was appropriately impersonal, and when I walked back into the street I was buoyed by my undemonstrative welcome to the city—I hate it when strangers pretend they like you. I stood on the corner and looked around. There was water off to my front and a big white boat racing a big gray cloud my way: I figured the boat for a ferry. A forest of skyscrapers loomed to my left, a hodgepodge of architecture that lay somewhere between offensive and important, which put it a cut above San Francisco's ungraceful spires. An object I presumed was the famous Space Needle jutted skyward to my right, and to my rear some nondescript buildings flanked something I would have guessed was a aqueduct if I'd been in ancient Rome instead of fin de siècle Seattle. A moment later, the aqueduct turned into a monorail.

The restaurant where I was to rendezvous with Peggy was in the direction of the skyscrapers, so I walked that way, wondering what I should say to her about, well, about us, knowing deep down that I shouldn't say anything at all, that words would make it worse. More alert to my interior landscape than to my surroundings, I roamed the city for close to an hour.

There weren't many people around, since it was Sunday, but there were several items of interest—a building that looked like a pencil balanced eerily on its point in defiance of gravity and good sense; an underground bus line as sumptuous as the Moscow subway but eerily abandoned nonetheless; several buildings that had once been grand but now were empty; and an artificial waterfall that wasn't as silly as it sounded. Every other window sported a sign that advertised espresso.

An assortment of ranters and ravers kept me on my toes, but there weren't nearly as many as used to occupy Civic Center Plaza or Union Square before the mayor launched his crackdown. I remembered that Seattle had passed a law that made it illegal to sit on the sidewalk. After an hour of meandering, I was tempted to become a criminal.

When I stopped to wonder what I thought about the place, I decided I was disappointed. Not that it wasn't spiffy, not that it wasn't clean, not that people weren't cheerful and even gregarious, just that it was generic. Nothing screamed Seattle. Nothing shouted salmon, or timber, or airplanes, or software, or whatever else made the city burst with pride. Seattle has been so much in the news of late, with so many touting its virtues, I suppose I'd expected too much and resented my gullibility. Maybe I'd see the light after Peggy gave me the grand tour.

I dawdled in a mallish enclosure called the Westlake Center long enough to be certain Peggy would arrive at the restaurant first, so she would have to wait for me and not vice versa. But just because the mall boasted an assortment of bookstores and gift shops and lingerie boutiques to divert me, it didn't mean they got the job done. By the time I opened the door to the Dahlia Lounge I was more nervous than I'd been since the last time a psychotic held a gun on me.

I spotted her right away, partly because she was the only person alone in a booth but mostly because I'd carried her image in my mind for six long years, examining it like an artifact during sleepless fits both late at night and early morning, until its conformation became indelible.

I looked at her, then looked away. Looked back until I saw that she saw me, then looked away again. Looked back, waved timidly, smiled, waved more vigorously, then headed in her direction, heedless of the hostess saying something at my back. My breath was high in my chest and my field of vision was the size of a dime. If I had fainted dead away or stumbled over a potted plant, I wouldn't have wondered why.

As I neared the booth I was buffeted by impressions—she was a little heavier, a lot grayer, a little paler, and a lot happier than when I'd seen her last. Her eyes preened with pleasure, her hair fell lushly in a short soft wave that looked expensively sculpted, her dress was a simple yet elegant suit—gray jacket with white windowpanes and black buttons, white top square at the neck and snug at the bodice, skirt just short enough to show a slice of thigh. Peggy had turned natty, if that was a word that applied to a beautiful woman—when she'd worked for me, natty wasn't in her budget.

Up close, some details asserted themselves, like the string of small pearls at her neck and the single gold hoop on her wrist and, as I felt more than observed when she slid out of the booth and embraced my hand in both of hers, the diamond the size of a crouton on her third finger left hand. We kissed each other, briefly and aridly, careful to preclude contact at breast or pelvis, then backed away and took a more languorous inventory.

"You're looking good, boss," Peggy said theatrically, a layer of brass masking whatever her urges were up to.

"Same to you, sweetheart." Whenever Peggy was around, I opted too often for Bogart.

She reddened and waved her hand. "Have a seat. Order a drink. I've already started," she added, pointing to the gold in her wineglass as we eased onto the benches.

A waitress drifted by and Peggy corralled her. "He'll have scotch on the rocks. Ballantine's." She looked at me.

"Right."

"Double?"

"Not unless I'm going to need it."

Peggy shook her head and the waitress drifted off. I leaned back against the padded booth and looked for ambiguity or ambivalence or even animosity. Thankfully, I didn't find any of those things, which made my smile grow fatuous.

Peggy was nervous, as was I, and in compensation was trying to be raucous and blasé. But behind her scripted sass was genuine pleasure, I decided, an unadulterated delight that we were together again, however clinical the occasion. That's what I thought I saw, in any case, and what I wanted to see as well. I hoped she saw the same in me.

I offered the cliché that came to mind. "It's been a long time."

"Six years."

"Seems like longer."

"I know."

All of a sudden her lip began to tremble and her eyes glistened until she blinked away the polish that forecasts a rush of memory. This time when she spoke, the words didn't come from a script.

"I hurt you when I left," she said softly. "I want you to know that I know that, Marsh; I'm sure it was a difficult time for you. Before we go further, I want to tell you I'm sorry."

I said what you say at such times. "There's nothing to be sorry about. You did what you had to do, and justifiably so. I was a jerk there at the end."

She waved away the indictment. "Just so you know that's not why I left. To hurt you, I mean. I just . . . everything was upside down. I'd done things that were *inconceivable* to me, things diametrically opposed to the way I wanted to live and the woman I thought I was, things that horrified and disgusted me. Disgusted *both* of us."

I started to object but she didn't let me.

"I could see it in your eyes. Your contempt. And worse, your disappointment. The bottom line was, I had no idea who I was or why I'd done the things I'd done, I just knew I had to get away so I could find out. And so I wouldn't see my mistakes reflected in your eyes."

It was painful to be described as her persecutor. To reduce the urge to counterpunch or to indulge in self-reproach, I examined the decor for as long as I could, then wrenched the issue toward its end. "Did it work? Did you find out what you needed to know about yourself?"

It took her a while to respond. "Not right away, but eventually. I'm not as bad as I feared or as good as I hoped, which I suppose is where most people come out if they bother to think about it. I think that who I am is pretty close to the person who applied for a job with you way back then, the one who told you she'd water your plants but wouldn't make coffee. Famous last words."

I smiled. "I haven't had a decent cup since you left."

We shared some mutual recollection and maybe a dollop of regret that issues were no longer that simple between us.

In the echo of our implicit truce, we sipped our drinks and inspected our fellow diners and tried to recover our balance. I glanced at the menu without absorbing it. The waitress returned, lingered, and left. Time was glutinous and thick with memory, combined pain and pleasure in a simmering stew that was too problematic to sample. When I looked at Peggy she was crying.

"There's no need to rehash it," I said softly. "It was a difficult time for both of us, but the good news is it's over. You're happy, right? That's what's important. What happened back then, and why, doesn't matter anymore. The only way it can do more damage is if we let it."

"But it changed my life. *Our* lives. We might have been . . . you know what we might have been."

"Leave it, Peggy. Just leave it. It might have been great or it might have been awful, but now it's just one more thing we'll never know. Like what was on the Watergate tapes."

After enduring my wit and wisdom, Peggy sighed and shrugged and threw off her mood. "I'll try to take your word for it." She dredged up a grin and glanced at the menu. "I assume from the phone call that your tastes in food haven't changed much."

"Not true. Sometimes I go gourmet."

"Which means?"

"Fig Newtons instead of Oreos."

"Fat-free, I hope."

I made a face.

She shook her head in exasperation and gestured with the menu. "I think you'll like the chicken."

"Fine."

"And I'll have the Walla Walla salad and salmon mousse."

"What are Walla Wallas?"

"Sweet onions. Some people eat them like apples."

I summoned the waitress and gave her the order. She obtained some details, including my request for another round of drinks, then went off to start the process of overfeeding us.

"Have you been in Seattle all this time?" I asked, just to be saying something.

She nodded.

"What made you pick it?"

She shrugged. "A year full of rainy days seemed appropriate at the time."

"Is Allison still dancing?"

Peggy shook her head. "Performance art. She adopts the roles of various people involved in the Hill-Thomas hearings, only reverses their race and gender."

"That could get to look a lot like a minstrel show, couldn't it?"

She laughed, though not quite on cue. "I'm afraid to ask. So have you gotten engaged or anything since I've seen you?"

"No."

"Not even once?"

"Nope."

"Must be a lot of broken hearts down there."

"Besides mine, you mean. Sorry," I said quickly when I saw that I'd hurt her. "So tell me about your fiancé."

"Why?"

"You know why."

She blinked as if her answer came in semaphore. "Ted's a banker, sort of."

"What's a 'sort of' banker do?"

"He's more like a venture capitalist."

"Venture capitalists tend to be rich, don't they?"

She couldn't quite meet my eye. "Ted inherited a lot of money and he's putting it to good use."

"Good for him. What's he look like?"

"He's tall, gray, and handsome. He golfs and collects Native American artifacts; there was a big write-up on his collection in the *Times* a while back. And he's very kind, Marsh. Conservative, and kind."

"That sounds like one trait too many."

She reddened as though I'd caught her shoplifting. "He's okay as long as I forbid him to watch Rush Limbaugh."

The subject was hot so I dropped it. "He was married before?"

She nodded. "He's been divorced for twelve years."

"His doing or hers?"

"His."

"Where's the ex-wife?"

She looked beyond me. "About four blocks from here. She's got a dress shop down by the market. Her home is out on Phinney Ridge."

"What market is that?"

"You don't know the Pike Place Market? It's our chief tourist attraction. I'd take you down there except I can't think of a single thing you'd find remotely interesting. Except maybe the bar at Il Bistro."

"Why that?"

"They specialize in single-malt whiskeys."

I smiled. "I'll check it out once I've finished the job. Which I can start as soon as I know what the hell it is."

Peggy wrinkled her nose and dabbed her lip with her napkin. "Can't it wait till after dinner?"

"Nina? Hi. It's Roan."

"Hey."

"How's it going?"

"I've been better. You?"

"I'm cool. Cleared sixty bucks on the Ave today."

"Great."

"So what did you do with the pus bucket?"

"I dumped him."

"When?"

"Ten days ago."

"For real?"

"For real."

"What'd he do?"

"About what you'd expect."

"He didn't, like, hurt you, did he? He gets pretty amped some-times. He pulled a knife on Mandy once."

"No knife."

"How about the scuzz who's been stalking you?"

"I haven't seen him for a while."

"You should tell the cops about it, Nina."

"Tell them what? That some old man has the hots for me? What are they supposed to do—give him a cold shower?"

"I guess. It's creepy, though. And speaking of creepy, there's some of Gary's stuff in the new Erospace show."

"Yeah? What stuff?"

"Just stuff. Political, I guess. That's what he's into now, right?"

"I guess so."

"Well, his politics seem pretty sick to me."

"Sick how?"

"You know."

"How would I know? I haven't seen the exhibit."

"But some of them are you. All of them, in fact."

"Couldn't have been. Some of the work I did with Gary was silly, but none of it was sick."

"You let him put stuff in you."

"What are you talking about?"

"There's all kinds of things sticking out of you in those pictures."

"What kind of things?"

"I don't want to validate it by discussing it."

"Come on, Roan."

"I'm serious. It's very upsetting to me. I don't see how you could let him do that to you. You must have been into some pretty heavy dope."

¤   ¤   ¤

THE MEAL CAME AND WENT. It was good, I guess, but then most meals are good except for inedible stuff like squash and sushi. We spent the time chewing and chatting like siblings—Peggy asked about people she'd known in San Francisco, including several clients who had become her friends, and I brought her up to date even though for several the status was less than optimum. For my part, I asked for details about her job, and her home, and her social life, and it was all very civilized and companionable, yet somehow beside the point. By the time we were helping ourselves to decaf espresso and flan, I found myself a trifle bored, the one reaction I hadn't anticipated.

When Peggy moved her dessert plate an inch toward the center of the table, I seized the chance to shift gears. "Enough with etiquette," I said, more gruffly than I intended. "Let's talk business."

I expected a halfhearted protest but what I got was equivocation, beneath a pair of skittish eyes. "All of a sudden it seems silly, bringing you up here like this. There's probably nothing you can . . . what I'm trying to say is, there may not be a problem. I think I got you here on a ruse, just so I could get some gossip and a free meal." She was trying to be jovial and indifferent but her expression remained overwrought.

"I don't want to bust your bubble, Ms. Nettleton," I said in keeping with her lead, "but there's nothing free about it." I patted my stomach. "This baby goes straight to the expense account."

It was a stupid and bogus joke, since the last thing in the world I would do was submit a bill to Peggy, but she took me seriously. "Of course. I didn't mean . . . should I give you a retainer or something? Of course I should." She hauled her purse to the table and began to paw through it. "Let me write you a check."

"No check."

She looked up. "I don't carry much cash."

I grasped her wrist and extracted her hand from the bag. "We'll settle up later."

"I just don't want you to think that I'm the kind of person who expects you to—"

"The only thing I think is that you're procrastinating." I waited until she looked at me again. "What the hell am I doing here, Peggy?"

She dodged my stare but answered the question. "You're going to help me find my future stepdaughter."

I raised a brow. "She's missing?"

Peggy nodded. "It seems so."

"How long?"

"Two months."

If you're from California, the word "missing" conjures one image above all others these days, that of bright-eyed Polly Klaas, the twelve-year-old who was kidnapped at random from her home in Petaluma and left dead near an abandoned mill by a life-long criminal who had no business being on the streets. That was the backdrop I had in mind, at least, as I began to pluck details from the mind and heart of my reticent client.

"How old is she?" I asked.

"She'll be twenty-five next month."

I was relieved that she was an adult, so at least part of the analogy was inaccurate. "Was she living at home?"

Peggy shook her head. "Not since I moved in with Ted. She had an apartment in the U District."

"U is for what? University?"

"Yes."

"She's a student?"

"Yes. That is, she was. Part-time, at least. She dropped out last term."

"Was she working?"

"Probably. I don't know where."

"Was she getting money from Daddy?"

"If she needed it, I presume she was. Ted doesn't deny her much."

The reference to her fiancé seemed to annoy her for some reason. Or maybe she was annoyed with me—most of my clients are at some point, at about the time I get to the heart of the matter.

I decided to sidestep the family for now. "What's her name?"

"Nina."

"Are you sure she's missing? She's old enough to have gone off on a toot by herself."

"Actually, it's quite possible that's what she *did* do."

"Go off on a toot? Why?"

"To punish us. Me, mostly," she added after a moment.

"Punish you for what?"

"For coming on the scene." Peggy looked at me with sudden intensity. "You were thinking kidnapping, weren't you?"

I nodded. "Ransom?"

She shook her head. "I'm sure it's nothing as dramatic as that. This is more a runaway, like all those other cases you used to have. Whatever happened with the Miller girl? Did you find her?"

"Not long after you left, her parents asked me to stop looking. 'We're no longer interested,' was the way they put it."

"God."

"I don't think God had much to do with it."

I drained my coffee and settled back in the booth and enjoyed a lesser degree of foreboding while wrestling with a stubborn degree of restlessness. A part of me wanted her problem to be more cataclysmic, of a degree that required heroics. Then I could impress her. Then I could remind her who I was. Then I could win her back and take her home with me. Not for the first time, I envisioned making love to a woman who was pledged to another man.

A waitress materialized and asked if we'd finished our desserts and cleared the table when we nodded. We both ordered a second espresso; I made sure she remembered mine was decaf. I can sip whiskey all night if I pace myself, but if I have an ounce of caffeine in the evening, I don't sleep a wink. Basically, I have the constitution of a five-year-old: a bag of Oreos never lasts me more than twenty-four hours.

I got out my notebook and pencil. "Let's start at the beginning," I said when the waitress was out of earshot. "What's Nina's last name?"

"Evans. Nina Becker Evans."

"Evans is her father's name?"

She nodded. "And Becker her mother's. Judy Becker."

I looked up. "Are you going to be Margaret Evans?"

She shook her head. "I'll still go by Nettleton."

"Are you in the phone book?"

"Only under Ted's name."

"You'd better give me your number."

She recited the digits and I jotted them in my book. When I'd finished, she issued a caveat. "Please don't call me at home unless it's absolutely necessary. I'll call your motel every evening at nine—Ted takes the dog for a walk then; he's gone for half an hour. If I don't reach you at nine, I'll call the next morning at eight—Ted leaves for work before I do."

"Why all the rigmarole?"

"I don't want Ted to know I've done this unless it turns . . . you know. Horrible, or something."

"I thought you were sure it *wasn't* horrible."

She closed her eyes and shook her head. "I can't be sure, Marsh. I don't know enough to be sure."

No one ever does. "Why did Nina drop out of school?"

"I don't know, but it seemed to be part of a general deterioration of her life. The process began in adolescence and accelerated when Ted and I started seeing each other three years ago. It peaked when I moved in with Ted last Christmas and he announced we were going to be married. Nina left school a month after I started living with her father."

"What kind of deterioration are we talking about?"

"The stuff young people are so damned good at—sex, drugs, hatefulness, irresponsibility."

"You make her sound pretty mutinous."

"That's exactly what she was, apparently. According to Ted, at least."

"What triggered it?"

She shrugged. "Ted makes vague references to her past from

time to time, as though something traumatic happened in her childhood, but if it did, I don't know what it was."

"Did she have run-ins with the police?"

"Not that I know of."

"When's the last you heard from her?"

"Not since she abandoned her apartment—no notice, no nothing, she just left it in her wake along with everything she owned."

"Do you know where she's living now?"

"No."

"Is there a boyfriend?"

"Not that I know of."

"But you think her snit has something to do with you."

"I'm certain of it."

"It's pretty hard to cast you in the role of the ugly stepmother," I said easily.

"Well, that's what I seem to be. In Nina's eyes, at least."

"Was there a particular bone of contention?"

She shook her head. "Quite the contrary. I tried very hard to make her like me; I didn't interfere in her life at all. I went out of my way to be nice, but for some reason she hated me anyway."

"Hate's a pretty strong word."

Peggy's lip quivered. "It's the word she used. To my face. More than once."

Peggy was on the verge of tears; I tried to tug her away from them. "Nina sounds pretty immature."

"She is. Unquestionably. I think most kids are these days. They're very spoiled, very used to getting their way, very used to ignoring authority without consequence. I think it's because the parents aren't around to impose discipline."

Peggy looked beyond me, at the traffic streaming by outside the restaurant, and used the kinetic blur to assemble her thoughts. "Nina is very verbal; very opinionated; very aggressive; very sanctimonious. And very beautiful. I think her parents avoided discipline because it turned into a war they couldn't win. It was easier to let their lovely daughter have her way. And I have to admit, based on her looks, it would be hard to imagine her acting as anything but an angel."

"Laissez-faire can be a formula for disaster, though."

Peggy nodded. "Kids need limits. They push till they feel them. When they don't feel any, they push harder. If there aren't any there, they fall down. Limits equal love; kids understand it better than adults do, sometimes."

I didn't have anything to add to her essay.

Peggy toyed with her spoon and overstirred her coffee. When she spoke again, her tone was thin and uninflected. "The person Nina's really angry with is Ted, of course. I'm just a stand-in for her daddy."

"What's wrong with Daddy?"

"Ted and Judy were divorced when Nina was twelve. A tough age for an upheaval, particularly for girls—they're very susceptible to rejection at that point. They're finally beginning to see themselves as individuals and just when they think they have a picture of who they are, they get slapped in the face by the person they love most in the world. Some kids never recover from it."

"Who took Nina after the divorce?"

"She lived with her mom at first. It went okay for a while, but they had problems once Nina hit high school—the relationship was turbulent. Ted was aware of the situation and tried to smooth things out—he saw Nina almost every weekend. There was a lot of bitterness toward him at first, but over time the relationship became quite strong." She paused. "Maybe to an unhealthy degree, because when I came along Nina acted more like his wife than his daughter—she definitely played the role of the wronged woman. I half-expected her to charge me with alienation of affections." Peggy's smile wasn't as disarming as it should have been.

"You're not saying there was anything going on in a literal sense."

She reddened as though I had slapped her. "Of course not. My God."

She stayed silent long after I apologized.

"The more I tried to be nice to her, the worse it got," she continued finally. "She even called me a slut one night when she showed up unannounced when Ted and I were preparing to . . . well, you get the picture. Once I moved in, she stopped coming by the house entirely. Her father had abandoned her again, at least symbolically."

"She and Ted haven't gotten together at all in recent months?"

"Up until two months ago they still saw each other regularly, but not in my presence. They had dinner once a week, Wednesday nights usually, at some nice restaurant. They made a big deal out of it."

"How do you mean?"

"They played dress-up. And drank champagne. And went to places like Canlis and Kaspar's and the Hunt Club. It was quite a production, usually."

"Sounds a little bent to me," I said, then quickly wished I hadn't.

Peggy started to object to my choice of words, then changed her mind and offered a concurrence. "It *was* bent. That's exactly what it was. What *she* was, at least."

"It sounds like a two-way street, Peggy."

The pain in her eyes was palpable. "I know it does. And it was, I guess. But it wasn't perverted, Marsh—Ted was just trying to keep his family together and that was the only way he could think of to do it."

"Did you say anything to him about his methodology?"

"Once."

"How did he react?"

"He told me I was being silly, that he was just giving a poor college student a night on the town once in a while. So he kept on fawning over her. And telling me to give her more time to adjust."

Peggy finished her coffee. "I don't mean to make him sound stupid," she said, even though that was what she'd done. "He was just determined to keep Nina's goodwill at any cost. Or almost any. He did tell me that if I insisted on it, he'd stop seeing her, at least so ceremoniously."

"But you didn't."

"Of course not. How could I?"

"But Nina took off anyway."

"Yes."

"Is she the only child?"

Peggy shook her head. "There's a brother. Jeff. He's two years younger."

"What's his attitude about all this?"

"He's pretty much written off the whole lot of us."

"What's he do?"

Peggy chuckled wryly. "Jeff writes a column for a local alternative newspaper called *Salmon Says*. What he is is a sex adviser."

"A what?"

"He tells people how to improve their sex lives. Ted hasn't spoken to him since Jeff did a column on anal intercourse. Which is probably the reason he wrote it."

To cover my embarrassment, I pecked at a small thread. "Does Ted have a will?"

"Yes, but I don't know what it says. Why is that relevant?"

"I haven't the faintest idea. Do you have a prenuptial agreement?"

She reddened and set her jaw. "This is none of your business; it has nothing to do with Nina."

That wasn't necessarily true but I didn't debate it. "Let's see if I've got it right. Nina lives a wild life that becomes even more rambunctious when you and Ted start dating. When you move in, she drops out of school and stops coming around the house but she and her father keep in touch. Then two months ago, she disappears altogether."

"Right."

"But you don't have evidence the disappearance was involuntary."

"No."

I shrugged. "Frankly, it doesn't sound that serious to me. Kids take off all the time. She'll show up next week with a nice tan and tell you she's been in Sun Valley for two months."

Peggy shook her head. "I don't think so."

"Why not?"

"Just a hunch."

I smiled. "I have to admit, you used to be a good huncher. But I don't see why the best thing to do isn't to give it more time."

Her outburst shoved me back against the booth. "Because my life is going to hell, *that's* why. It's all he can talk about. All he does with his free time is *look* for her. We haven't done anything but search for Nina in weeks—he says he can't marry me until he finds her."

Her fists were white and her words were raw with ire and insult. The admission that her relationship was in extremis had cost her a lot.

"Has Ted called in the cops?"

"No."

"Why not?"

"Because he's afraid he might get his precious Nina in trouble. She did lots of drugs for a time. Ted's afraid if the police nose around, they might find evidence to charge her with something."

"Has Ted hired his own investigator?"

"I don't know; it's possible. He's as desperate about this as I am, though not quite for the same reason." She reached out and grasped my hand. "Will you look into it, Marsh? It would mean a great deal to me if you could find her. You can probably do it in a day—she's just gone off to pout somewhere."

I met her look. "You must think it's worse than that or I wouldn't be here. What I don't understand is why."

"I just want Ted to have his daughter back. Why is that so awful?"

"It isn't awful at all, if that's all there is to it."

Her eyes danced away. "What else would there be?"

"I have no idea," I said truthfully. "Do you have a picture?"

Peggy reached in her purse and gave me a photograph. It was an informal snapshot of an extremely pretty young woman wearing shorts and a halter top, leaning against a car and eating an ice-cream cone. Her pose was casual but self-aware, as though she knew exactly how to make herself look innocently provocative, exactly how to make the cone seem unwittingly symbolic, exactly how to seem sinful.

I put the picture in my pocket and looked at my watch. "It's only eight. We could go somewhere for a nightcap."

Peggy hesitated, then shook her head. "I should get home. Ted gets nervous when I'm out late."

I was tempted to tell her Ted needed to get used to it.

Twenty minutes later, I got a drink on my own, the sole customer in the generic lounge adjacent to the motel, and spent the rest of the evening imagining Peggy Nettleton coming to the end of her day in bed with another man.

CHAPTER 5

Shrouded in a polyester scarf and formless shift, eyes erased by pseudo-Claiborne shades, she loiters across the street until the gallery is full to bursting. Then she enters surreptitiously, joining a group of three as if she completes the quartet even though the others are strangers, these casual consumers of erotica, these corrupters of her trade.

When the woman of the trio frowns at her impolitic proximity, Nina heads for a crowded corner near the door to the storeroom, aware as she edges through the mass of humanity that is attaching itself like lichen to the fecal equivalents displayed on the walls that she is known to a dozen people in attendance, so her guise is being road tested. Shoving the dime-store sunglasses higher on her nose, she wanders toward a place of refuge near a group of disapproving strangers adjacent to the rear partition. Slowly, she begins to relax; slowly, she trusts her costume; slowly she feels invulnerable. Eagerly incognito, she seeks what she has come to find.

His name is computerized and enlarged and tacked to the north wall, above a series of six matted but unframed photographs that bear his splashy stamp. Several people are gathered nearby and one of them, a woman in Levi's and Greenpeace T-shirt, seems antagonized by what she has seen. Her companion has the look of weary tolerance that indicates he has been embarrassed by his lover's outbursts so frequently that he has concocted an antidote in the form of an unimpeachable nonchalance that is subject to whatever interpretation one wishes to attach to it.

When the space is free, Nina fills it. One by one, she looks at his treasons. One by one, her body temperature mounts, one by one her pulse accelerates to an ultra-high frequency, one by one a white-hot singe of rage inflames her as she sees the extent to which Gary Richter has defiled her, made a shambles of her devotion, used her body not as a molten vessel but as a chamber pot for his treacly eroto-politics. She is afraid, for just a moment, that she is going to faint.

¤   ¤   ¤

I STARTED MY SEARCH for Nina Evans first thing in the morning, at the place where she used to live, which was an eight-plex apartment near the corner of Fifty-second and University, just north of the University of Washington campus. The people up and at their lives at 9 A.M. didn't include the manager of the Pacific Apartments. He lived in Unit 1, so the sign by the door informed me, and was apparently a dedicated sleeper. By the time he answered my summons, my thumb ached from pressing his bell.

The apartments were arrayed on two levels in a horseshoe configuration that extended back from the phony stone facade and corrugated tin fence that fronted the building on the street. The set pieces perched on the veranda that provided access to each unit ranged from various forms of plastic furniture to a greasy Suzuki motorcycle and a bedraggled cactus that looked homesick for Arizona. The manager made do with an overstuffed chair that slumped like a drunken sailor outside his door and was bloated with moisture and rotted with age. From the polka dots on its back and arms, I guessed sparrows made more use of it than he did.

The man who opened the door wore khaki shorts that fell to his knees and a Husky T-shirt he had rendered sleeveless for reasons not evident from his biceps. His eyes were lidded and unfocused, as though he'd left his glasses or his amphetamines by the bed. His feet were bare but for a layer of soot ground deeply into the soles. His beard was soggy and his hair was wet and matted. The general effect was that a thunderstorm had let loose inside his bedroom and he hadn't had time to towel off.

After I introduced myself, he made an assumption. "You're the guy from twelve, right? Well, I ain't going up there, I don't care how much it's backed up. I told her if it happened again she had to ream it out herself. Last time I ran a snake down there I pulled out a hair ball the size of a weasel. She's got to stop barbering in the bathtub, man."

"I'm not from twelve," I said as soon as I could manage it. "I'm here about Nina Evans."

He blinked to switch circuits and picked his nose to refocus. "Nina? Yeah. Yeah. I'm tracked. What about her?"

"I was wondering which unit is hers."

"Why do you want to know?"

I smiled. "Business."

"What kind of business?"

"Personal business."

"You got the back rent?"

I shook my head.

He sniffed and ran his tongue across his teeth. Whatever he encountered made him pucker. "Are you, like, official or anything?"

"I'm officially unofficial. What unit is hers?"

"None of them."

"I was told she lived here."

"She did but she don't. Just like I told her old man."

"Her father was asking about her?"

He nodded. "Month ago. What is he, a preacher or something?"

"Why do you ask?"

"Guy made me feel like I was shit in a suit. He's worse than *my* old man, for Christ's sake, and that takes work. Know what he gave me for Christmas?"

"Mr. Evans?"

"My old man. A subscription to fucking *Forbes*. Might as well have given me a subscription to *Ladies' Home Journal*, the bastard."

It was time to end the soliloquy. "What did you tell Mr. Evans about his daughter?"

"I told him what I knew, which is that she used to live in three but didn't pay for April. I didn't hear nothing and didn't see her around, so on the tenth I posted a notice to quit, and rented the unit May one. You got a problem with that, you can talk to my lawyer but it won't do no good. I never had an eviction voided yet."

"Did you see Nina again at all?"

"Nope."

"She have money on deposit?"

"Six hundred last month's rent; eight hundred damage and security."

"Pretty steep deposit."

"Steep, shit. Half the time they barely leave the Sheetrock. I lose my ass on refurbishment, let me tell you."

"Do you own the building?"

"Yeah. Well, technically I'm partners with the old man, that way he can tell the boys at the club his son's in real estate." His grin was pitiless. "The charade works till I show up on the first tee to give him his take. Last time he hit a duck hook that cold-cocked some skirt on the next fairway." His smile turned giddy. "Yeah, whenever I'm around the old boy uses too much right hand."

I tried to get him back on track. "Did Nina tell you she was going to be leaving?"

"Nina didn't tell me nothing. Not lately, she didn't. All of a sudden, I wasn't worthy of attention."

"Why do you say that?"

"She and her new pal thought they were so cool they cracked. Looked at me like I was scum squared."

"Who was this new friend?"

"Don't know. Never got introduced."

"Can you tell me anything at all about him?"

He shrugged. "Actor, maybe; dressed the part, anyway. Nina always hung around with arty types. If he was an actor he was a rich one—cool duds, cool car, cool customer. Maybe he was one of the guys from 'Northern Exposure.' The TV series? They tape over the pass in Roslyn but they hang around Seattle a lot."

"But you don't know that for sure."

"Hell, no. Like I said, no one introduced me."

"Was Nina an artist herself?"

"She wore black. That means she's creative, right? Poet. Painter. Whatever. I got no time for it myself. Art's the *new* opiate of the masses, man: TV, movies, rock and roll—brainless drivel to keep the people's minds on money and sex and off of exploitation."

"What exploitation would that be?"

"Economic oppression, man. Tax laws, S&Ls, stock options, junk bonds—Generation X works in a fucking franchise while Yuppies live like potentates. America's worse than Brazil, for Christ's sake."

"Have you been to Brazil?"

"No, but I been to Rainier Valley. Same difference."

He didn't quite convince me. "Did you ask the other tenants if they knew where Nina had gone?"

"Hell no. I got the deposit; I got her rent; I got stuff I can sell to cover my losses. What do I care where she went?"

"So for all you know her next-door neighbor knows exactly where she is."

"Her next-door neighbor is a power lifter—what he knows is 'roids. Anyone knows where Nina is, it's Willie."

"Willie who?"

"Willie Gamble. Unit 4."

He started to close the door but I stopped him. "You said something about selling her stuff."

"Yeah. She left a bunch of crap behind. She doesn't show in a month, I sell it to a junk dealer. So what?"

"Can I see it?"

"Naw, I . . . hey. You got business with Nina, maybe I'll sell it for what you owe her. Sort of an informal garnishment, if you get my drift—keep the lawyers out of it, more for everyone that way. I'll give you a good deal, man—I need to clear the space."

I pretended to think it over. "I guess it wouldn't hurt to take a look," I said reluctantly.

He led me to the back of the building and opened the steel-wrapped door to the basement. There was an oil furnace and two giant water heaters down there, along with a host of junk presumably accumulated from flighty tenants like Nina: bicycles, skis, bowling balls, exercise equipment, even a dollhouse and tricycle and jungle gym. At the far end were two rooms locked with padlocks and labeled STORAGE with a Magic Marker.

The manager opened the door on the left, flicked on a dim light, and stepped aside. "Hers is in front of the Ping-Pong table. You see anything you like, make an offer. I'm easy, like I said, but you do your own hauling. I'll be down by the boiler; fucker's losing pressure again."

The manager was an interesting blend of socialist urges and capitalist behavior—his daddy hadn't been entirely ineffective. I entered the windowless cavern and rummaged around in Nina Evans's abandoned property.

It didn't take long to conclude that she hadn't been kidnapped. The stuff in storage was mostly junk—trashy novels, broken furniture, dented appliances, ripped bedding, unfashionable clothing. There was a lot of it, to be sure, but it was still junk: no stereo, no TV, no CDs, no jewelry. The only items that retained utility were large and unwieldy—couch, chair, dresser, desk—which indicated Nina had skipped with the things she could carry unobtrusively and without help. If it wasn't portable, it got left.

Just because it was junk didn't mean it didn't contain a clue to her whereabouts, however, so I made a pretense of inspecting the treasure trove more closely. The manager didn't worry that I was a thief—he was still berating the furnace.

The most promising resource was the desk. It was one of those pressboard jobs you buy at Kmart or Target, painted green, bearing the scars of knife cuts and cigarette burns and tattooed with doodles in ballpoint. The doodles didn't reveal anything other than a preoccupation with daisies and diamonds and the drawers were empty except for several scraps of paper, most of which seemed to be trash, and some fairly recent issues of *Modern Photography* and something called *New Media*. The only other objects of interest were some dull X-Acto blades and a flattened tube of rubber cement—I guessed Nina had been mounting some pictures.

I abandoned the desk and moved to the books. I riffed quickly through them, but nothing fell out except a bookmark from the University Bookstore and a flyer from a tanning parlor. There weren't any notes in the margins either, except on the title page of a novel called *Exposure* was the word GARY, written in pen and ink and traced over and over until it was thickened into boldface. Below Gary's name was a drawing of something dark and dangerous that looked like the profile of a pistol.

I pawed through the clothes and cookware and linens. There were stains on the sheets, but I guessed their source was menstrual, not criminal. There were holes in some of the clothes, but I guessed they were normal wear and tear. There was some white powder in one of the drawers, but it tasted more like talc than cocaine. Otherwise, nothing turned up except mildew.

I collected the scraps of paper in a pile and went through them more carefully. One was a cash machine receipt from Seafirst Bank dated March 16, not long before Nina had disappeared. I jotted down her account number and balance—$5,435.27—which seemed a bit large for a woman who bought cheap desks and used dented cookware. Another piece of paper was a sales receipt from a place called Intimates. The date was March 18; the amount was $367.17. A third was a business card from something called DigiArt, with an address on Western Avenue. The rest of it was dross.

I found the manager and told him I couldn't use any of Nina's stuff. Since he was still warring with the boiler, he didn't try to renegotiate. I headed for Unit 4.

The woman who answered my knock was such a contrast to the phlegmatic manager she seemed like an interloper. Bright-eyed, kinetic, eager to the point of evangelism, she looked at me so intently I began to feel like some sort of savior except I suspected she'd already found one.

Everything from her short brown hair to her short white skirt jiggled and jumped as I told her who I was. "Hi, Mr. Tanner," she responded happily.

"Hi. Is Willie here?"

"*I'm* Willie."

"Sorry, I just assumed—"

"It's all right. Everyone does. But, like, I *refuse* to go by *Wilma* anymore—no one should be a Wilma at my age, do you think?—so Willie's what I'm left with. If you're collecting for charity, I'm basically broke. They laid me off at Tower. I was too peppy, they said; plus I was, like, the only one there who was into Mariah Carey."

I smiled. "I'm not collecting for charity, I'm looking for Nina Evans."

She glanced to her right, in the direction of Nina's former abode. "Nina's not here anymore."

"I know she isn't. I thought you might know where she went."

She seemed puzzled. "Why would I?"

"I heard you were friends."

She shook her head. "Not really. I mean, I knew her to speak to and everything, but she was, like, way too cool for me. Especially lately."

"What happened lately?"

Her round face elongated with uncharacteristic censure. "She made noise, for one thing. Coming and going at all hours, waking me up in the middle of the night—I was, like, bummed about it, since I need my eight hours to feel good about myself. I didn't *say* anything, of course, because I don't do confrontation. But I *wanted* to."

"Are you a student, Willie?"

"Sure. Almost everyone around here is."

"Was Nina a student, too?"

"She used to be, but she dropped out."

"What was she studying?"

"Art, I think. Or maybe art history. There was always a lot of those types coming around. They acted like I was some sort of Jell-O mold if I didn't know where she was. But I was, like, I'm not her *mother*, you know?"

"Why did she drop out of school?"

"She said she was bored."

"It doesn't sound like she was bored, what with all the activity."

"She had some new friends, I think. I don't know who they were, but they were rich, I know that much. One of them drove a car that was to die for."

"What kind of car?"

"Convertible. Black seats, black top, black everything. I'm, like, why don't guys like that ever hit on *me*? Not really," she corrected quickly, in case I got the wrong impression.

"What make was the car?"

"I'm not sure. Foreign, I think. Like maybe a Porsche? Is that foreign?"

I told her I thought maybe it was. "Do you know any of her friends' names?"

She shook her head. "She used to hang out at the Brooklyn, I know, so you might try there."

"What's the Brooklyn?"

"The Last Exit on Brooklyn. Next door."

"I thought this was University Avenue."

"It is. The Brooklyn used to be on Brooklyn, but they lost their lease and moved up here. The Brooklyn and the Blue Moon are the hippest places around that I know of, so you might try there, too. Sorry I'm not real helpful, but I'm not into creativity myself. I mean, I'm, like, just sort of happy the way it is, you know? People sort of hate me for it, but I can't *help* it. I just don't think life is all that *awful*. That's not, like, immoral or anything, do you think?"

I told her I didn't think being happy was ethically suspect.

CHAPTER 6

Her Americano has turned tepid; her fellow patrons are reduced to two, both of whom look as depressed as she is. Maybe she should go on Prozac, like everyone else in the Western world except sorority girls and fundamentalists.

What should she do? What can she do, except give in to the impulse she always has when confronted by a masculine adversary, which is to win him with her body, to give him what he wants. No. Not this time. This time, she will fight with other weapons.

But how? She has neither money nor power nor the courage to fake such armaments. She has no friends who are influential, no friends, in fact, who are not linked, through the network of artists and photographers that haunts the bistros of Fremont and the U District and Capitol Hill in search of means to underwrite its talent, to her tormentor. Plus, how can she fight him if she can't even find him? She has called his apartment a dozen times, and gone by half that number, to vent her spleen or commit a felony, but she still hasn't caught up to him.

She sips the dregs and makes a face. Maybe it's not as bad as she thinks. Her face isn't all that obvious, after all, and there are certainly enough diversions from that part of her anatomy. Maybe no one but Roan suspects it's her up on the wall at Erospace, and Roan can be bought off. Maybe someday she will smile at it in the carefree way the guy taking the seat across from her is smiling.

"Hi," he says. Entry-level hustle.

"Hi, yourself."

"Are you Nina Evans?"

"Maybe. Who are you?"

"My name is Chris."

"Chris what?"

"Chris is enough for now."

"Why the dodge? Are you famous or something?"

"Not significantly."

"That's rather coy. Should I have heard of you?"

"I have some notoriety in certain circles."

She shakes her head. "Notoriety is what I don't need at the moment."

She signals for another Americano, which gives her time to decide what she wants to do about this guy. He's cute, for one thing. And sophisticated, for another. And he looks prosperous. She has a use for all three attributes.

"I admire your work," he says gently, as though she is working now.

"What work is that?"

"The Drew show, for one."

"You saw that? How did you hear about it? Are you a pal of Gary's?"

He shakes his head. "I knew about the show because I've been following your progress for quite some time."

"Great."

"You're marvelous, you know."

She smiles. "I know. But thanks." In a burst of resolution, she decides this isn't the time or the place to submit to this stuff. "Look. I've got things to do. What can I do you for, Chris?"

"I'd like to discuss your coming to work for me."

"Doing what?"

"Doing what you do. I'm looking for a suitable subject for a project I'm planning, and I think you might be just the ticket."

"Suitable for what, exactly?"

"It would be much like the work you did for the Drew, but different in some ways, too."

The Drew had collected Gary Richter's best work and consequently hers as well. Black and white; figure only; abstract yet sensuous; classic yet postmodern. The reviews had been generous—Gary had parlayed them into half-a-dozen minor jobs.

"You're a photographer yourself?"

"Of a sort."

"This isn't for some sex book, is it? I don't do core. Hard or soft."

"I guarantee this is legitimate."

His eyes are so kind she is tempted to hear him out, but unfinished business remains with Gary. The Erospace images are still too vivid for her to want to work again, even with a person as unthreatening as this one.

"Not interested," she says. "Sorry."

He responds didactically, as if he is her academic adviser. "If you're selected as our subject, it will be the most profitable position you've ever held."

She is quickly tempted, but something about his archness puts her off. "Maybe some other time," she says.

He reaches into his pocket and hands her a card with some technobabble on it and a phone number and address on Western. "Call me if you change your mind. If I don't hear from you in two weeks, I'll go with someone else."

"Two weeks," she repeats, then looks at him, then looks at her watch to check the date.

¤   ¤   ¤

THE LAST EXIT ON BROOKLYN was no more déclassé than the Caffè Trieste or the Bohemian Cigar Store, the North Beach joints where Charley Sleet and I hung out, but it was bigger than either San Francisco establishment and served a wider variety of food and drink. The hand-lettered sign out front announced that the place had been founded in 1967 and that it claimed the title as the city's oldest coffeehouse. I wasn't in position to argue.

Coffee had assumed totemic proportions in Seattle, I'd read, so the variety of options on the menu was daunting—Doppio, Americano, Medici, Panna—but the beverage of choice was a latte, it seemed, so I ordered the cheapest version they had, which wasn't all that cheap. Then I looked around until I spotted a seat at a table against the west wall, beneath a mural that featured tropical birds and monkeys.

The seat turned out to be a picnic table that had been painted with green enamel by way of conversion to indoor use. It looked neither sanitary nor comfortable but it was the only unoccupied space in the place so I wedged myself onto the bench and took my first sip of a latte. Mostly what I tasted was warm milk beneath a skim of itchy foam—the object of Seattle's ardor had less in common with java than with baby formula.

As soon as I could without being obvious, I scoped out the crowd, which was mostly young though not exclusively so. In fact, the Last Exit seemed to be frequented by two distinct groups—college students and unreconstructed hippies. The older crowd wore ponytails if they were men and buzz cuts if they were women; the young ones were of opposite inclination. The old ones wore multicolored costumes that smacked of verve and celebration; the young ones wore threadbare flannels and perforated denims that smacked of enervation and depleted self-esteem. The old ones had age spots and sun blotches; the young ones had tattoos on every dermal surface including neck and scalp. The old ones had maybe a single earring, the young ones were pierced at every point that was pierceable—lip, nose, ear, eyebrow, and God only knew where else; I'd heard rumors they even pierced their scrota. I couldn't help wondering how those kids were going to feel about those indelible tattoos when they got to be my age. The perforated scrota would be less of a problem.

My waitress was so deferential I doubted she had a historic perspective on the place. When I told her I was fine with what I had, she seemed pleased that I had reached a state of grace rather than disappointed that she wasn't moving product. A month from now, she'd be pushing Doppios and puff pastry on anyone with the temerity to make do with drip.

The waiter busing the next table with a sullen indelicacy was sufficiently lethargic to peg him as a more productive source of information. When he drifted my way, I dared a generic question. "Hey," I said when I caught his eye. "How's it going?"

He swiped at my table with a sodden rag. The poster above his head read, AMERICANS BOUGHT 8 MILLION GUNS IN 1993—FEEL SAFER? "I'm adequate, man," he muttered. "You?"

"Same here. Seen Nina lately?" I continued, as if we'd shared the subject previously.

"Nina who?"

"Evans. Nice-looking. Artist type."

"They're all artists if they don't have a job. What do you want her for?"

"Got work she might be interested in."

"What kind of work?"

"Art work."

He inspected me more closely; I think he branded me a narc. "Don't know the lady, man. Don't know you, either."

"This isn't about trouble. This is about money."

He shrugged. "So maybe you could leave a note." He pointed toward a board on the wall by the door, a feathery collage of writings from personal messages to business announcements to handmade ads for everything from massage to music lessons. "Or run an ad in the *Salmon*," the waiter added with what sounded like sarcasm.

"Nina's brother works for the *Salmon*," I said, to show I knew more about her than a narc would. "Jeff. I talked to him about her but he blew me off—he and sister don't get along."

My fable made the waiter reassess. "*That* Nina," he said finally. "I was thinking of the other one."

"So do you know how I can reach that Nina?"

"She's got a crib in the place next door."

"Not anymore, she doesn't."

"Then I'm tapped. Come to think of it, she hasn't been in for a while."

"When you saw her last, who was she with?"

"You mean other than Richter?"

"Yeah. Other than Richter."

He thought about it. "Girl named Roan, sometimes. And some guy I've never seen before tried to hit on her a while back. They're the only ones I can think of."

"Where can I find Roan?"

"Hawking on the Ave."

"Hawking what?"

"Jewelry."

"How about Richter?"

"Gary? What about him?" The waiter had turned suspicious— I'd asked one question too many.

I took a chance at indirection. "He still in the old place?"

The gambit didn't work. "Far as I know," he said indifferently. "I heard he came into some bread, though. Movie money, or something."

Someone across the room yelled, "Hey, Lance. Order's up."

Lance pocketed the rag. "Catch you later, man."

By now I was attracting enough stares to know that my time in Brooklyn was up. I left a big enough tip to encourage my waitress to retain her family values, then strolled south toward what the natives apparently called the Ave.

The portion of University way south of 47th Street was Seattle's version of Telegraph Avenue, a tattered strip of record/pizza/ health/copy/computer/book/sports/ and Middle Eastern import stores that paralleled the campus one block removed from its western border. Like Telegraph, the street seemed to meet the needs of the students and, more precisely, those of the auxiliary community of intellectuals and idiots that leeches onto a college campus the way whorehouses leech onto an Army post. I strolled the Ave and took inventory.

The usual stew of commercial establishments was in evidence, spiced with the ubiquitous espresso carts. I saw more Asians than Caucasians, more skinheads than frat boys, and more women than men. I might have been back in the East Bay.

When I reached a string of sidewalk vendors huddled together for warmth, I asked the first one I came to if she knew where I could find a woman named Roan who sold jewelry. The woman was rail-thin and nappy-headed; her shirt was short-sleeved and diaphanous and she was trembling like a rabbit from the cold.

She pointed south. "Roan usually works the next block."

"Which side?"

"This one. Everyone likes sun but the candlemakers."

The sun she referred to was not in evidence. "What kind of jewelry does she sell?"

"Silver, mostly. Some pewter. She tried gold a while back but she's too wired to work it right."

"What's she look like?"

"Roan? She's tall. Taller than you, I bet." She seemed to regard it as a feminist achievement.

"Be hard to tell tall if she's sitting down," I pointed out.

Helpful in the way most of the natives seemed to be, she trolled for another detail. "She's got a silver nose ring," she said finally, as though it was an incidental accoutrement hardly worth mentioning.

I glanced at two girls strolling past. "So does half the town."

"She's got a tattoo of a bee on her tit, but you'll only see it if she likes you." Her grin turned mischievous and her lips stopped quivering; double entendre warmed her up. "When she got pregnant, the bee looked more like a B-52."

I laughed.

"Ask around. You'll find her if she's here. Roan's been on the Ave longer than anyone."

I thanked her for the information. As I started to leave, she reached for one of the objects on the walk beside her and raised it for inspection. "Need a wallet, mister? Calfskin; hand-tooled; triple fold. Makes a nice gift."

I told her I didn't know anyone who had anything to put in it.

Roan wasn't hard to spot. She was sitting cross-legged on a dingy blanket in the middle of the next block, her long legs barely leaving room on the blanket to display her wares, her long arms crossed for warmth on her chest. Her dress was dark and shapeless, a muslin drape long enough to cover everything but her toes. For ornament she was featuring earrings and finger rings and nose rings, with a necklace and bracelets as well. Similar jewelry was clustered near her on the blanket, as though she'd birthed a hundred silver children.

The designs were simple yet arresting, suggesting droplets of rain and pools of water. In Berkeley, the sidewalk stuff is mostly unremarkable—I suspect a family in Mexico makes it all and the local vendors sell it on consignment. Roan's output was a cut above, but a degree or two short of elegant.

I told her she had nice stuff. She thanked me. The woman selling dried flowers on the next blanket said something about the cop on the corner and Roan turned her way and laughed.

When she turned back, she said, "He gives us an hour, then rousts us. Fucking city attorney thinks we're a threat to civilization. We *are* civilization," she added bitterly, then asked if I was looking for anything special.

"I am, but you don't seem to have it," I said with what I hoped was a disarming smile.

"What's that?"

"Nina Evans."

Roan frowned and recrossed her arms. The wings of the bee peeked over the front of her bodice. "What do you want with Nina?" she asked with chilly reserve.

I repeated my earlier lie. "To talk about a job."

"What kind of job? Modeling?"

I nodded.

"Paint or photography?"

"Pardon me?"

"Are you a painter or a photographer?"

I took a stab. "Painter."

"Nina doesn't do paint."

"Yet," I bragged.

Roan squinted into the suddenly emergent sun. "Rhonda does paint." She pointed. "She has the pinecone candles across the street."

"I'll check her out later, maybe, but I hear Nina is special. I'm betting I can convince her to diversify."

Roan shook her head. "I doubt it."

"Do you know where I can find her? I can't seem to raise her at her place on Fifty-second."

"I think she moved."

"Do you know where?"

She shook her head with what looked like sadness and maybe a little irritation.

"Do you know anyone who might know where she is?"

"Only the asshole."

"Which asshole is that?"

"Gary Richter. Nina used to pose for him even though every-one told her he was shit with lips. She *saw* what happened to

Mandy, but she went ahead anyway. Well, she learned her lesson, didn't she?" The conclusion carried a trill of triumph.

"What happened to Mandy?"

"Gary stole her soul and did the same to Nina." Roan turned toward another customer, but my presence brought her back. "If you want to see how, take a look at Erospace."

"What's Erospace?"

"Gallery on Brooklyn. Across from the pharmacy."

"Thanks. Where can I find Mandy?"

"Somewhere near the doorstep to hell." She narrowed her eyes and lowered her voice. "You're not the guy who's been following her, are you?"

"Nina?" I shook my head. "What guy?"

"Old. Grungy. Smells. He's been hanging around her for months."

"I'm not him." I gave her my name and pulled out a motel card and presented it. "If you see Nina or the creep or Mandy, will you call me?"

Roan shrugged and stuck it in her purse. "You need any jewelry, mister? I'm on sale today—twenty percent off. Makes a nice gift for the special woman in your life."

I thought of Peggy and her man, and Betty and hers, and then I thought of Eleanor. Then I told Roan that at the moment I didn't have any women in my life who were old enough to wear it.

CHAPTER 7

After a week of searching she finally finds him. Finds him, then follows him, to see where he is getting the money for the car and the clothes and the equipment that have blossomed in his life. One evening in April, she trails him out of the Triangle Tavern, down to the edge of the lake, then east toward Gas Works Park. At the pace of a dawdler, he leads her to a secret lair.

The new place is as different from Gary's studio in Fremont as diamonds are from coal. It sits atop a brand-new building nestled between the Harbor Patrol and a shipyard full of rusting fish processors with names like Yardarm Knot and Dakar. The gleaming white structure is as incongruous in that neighborhood as is Gary's presence in it.

She returns three nights later. Because he is new to the job, the super lets her in, on the premise that she is Gary's latest model just off the plane from New York, a guise furthered by her lie about his sainted mother's heart condition and by the aged super's appreciation of a pretty face. As he lets her in the apartment and wishes her a pleasant stay, she stifles an exclamation at its opulence.

The place is fit for a playboy—sleek soft furnishings, exotically contoured lamps, gleaming sets of stemmed glasses, sumptuous oriental rugs, plus a view of the lake and the boats and the mountains and the vertical lights of downtown. All of which is the least of it. What he also has is a windowless room in the back where he does the work she has suspected him of.

The lab is crammed to the ceiling with stuff—when she flips on the light they seem to jump at her, the hulking beige machines, like animals too long in a cage surging toward a friendly face. There are computers and monitors and workstations and printers and enlargers and half-a-dozen devices she's never seen before, along with bottles of developers and toners and bleachers and fixers, stacks of variable contrast papers, and enough film to fill a refrigerator. It is as different from a conventional darkroom as Gary's encrusted kitchen is from this one, which is out of Martha Stewart.

She pokes around in a daze of wonder, looking for something inchoate. She avoids the machinery in favor of something she can understand, which is books, but they are either art books or computer manuals: she suspects the latter are the source of the images at Erospace, that they offer instruction in the black magic that taught Gary how to put innocence and art in one end and come out with obscenity and evil at the other, but she hasn't the time to decipher them.

She heads for the filing cabinets, which come in a rotary design that presents a series of trays that revolve in the manner of a Ferris wheel. She spins the cylinders, examining the labels as the drawers pass by. She is not surprised when she sees her name, nor when her tray contains copies of the Erospace prints as well as lesser libels of that ilk. When she finds nothing worse than what she has seen already, she is relieved.

Similarly, she is not surprised when she comes across a drawer marked Mandy. She expects more of the same within it, but when she examines the contents, she recoils. Finally she knows what has savaged Mandy's life, what has reduced her from debutante to stripteaser to junkie to probably worse by this time.

Poor Mandy.

Poor Jeff.

She leans against the wall for support, her legs liquid beneath her. She has projected Gary Richter as capable of anything, but she has not considered this. She is furious, then terrified. The aura of the room is foul, an ominous fluorescence of a force that is sick and insidious, of a world that is ruled without regard for dignity or compassion by men who see such concepts as territory vulnerable to conquest.

She is tempted for a moment to destroy as much as she can, but she fears the consequences. She fears Gary, she fears his machinery, she fears the men who paid for it, she fears she will wither unto death like Mandy.

She gathers up the worst of his wares, then escapes as quickly as she can.

¤　　　　¤　　　　¤

THE EROSPACE GALLERY was on Brooklyn Avenue, two blocks above Forty-fifth, between Top Video and the Weaving Works. A subtitle painted in bloodred calligraphy on the bottom of the window read, "A Gallery of the Sensual and Erotic Arts." When I shoved on the door it was locked; the fine print told me that was the norm for Mondays.

I was about to head back to the car when I saw movement in shadows at the rear of the gallery. I pressed my nose to the glass and squinted. A light flashed on behind a rear partition and a woman walked out of one room and into another towing a vacuum cleaner the way golfers tow carts. I knocked on the door a single time, then rapped more insistently when there was no response, my drumming implying that I was such an important personage I had a right to off-hours admission. All of a sudden a pretty but mistrustful girl was framed in the glass of the doorway.

She was young and blonde and as unsure of herself as she was of me. Her green hospital shirt was smeared with grease and grime and her denim cutoffs had various messages spelled out in pen and ink. The only one I could decipher without being lewd declared, "Kurt Lives."

She brushed at her bangs with the back of her hand. "We're not open," she said nervously, opening the door an inch to transmit a message that was already inscribed on it.

I adopted an officious tone and informed her that I was aware of that fact. "However, I was told that a woman named Evans would be in attendance today, regardless. A Nina Evans, to be precise."

"Sorry. I'm the only one here and I'll only be here twenty more minutes."

I became befuddled. "How odd." I tried to become more imperious but I was handicapped by my attire, which wasn't far removed in either cleanliness or cost from what the young woman was wearing. "May I know your name, young lady?"

"Why? Are you going to report me? I *need* this job, mister. No one's hiring except Burger King and I worked so long for McDonald's I still smell like a french fry." She sniffed as if to prove the point.

"I'm sure a report to your superior won't be necessary. I merely wish to address you more appropriately."

"I'm Sharon."

"Well, Sharon, I'm afraid I have a problem. I'm from out of town. I got in late last night, did some business downtown early this morning, and I have to catch a plane for Miami in three hours. I very much want to see the exhibition before I leave, and I was assured that Ms. Evans would be available to show it to me, an erstwhile docent, if you will, even though it is not the usual hour. But you say she is not on the premises."

Sharon shook her head agreeably. "I'm definitely the only one around."

"Then we'll have to improvise, won't we?"

She frowned. "I don't play an instrument or anything, if that's what you mean. I do karaoke sometimes. When I've smoked enough bud."

"I wasn't making a musical reference, although I'm sure you are a charming songstress, I was merely trying to decide how to proceed for the benefit of all concerned. You see, based on what I've heard about the exhibit, I have come prepared to make a significant purchase. Perhaps you know of my interest in this area. In my home in Miami I have one of the finest collections of twentieth-century erotica in the southeastern United States."

Sharon shook her head. "Sorry. I don't know that much about erotica. I guess I don't get it. I mean, my boyfriend keeps bringing home X-rated videos, but they don't light me up."

"I believe erotica is primarily a masculine enterprise, although anthologies of women's erotic literature have come to market with success in recent years, so perhaps I'm mistaken. One never knows what women will enthuse over these days, does one?" I looked at my watch. "Under the circumstances, it seems sensible for me to wait inside. That way, I can examine the exhibit and make my selections so I'll be ready to negotiate price when I get back to Miami."

Sharon was dubious. "I don't know. They told me to keep the door locked."

"Surely you don't fear any sort of mayhem on my part. I'll keep out of your way and let you do your work." I reached for my wallet. "I'll pay twenty dollars for your trouble. How's that?"

"I don't know," she said again. "Maybe I should call Fran."

"And Fran is . . . ?"

"The manager. She's the one that hired me."

"Ah. Well, you're certainly free to call the estimable Fran if you like, but there's really no need to bother her, is there?" I looked at my watch again. "Tell you what. If Ms. Evans isn't here by the time you finish your work, I'll leave a note where she can reach me in Miami and a list of the works I'm prepared to dicker over, then I'll be on my way. How's that?"

"Well . . ."

"If I leave without seeing the exhibit, the gallery will be out a sizable sum. You don't want that burden on your shoulders, do you, my dear?"

"No. I sure don't."

"Well, then."

She yielded, of course. The nice ones always do because the nice ones are taught from an early age that it's more important to be nice than prudent, and that sort of upbringing keeps them in trouble the rest of their lives.

I entered the gallery and turned on the lights and wandered the exhibition armed with ersatz expertise. I was looking for a way to get access to the personnel records, to see if they contained a reference to Nina Evans as Roan had implied they would, but Sharon needed some time to get used to me. So I made like the collector I was pretending to be and perused the stuff that Erospace was passing off as art.

The exhibit was titled "Politics or Pornography?: An Exploration of the Frontiers of Free Speech." It was quickly apparent that the frontiers in question were exclusively sexual—the art was explicitly lusty if not literally pornographic. In a variety of mediums—painting, sculpture, photography, and video—an attempt had been made to suggest that politics and sex were not polar opposites but rather a joint venture that had as its object the elevation and enlightenment of its audience. The problem was, most of the work on display undermined rather than augmented the thesis.

The major portion of the art was awful—blatant, humorless, clichéd, and that most deadly of deficiencies: boring. I was examining a photograph of a particularly buxom woman with a tattoo of Newt Gingrich on one of her breasts and Ross Perot on the other when the photo next to it caught my eye.

It was the first of a series, black and white, matted but not framed, of a naked woman in various positions of subjugation, accompanied by instruments of violence and sedition. For the moment, the pictures were less interesting than the name of their creator: Gary Richter, the man both Roan and Lance had spoken of so disparagingly, which seemed to indicate that Nina was not an employee of the gallery as I'd assumed, but was the model for the photos on display under Gary Richter's byline.

A biography of the artist was posted next to the pictures. Richter had been born and raised in Seattle and had been introduced to photography while working on the student newspaper at Lakeside School. After a brief stint as a photojournalist at *Salmon Says* and then the *Seattle Post-Intelligencer*, he had become a professional arts photographer, with shows in galleries from Seattle to L.A. to Austin. Richter was thirty-two, his primary artistic interests were the interplay of sex and politics, and the photos on exhibit were part of a larger body of work exploring the historical symbiosis between the female form and political propaganda.

There was a picture of Richter attached to the bio—he was thin and gangly, weak-chinned and petulant, with an overweening arrogance that was at least as off-putting as it was calculated to be. I was hoping to get an address for him from the bio as well, but all it said was that he worked out of a studio in Fremont, wherever that was. The name of the model wasn't mentioned either, which was understandable, but I was certain I knew who it was even though her face wasn't clearly displayed in a single picture.

I examined the photos as closely as I could, to see if there was a way to identify her for certain. Posed in a variety of positions, some slack and degenerate, others stark and aggressive, the model's matchless figure was rendered scandalous by her accessories. In one, a flag rose out of her upraised buttocks as she crouched at the foot of a helmeted soldier in a parody of Suribachi. In another, her bright white flesh had been defiled with black swastikas and other supremacist slogans. In a third, she performed fellatio on a chrome-plated semiautomatic pistol that usurped the place of the penis on the headless man before whom she knelt in rapture. In yet another, the model's legs were raised and spread and at the vortex an all-too-realistic combat knife seemed buried to the hilt in her vagina.

It was repulsive, certainly, and not particularly thought-provoking unless you think the "Piss-Christ" that raised such a flap with the NEA is thought-provoking. But the technical aspects of the prints seemed adept, and the model, well, the model was as flawless an example of the genre as I had ever seen. When I transposed the face of Nina Evans from the snapshot in my pocket onto the shoulders of the woman in the photographs, the result was both breathtaking and bewildering. No wonder Daddy liked to dress her up and take her out to dinner. And no wonder the people who loved her were worried about her.

Suddenly, Sharon was at my side. "It's noon," she said quietly. "I don't think she's coming."

I looked at my watch. "I think you're right." I pointed. "What can you tell me about these pictures?"

She resisted inspection of the object of my inquiry. "Not much, I guess."

"Do you know the photographer? Mr. Richter?"

"Only what it says up there."

"Where's this Fremont place where he has his studio?"

"It's over by the Ship Canal."

"Which is?"

"That way." She pointed in a direction I thought was west. "Take Fiftieth across the freeway and under Aurora, then turn left on Fremont Avenue North. Fremont is just before you cross the drawbridge."

I thanked her for the information. "How about the model? Do you know who she is?"

She shook her head.

"She's never come to the gallery to see herself on exhibition?"

She shrugged. "I'm not here during normal hours."

I gave her an avuncular pat. "Do they keep a file on the artists they exhibit? They must," I concluded before she answered.

"I don't know anything about it if they do; I'm just a maid, mister. And I've got to go. My boyfriend and me are going to the Two Eleven to shoot pool."

"I'll just have a quick peek in the office before we leave. I'm prepared to buy the entire set of Richter photographs if I'm satisfied that he's a serious artist as reflected by his past work and current price structure."

She cast her eyes in a nervous search for aid. "I can't let you go poking around and stuff."

"Sure you can."

"No, I can't. They told me not to go *in* there."

"You don't have to."

She shook her head. "It's not right. That's private."

"I have a right to know what I'm buying, do I not?"

"They're all right there." She pointed at the pictures with delicacy. "Seems to me you should know if you like them or not without snooping in any files. I mean, they're good or they aren't, right? And you're an expert so you should know. Right?"

"You don't understand collecting at all," I said with a spray of condescension. But of course she understood it perfectly.

CHAPTER 8

She is so used to doing business in lofts and hovels she is convinced she has misread the card, that she is in the wrong part of town and that he will laugh when she reveals her mistake. Then she fears she is being tricked, that his purposes are perverted and sick. It is silly, probably, but not as silly as it used to be, given what she has learned about Gary.

The building is an expensively restored brick structure that bears the name The Luckness Building, a block from the waterfront in an area of shipping warehouses and chandlery offices that have been converted to more modern uses. She checks the directory and finds him quickly—Chris Wellington, third floor. There is no title; no job description; no clue. She looks at other entries; the rest of the offices are all rented by DigiArt.

The outer office contains a reception desk, a potted plant, a chair, a painting, and a love seat. All are fresh and functional, and entirely uninspired. A computer on the desk emits light and white noise but there is no one tending it. There is music in the air—Dire Straits. The room feels ominously empty, abandoned in the throes of disaster—she thinks briefly of the end of the world, and sighs. At this point, that might come as a relief.

She sits, then stands, then sits, then walks to the desk and looks down. The monitor displays a screen saver with flying toasters. There is no book or paper in sight. There is no photo of family or *souvenir of the vacation in the San Juans. There is just a sign that says,* PRESS # FOR INNER OFFICE INTERFACE. *She does so.*

A second later, Chris emerges from behind an inner door. He is wearing Levi's and a white shirt with a banded collar. He is so crisp and clean and cheerful she is reminded of a cleric just off the plane from seminary. She bets herself that he's Catholic. Still.

"You found me," he begins.

"Not where I expected, however."

"What did you expect?"

"One of those dives down by Cyclops and the Millionair Club."

"I spent quite a bit of time in that neighborhood, as a matter of fact."

"Doing what?"

"Struggling."

She looks around. "Looks like your struggles are over."

"Not really," he says. "They've just changed their names. Why don't you come inside?"

He leads her to the inner sanctum, which makes the reception area seem chummy by comparison. It is so stuffed with electronics she immediately thinks of Gary's lab and experiences a flutter of foreboding. There is much of the same stuff here—computers and monitors and their cohorts stacked on shelves, on tables, on boxes, on the floor, on each other. But there are differences as well—a large glass rectangle of indeterminate purpose is suspended from the ceiling like a stiff black banner, half-a-dozen video cameras are perched atop tripods like vultures waiting for news of carrion, other cameras of all models and makes peer out from nooks and crannies like young marsupials. The monitors glow with different images, the printers spit out paper that snakes across the room— there is so much to see that nothing registers.

When she spies a chair she collapses into its innards, making it her cocoon. "What is this place?" she asks nervously.

"This is my studio."

"What do you do in it?"

"I make digital art."

"You must be good at it."

"I am."

"Where do I fit in, exactly?"

He sits on a stool across from her. "We're looking for a figure model. If you're the one we select, you'll be required to sign a personal services contract with DigiArt and be on call at all hours, to work when and how requested, to be available at a moment's notice. We will provide room and board and transportation and off-duty entertainment as well. Neither the nature of your work nor your whereabouts may be disclosed to anyone during the course of the project. It will be not unlike joining the Army and being assigned to Special Forces."

"You're kidding."

"Not a bit."

"You'll get me a new place?"

"Right."

"Where?"

"We'll let you know."

"Why the secrecy?"

"Because nothing like this has ever been done before."

"Nothing like what?"

He smiles. "We'll let you know."

"Remind me again of my fee."

"Five thousand dollars."

"A month."

"A month."

"For how many months?"

"That depends on several things, including how well you do the job. A salary for six months is guaranteed."

"When do I have to decide whether I want to do it?"

"After we decide we want you."

She leans back in the chair and exults. It is an answer to her prayers, she realizes, an expense-paid refuge from the fallout from the show at Erospace, from the odd old man who has been stalking her, and from the newly potent aura that emanates from Gary Richter.

She twists his way and smiles and offers a look at her legs.

¤   ¤   ¤

SEATTLE IS DIVIDED into neighborhoods, I discovered, each with its own name, boundary, commercial core, and socioeconomic stamp. Fremont was hippies, the girl in the gallery had told me with surprising distaste. Since it was the nineties, not the sixties, I assumed she was exaggerating, but when I got to Fremont I changed my mind. It was North Beach after the war and before the Chinese, with a little less of Little Italy and a little more of Pittsburgh.

The hallmarks were a drawbridge over what looked to be more a canal than a river, a life-sized sculpture of some commuters waiting in line for a bus, and a coffeehouse that called itself Still Life in Fremont. Of the available options, the coffeehouse seemed the best bet, which caused me to wonder whether my entire investigation would take place within arm's length of an espresso machine.

I stood in line for coffee and a muffin, eyeing the art on the walls, wondering why so many places make you stand in line for food. When I got to the register I asked the woman if she knew a photographer named Richter. She said she didn't. I asked if anyone else might know. She pointed to a woman carrying some dirty dishes toward the kitchen. "Glenda knows everyone. She's been here, like, forever."

"How long is that?"

She shrugged. "A year, maybe."

Forever ought to do it. I took my coffee and muffin to the table Glenda had just bused and waited for her to come back. When she did, I waved her over and asked how she was doing.

"Same old same old," she said without much interest in me or her state of mind. "What can I get you?"

"Gary Richter."

"What?"

"I'm looking for Gary Richter. Seen him around?"

Her face darkened. "Yeah, I seen him. I see him again I'll kick his balls up to his throat."

"Why?"

"He treats people like shit. Especially women. Especially women who work for him."

"Models, you mean."

Glenda glanced at a woman sitting at a table across the room, staring into her coffee as though it had spawned some new life forms. "I got to chop lettuce. Take it easy."

"You, too."

After Glenda walked behind the counter and disappeared into the kitchen, I walked over to the woman doing a treatise on the contents of her cup. "I hear you used to work with Richter," I said casually.

She looked up. "So what?"

"I'm looking for models myself."

She measured me up and down. "You don't look much like an artist."

"What's an artist supposed to look like?"

"For one thing, he's not likely to be wearing wing tips."

I smiled. "Maybe I'm a society photographer."

"And maybe I'm Cindy Crawford. Get lost, mister. It's not cool to hit on women this time of day."

"It's also not cool to be so morose."

"In Seattle it is."

"You're too smart to buy into that."

"How would you know how smart I am?"

I pointed at her Jane Hamilton novel.

She managed a grudging smile. "So what is this, an outreach or something? Are you some sort of street preacher?"

"I'm just trying to find Gary Richter."

"I suppose it's too much to hope you're a hit man. Or a cop," she added as she looked at me more closely.

"Why should a cop be interested in Richter?"

"Because he's an insult to every woman who ever lived."

"Insults aren't illegal."

"Richter's should be."

"I keep hearing he's a jerk, but no one gets very specific."

"Specifically, he tried to get me to peddle my ass to some rich guys in Bellevue. And that's all I've got to say on the subject."

"If you tell me where can I find him, I'll get out of your hair."

She pointed. "Studio's on Thirty-fifth, just past the brewery."

"What brewery is that?"

"Redhook. You must be from out of town," she added when she saw my blank look.

"I am."

"Where?"

"San Francisco."

"Yeah? I spent a year there one weekend. Grateful Dead in the park, ate something gooey they were passing around and woke up naked in the back of a van that was parked way too close to the airport. Only one with me was a fifteen-year-old kid who looked like Mick Jagger and swore he hadn't fucked me. I'm glad I don't know what went on that night," she added after another look inside her cup.

"Maybe that's what got you interested in modeling."

"What got me interested in modeling was hunger. Why am I *telling* you this?" she demanded rhetorically.

I knew better than to answer the question. "What's the address on Thirty-fifth?"

"Just look for the bathtubs. He's number eight upstairs."

"Thanks. What's your name, by the way?"

"Fiona."

"Fiona what?"

"Fiona bored."

She returned to whatever she saw in her cup. I thanked her for her time and took a stroll.

Thirty-fifth Street took me five blocks west of where I was parked, down by the brewery and its satellite, the Trolleyman Pub. Beyond the brewery were some offices and a warehouse for Pet Foods. Across from the warehouse was a concrete structure that was sufficiently funky it had to be a warren of artists. Next to the building was an art gallery. Next to the gallery were the bathtubs.

There were two of them, stuck vertically into the ground so they looked like concave shields, or a set of urinals, or tympana, or something else of indeterminate significance. What they seemed to be were gateposts bestride the entrance to an open space that sported a menagerie of stone and metal sculpture that had most likely been crafted in the studios that surrounded the lot.

The apartments combined both studios and residences. The exteriors were decorated according to the style of their occupants—some with abstract sculpture in the windows, others with chiseled mounds of stone and glass out front, several with elaborately colored door panels, some emblazoned with somber aphorisms in the manner of Jenny Holtzer, such as the one that read, LIFE MUST IMITATE ART, WHY ELSE WOULD I BE BENT OUT OF SHAPE?

Number 8 was upstairs. Its only decoration was an eight-by-ten glossy taped to the door at eye level, a reproduction of Marilyn Monroe's nude calendar photo. When I knocked on the door, nothing happened.

The windows of both Richter's studio and the adjacent apartment were covered with black plastic. The street and sidewalks were empty; nothing was moving but clouds and a yacht down the distant canal. There being no reason not to pry, I did so, with the aid of a credit card and some muscle.

When I closed the door behind me I created something close to absolute darkness. As I flipped on the light to erase it, I inhaled a bouquet of scents that was a mix of sweaty socks and stale beer and something far more toxic that probably had to do with photo chemicals. When my eyes adjusted to the light, I got a surprise.

Gary Richter was living in his studio, all right—the far end of the room was an atoll of clothing heaped around a lumpy futon and decorated with chunks of coral that turned out to be terminal sneakers and empty beer cans. But the mess at that end of the room had been created by the artist; the mess in the work space was otherwise: Richter's space had been tossed, by person or persons unknown. I listened for sounds of interest from outside and when I didn't hear any I got down to business.

The desk was a former card table, legs folded under, that rested on a pair of flimsy file cabinets whose contents had been scattered around the room like dozens of manila playing cards. The top of the desk was cluttered with bills and receipts and the similar effluvia of life, but any semblance of order had been shattered. Containers of pencils and paper clips and stamps had been dumped into the mix as well, but robbery hadn't been the motive since at least five dollars' worth of quarters was in evidence in a ceramic cup, presumably destined for parking or the laundry.

The only thing that jumped out at me from the jumble on the desk was a brochure from something called the Photo Academy. Its list of classes ranged from Basic Black and White to something called Cibachrome Masking. Richter appeared on the list of instructors opposite two courses—Form and Figure and Advanced Light Control. The bio under the heading Featured Photographers didn't tell me anything I didn't know already.

I noted the address of the school in my notebook, then pawed through what had formerly been the contents of the file cabinets.

Mostly they were folders containing his stock-in-trade—photographs of nude women in a variety of poses from the artful to the erotic—covering the entire spectrum of propriety. I guessed that sort of schizophrenia was common to the business, the way poets writing porn is not unknown to literature. But the purpose of the intruder hadn't been to collect modern art—there were easily a hundred photos in view that had slipped from their folders as they'd been tossed aside as unimportant. Some were quite good to my uncultured eye, better than a lot of the stuff I saw on the occasions when I perused copies of *Modern Photography* on the shelf of the local library. But the intruder hadn't been interested. The reason was probably significant.

I leafed through the pictures and the file folders with care, but there was no clue to the purposes of the thief, just an overabundance of flesh. Some of the pictures were familiar—I'd seen several of the models on the wall at Erospace next to the names of other photographers, and I'd seen one of the models a few minutes earlier at the Still Life in Fremont Café. And some of the pictures weren't nudes at all, but rather formal portraits of dozens of clean-cut young people of what I guessed was high school age—I couldn't figure that one at all. When I looked for pictures of Nina Evans, I couldn't find any.

The only other files contained business correspondence and expense and income data. I looked through them without knowing what I was looking for, noting Richter's communications with magazines from *Stud* to *Mirabella* and with outlets from Erospace to something called the Craig Butera Gallery. He spent a lot of money on equipment and he earned a decent living from the sale of his work as evidenced by copies of his tax return. His business income on the 1993 Schedule C was $27,452. Good, but not great—Gary must still be on the hustle, and no doubt sending stuff to *Hustler*.

I made a search for an address book or Rolodex, but didn't find either. What I did find was a file full of releases signed by his models that allowed Richter to do with their images what he would, apparently without restriction—I shuddered to think why anyone would sign such a thing. I made note of the models' names, then returned the releases to their folder.

I looked through the closet and chest of drawers and kitchen cabinetry as well, but there was nothing in any of them that wasn't expected and nothing from the saucepans to the boxer briefs that couldn't have used a good washing. There were some oddities among the ruins—a jar of Vaseline I assumed was a sexual lubricant until I remembered that photographers sometimes smear jelly on their lenses; a variety of development chemicals but no enlarger, which indicated his darkroom was elsewhere; a host of lighting devices; and a nest of filmy lingerie heaped in a cardboard box, ready for the next assignment from *Swank*.

And two last items. One was a thirty-eight police special that was stuck inside a pillow next to the futon. When I sniffed I didn't detect the fumes of recent discharge, but that didn't mean it hadn't happened. The other item was a stone, small and flat and pointed, lying on the floor by the door. I didn't realize what it was until I picked it up—an arrowhead, jagged and sharp and lethal. When I put it in my pocket, I experienced a detectable pang of wrongdoing.

My final stop was the west wall, where Richter had hung his harem—a dozen photographs, wrapped in plasticine, arranged in a rectangle, stuck to the wall with pushpins. Each was of a naked woman, and each woman faced the camera in a formal pose that was made ludicrous by her facial contortions. The women mugged, they sneered, they looked cross-eyed, they looked like fish and squirrels—Richter seemed to have a sense of humor. But what was more noticeable than what was tacked to the wall was what was missing. There was a hole in the comic collection, a void in the upper-right quadrant: one of the models had been edited out; I was certain it was Nina.

CHAPTER 9

"So what do we do now?" she asks.

"I videotape you, then interview you."

"Interview? What kind of interview?"

"Something to see what kind of person you are and what kind of mind you have."

"What is this, Miss America or something? What difference does it make what kind of mind I have? I'm here because of my body and we both know it."

"The mind-body distinction is passé; we believe that spirit and flesh are one and that in the right hands the camera reveals both the inner and outer selves. We want both to be unexceptionable."

She is tempted to dispute him, to declare that her mind and body travel separate paths that often result in painful collisions, but she opts not to because she is not sure how much of herself she wants to reveal to him. So she shrugs. "What do I do now?"

"Go stand by that wall."

She plucks at her T-shirt. "Off or on?"

"On, for the moment. We'll do dressed first, then nude. Nothing fancy—just basic position and movement. We're only interested in infrastructure at this point."

"You saw my infrastructure at the Drew exhibit."

"I did; he didn't."

"Mr. Big? The guy who's behind all this?"

"Mr. Big. Right. Now, if you'll sign this release, we'll get right to it."

Again, she thinks of Gary. "I don't like releases."
"And we don't like lawsuits."

¤   ¤   ¤

IF GARY RICHTER didn't already know his place had been tossed, he would certainly know it the minute he set foot in the door and if he had any sense, he'd go to ground until he found out what the invasion was about. I was out of my element—Seattle's streets and alleys were as foreign to me as London's, while a guy with as many enemies as Richter would know them all—so the chances of running him down weren't good. I went out the door, made sure it locked itself, then took six steps to my left and knocked at the adjoining apartment.

The man who answered was wearing shorts and an eye patch and looked as if he had been out in the yard playing with mud. When I remembered the conglomeration in the next lot, I guessed he had been throwing a pot.

"What?" he demanded with the egoism common to most great artists and too many lesser talents.

"I'm looking for the guy next door. Gary Richter," I added when he didn't say anything. "Know where he is?"

He blinked his single eye. "No idea."

"Know where he has his darkroom?"

"No idea."

"Do you know the whereabouts of a woman named Nina Evans? She's a model who was working with him."

He lifted the patch and massaged the drumhead of skin that stretched across the socket. "No idea."

I smiled at his attempt to disgust me. "I wonder if you happen to know who trashed his place."

A brow soared like a tern lifting off a log. "His place is trashed?"

"Yep."

"Good." He grasped the door and began to close it. "Does that take care of it?"

"Not nearly," I told him, then flipped my adopted card into the depths of his studio before he could close the door in my face.

When I got back to my car I cast about for other leads; the only one I came up with was the Photo Academy.

The offices were in the shade of the monorail track near the corner of Fifth and Denny. As I walked down the block a train passed overhead, smooth and silent and untroubled by the sludge of street traffic. It seemed like a good deal; I wondered why no one was riding it.

Fittingly enough, the school had a photo gallery in front with offices behind a counter in the rear and classrooms up and down a set of metal stairs that were attached to the back wall. While I waited for the woman at the counter to finish telling a man about the policy on refunds in case he decided not to continue the course, I browsed through the exhibit in the gallery.

In contrast to Erospace, the offerings were pretty tame. The title of the show was "Seattle Scenes," and most of the photos depicted the out-of-doors: mountains and trees and streams; tugboats and houseboats and ferries; gardens and markets and malls. In contrast to the colorful landscapes, a series of black-and-white shots caught my eye from across the room.

Even here, Gary Richter was an iconoclast. His subject was a stripper; in each snapshot she was in a different state of dishabille, wearing an expression of weary wantonness. The marquee above a shot of her reporting for work in her street clothes read, THE BLITZ CLUB. In the third picture of the series, the lady was naked except for her high heels and was tickling herself with a boa. Her mons was shaved and the bulb of naked flesh was tattooed with a garland of leaves and flowers. What will they think of next?

When the woman had finished her spiel, I approached with an

impromptu scheme. "Are you here for the fall schedule?" she asked when I reached the counter.

I shook my head. "I'm here for some help."

She looked disappointed. "I'm not an instructor, I'm afraid. The staff won't be in till evening."

My sheepish expression was only partially fraudulent. "I got married a few weeks ago. Second time."

"Congratulations. I'm getting married in December myself."

"Hey. Great. I hope you'll be as happy as I am."

"Thanks. So how can I help you?"

"It's kind of awkward. Maybe even weird. What I want is a really nice portrait of my wife. Not portrait, exactly, but study. You know." I blushed and fidgeted.

"Study?"

"Figure study. You know. Nude. Maybe a series: front, back, and side. Triptych. Is that what they call it when there's three? She's so damned beautiful, I want to . . . well, you know."

Her look made it questionable that anyone betrothed to me would do justice to a camera lens. "I'm still not sure how I can help you. You want to learn how to do it, is that it?"

I shook my head. "I want to hire someone. A pro. But I don't know who to send her to. I don't want some sleazeball, obviously, or an amateur just in it for kicks. I want someone serious and professional and not too expensive, who'll do a nice job and get everything out of Edna she's got to give. She's shy. I mean, she wants to do it and everything, but she's nervous. She's Lutheran," I added, as if that would explain everything.

"Maybe a female photographer would be best. We've got several wonderful women on staff, I'd be happy to—"

"I asked Edna about that. She said she preferred a man. A woman would make her even more nervous, she says."

"Why?"

"She says a woman would be too critical, that a man would

understand what we were trying to do and not pass judgment on . . . anyway, someone told her about a guy named Richter. They said he was good and they gave me the number of his studio but I haven't been able to reach him. I figured he'd probably moved and when I saw his name on your brochure, I figured you could tell me how to get in touch with him."

"Gary Richter. Yes. He's one of our instructors. But I'm not sure I can—"

"I'm prepared to pay full rate if he and Edna decide to give it a go. If he's teaching here he must need the money."

She bristled. "Our instructors are highly successful photographers. They teach in order to give something back to the profession and to encourage others to pursue a career that they themselves have found fulfilling."

"I didn't mean he was a loser, I just—"

"Are you still obsessing on Richter?"

The voice was low and resonant and issued from a woman who had come into the gallery without my noticing. I'd seen her two hours earlier, in the café in Fremont, taking stock of her cup and her life.

"Hi," I said.

"Hi."

"Fiona, right?"

"Right."

She had gotten spiffy in the interim—black tights with a red silk shirt over the top, an oversized shirt with black dots all over it. Her complexion was dark, possibly Middle Eastern; her hair was wound on the top of her head in a way that showed off an elegant neck and finely chiseled ears. Her legs were long and thin and straight, the base of a dancer or model.

I grinned. "You're the one it was too early to hit on."

"Yeah. I was rude, wasn't I?"

"I'm used to rude. I hardly notice anymore."

"Well, I apologize. I'd just lost an Eddie Bauer shoot I was up for, and I was pissed. I guess I took it out on you."

I opted to maintain my charade. "Then you can help me find Richter? To do the nudes of my wife?"

"If you're really who you say you are, which I doubt, you don't want him."

"Why not?"

"Gary Richter is a carnivore," she said, with at least as much savagery as the words implied.

"What do you mean, carnivore?"

"I mean he preys on women. He uses his skills as bait, and lures them into a professional relationship, then maneuvers them into a position of need and subservience. He devours them, he chews them up and spits them out, he treats them like raw meat when he's not treating them like garbage." She gathered breath for one last lambast. "Gary's a control freak, a sadist, a misogynist, and a liar. He's the last person on earth you should find for your wife."

A phone rang at the close of the diatribe and the woman behind the desk broke off her thrall and went to answer it, reluctant to forgo the next installment of the assassination of Gary Richter.

I looked at the woman in the red shirt. "Have you got a few minutes?"

"Why? I've told you all you need to know about the man. There are plenty of other photographers who—"

I lowered my voice. "I'm not looking for a photographer; I'm looking for Nina Evans."

She frowned. "But you said—"

"I'm a private detective. The things I say are only true in context. I'd like to buy you a cup of coffee and discuss Mr. Richter in more detail."

She glanced at a clock on the wall. "I'm the model for the five o'clock class, so I . . . hell. Sandy was late last week, and she always lectures them for twenty minutes while I sit on my stool freezing my ass off. There's a café around the corner. The legendary Five Point."

"I'm afraid I'm not up on the local legends; I've only been in town twenty-four hours."

"Where from? Wait. I remember. San Francisco."

"Right. Where you got hijacked by a Dead Head that looked like Mick Jagger."

She reddened and grabbed my arm and led me around the corner to the Five Point. Along the way we met Kitsap the Indian, in the form of a bronze statue of him with his hand extended toward the first ship that sailed into Puget Sound, in the year 1792.

The Five Point housed a bar to the left and a restaurant to the right. The banner in the window declared it was Seattle's oldest family-owned restaurant—Seattle people liked to commemorate themselves. The pictures on the walls were of luminaries posed next to Kitsap, who didn't seem pleased with his groupies.

We sat at the counter and ordered. The Indian behind the cash register was wooden, not bronze, but he didn't look any happier than Kitsap—I had a feeling I was about to be scalped. When I looked at the TV for diversion, what I saw was a laundromat. They take their soap operas literally, apparently.

"The coffee's not great," Fiona said when the waitress left. "But I'm sick of Starbucks' overroasted shit. So you're looking for Nina Evans," she segued smoothly.

I nodded. "Know her?"

"Some. Mostly I know her stuff. She worked with Gary, too, which means we're in the same club. Sort of like Holocaust survivors."

"So you weren't friends."

"With Nina? No chance. She kept to herself, pretty much, plus I did fashion and cheesecake and trade shows so I wasn't a serious artist as far as she was concerned." The words were clipped and sardonic.

"Tell me more about Richter."

She shrugged. "A hustler with talent. Lethal combination."

"Do you know where he does his darkroom work?"

She shook her head. "He used to have a place out by Shilshole but he had to give it up."

"Why?"

"Couldn't afford it. But I heard he came into some money. Someone saw him driving a Porsche."

"Black?"

"Red. Why? You don't look like a Porsche man."

"What does a Porsche man look like?"

She glanced out at Kitsap. "Like him only with lots of gold chains."

"Was Richter involved with the porn industry?"

"He sells to them, if that's what you mean. The magazines, at least."

"Is that mob activity in this part of the country?"

"No one ever talks about it that way. Not to me, at least. Of course I'm not a candidate for that market anymore."

"Why not?"

She glanced down. "They like thirty-eight triple Ds. Minimum." She looked up. "You look like you expected a more philosophical answer."

"Not really."

"Hey. If I had the tools, I'd use them. Men like naked women. If all they do is look, I've got no problem with it."

"And if looking makes them do something else?"

"Like what? Beat off?"

"I was thinking of sexual assault."

"There's been no proof of a connection despite what redneck preachers and Andrea Dworkin want you to believe."

I didn't know if she was right or wrong; I doubt if she did, either. In the Information Age, truth tends to get lost. "You implied Richter wanted you to prostitute yourself," I said.

"Yeah, well, I was exaggerating a little."

"There must have been something."

"All he wanted me to do was go to some parties."

"What kind of parties?"

"Parties with guys who like to hang out with pretty women. I told him right off I wasn't interested."

"Did he try to get all his models to these parties?"

"Probably, but I don't know for sure. The girls didn't talk much. Attractive women tend not to like each other."

I didn't know if she was right about that, either. "If someone was after Richter, who do you figure it would be?"

"Most likely a model or one of their boyfriends. Gary hits on women the way birds peck at seeds—it's genetic. He only teaches at the academy so he can recruit students to pose for him. But if he's in trouble and it's not something like that, I don't know. Could be the mob, I guess, if he stiffed them or something. Of course anyone who dealt with Gary for five minutes despised him, so it's a long list."

"You don't know of a specific grudge?"

She shook her head and her brow furrowed. "What's happened to him? He's not dead or anything, is he?"

"Not that I know of. Why?"

"He owes me money on my last shoot. I'd hate to think someone got to him before he paid off."

I thought of the mess in Richter's studio. "What's with the pictures of young kids I saw in his place?"

"School pictures. Gary's the photographer for the best private schools in town—Lakeside, Bush, Carlile. He gets a pretty penny to make the rich kids look glamorous, which is why he keeps his T&A work under wraps."

"Is his stuff valuable? His art photographs?"

She shrugged. "He always has good drugs; he gives his models nice presents in the initial stages of the hustle. So yeah, his stuff is worth something. Some of the shots he took of me are in SAM, and some are in Magnolia and Laurelhurst, too."

"SAM?"

"Seattle Art Museum. Magnolia and Laurelhurst are two of the upper-crust neighborhoods in town."

"Do you know where Richter might be if he isn't in his studio?"

"Sponging off his girlfriend, maybe."

"Who's she?"

"Don't know."

"How about the stripper?"

"Who? Oh. The exhibit. That's Mandy."

"Who's she?"

"She worked for Gary for a while. When they broke up, she took it hard."

"Where does she live?"

"No idea, but the last time I saw her, she looked like she wouldn't live long."

"Drugs?"

Her eyes flattened. "Everything."

"Is the Blitz Club a strip joint?"

"Never been in the place, but that's what the ads say."

"Did Nina ever do Blitz type of work?"

Fiona shook her head. "Nina was serious about modeling. It wasn't just a job for her; she really thought it was art."

"Was it?"

She started to say something cynical, then seemed to change her mind. "Once in a while it was. Even with Gary, once in a while it had something to say. Once it a while it seemed important."

CHAPTER 10

When she is dressed, she experiences an unaccustomed dread as she waits for Chris to repack the camera in its case.

"So how'd I do?" she asks, knowing from the alacrity with which he had moved her through balletic positions and gymnastic movements that he had been as captivated by her lines and energies as Gary had been.

In the middle of the shoot, when she had decided that she really needed the job, she had begun to assert herself. Swimming in the air and light, casting strange new shadows on the backdrop, she had cast a spell with the aid of only effort. His eyes were enameled with awe as they ducked behind the camera and nestled against the viewfinder, which followed wherever she led it.

"You did fine," Chris replies with studied nonchalance. "Excellent, in fact."

"Good. So what now?"

"I ask you some questions."

"Is the question bit really necessary? I thought if the shoot went well enough I wouldn't have to, you know, be treated like a game show contestant."

His smile is insufferably paternal. "Why are you trying to hide from us, Nina?"

"Don't be silly."

"Then why are you resistant to the interview?"

"Because it's not what I do; it's not who I am; it's irrelevant."

"Not to us."

"What's with this us? All I see is you. Who makes you us?"

"I told you, I can't discuss that."

"What if I won't go ahead till I know?"

"Then we'll find someone less inquisitive."

"Okay, okay. Will you tell me some day, at least? Before the thing is over?"

"I'll ask him. That's all I can say. The nature of his involvement is entirely up to him—he does what he wants when he wants to do it and what he wants is usually unpredictable."

She makes a prediction anyway. What he will want is me, she whispers, though only to herself.

¤ ¤ ¤

I WENT BACK TO THE MOTEL to reconnoiter and take a nap. When I got to my room the message light was blinking. I assumed it was a call from Peggy, but the desk clerk told me that a package had been delivered for me about an hour ago and I could pick it up in the office at my convenience.

The package turned out to be a manila envelope with my name written on the front in the thick black strokes of a Magic Marker. The slant and script were familiar, but I waited until I was back in my room to make sure.

There were two items in the envelope. One was a note from Peggy: "I need to see you; something upsetting has happened. Please come to the house at nine. Wait for Ted to leave with the dog, then walk down the drive and knock at the door to the sunroom. *Please.* P.S. This is the paper Jeff writes for—his column is on page 12. See you tonight."

The other item in the envelope was an issue of *Salmon Says*, dated the previous Monday. I took it out and paged through it.

The *Salmon* was typical of its genre. Iconoclastic and raunchy, it was filled with weird comic strips and primitive cartoons, irreverent reviews of bands and books and movies, and ads for places like Funk You funky threads, Skin Art Tats—by which I assumed they meant tattoos—and Positive Affinities, a dating service for people who were HIV positive. There were lots of ads for fare in the local clubs and a letters section full of rants about everything from the attributes of Generation X to the corruption of the Seat- tle scene by the money spread around by big record labels. The personals section featured the usual Girls Seeking Boys and vari- ations thereon, but what was new to me was a rather jarring sec- tion called Other Options, in which sadists and masochists sought others of their stripe and heterosexual couples looked for a third participant in their wanton activities. I wondered if the ads were for real and decided they probably were.

Jeff Evans's column was entitled "Taboo" and it began with a confession: "I've never successfully beat off. That is, I've never pounded the pud with sufficient skill to come all over my sheets or my jeans or whatever. Never, that is, until I talked to Paul. Paul is the Mozart of Masturbation. Paul could get the Pope turned on to self-abuse (if he isn't already). Beating his meat to a fare- thee-well is Paul's life's work—he is the best there is at what he does. He is the King of Come, the Oracle of Onanism."

Jeff went on to describe a variety of techniques, most involving mundane appliances available at something called the QFC. Sat- isfaction was guaranteed or Paul would come to your house to instruct you himself with proven hands-on methods. By the time I neared the end of the piece I was laughing. But then I stopped.

A portion that was clearly serious came in the final graph. After wrapping up his ode to autoeroticism, Jeff stuck on an addendum: "And as always, Mandy, I love and want to help you. Please call when you can. None of this has to happen." With that, Jeff Evans signed his name, in a singular, splashy stroke.

I put the note and the *Salmon* back in the envelope and lay down on the bed to rest. The room was a clone of all such rooms, barren of charm and lacking in stimulus, predictive of only perdition. You are confronted with too many aspects of yourself in rooms like this. There are too many mirrors, there is too much time, there is too little in the way of diversion, there is too much that is alien and too little that is friendly. It takes a better man than me to find solace in such an environment; the only antidotes are sleep or defection. I closed my eyes and opted for the former.

I hadn't gathered enough information to learn where Nina Evans was hiding herself or perhaps was being hid, so I didn't have enough ingredients for deduction. But thanks to the photos I'd seen at Erospace and in Gary Richter's studio, I had plenty of stimulus for the more carnal creases of my brain. Not long after I lay down, I reached the suspended state of inhibition that lies between slumber and wakefulness and found myself in the middle of an erotic entanglement that was a candidate for the walls of Erospace itself.

Usually I welcome such dreams at any time in any guise, since they make up a significant percentage of my sex life, but it was five in the afternoon and I was fully dressed, so it was probably fortunate that a door banged shut down the hall and roused me in time to prevent me from making a mess of the sort that Jeff Evans had written a column about.

I got up, took a cold shower, got dressed again, paged through a copy of the *Seattle Weekly* that I'd picked up down at the desk, and decided on a place to eat. The place turned out to be on the edge of Pioneer Square, a refurbished part of town down by the bay and the Kingdome that was populated by what passes for chic in every reclaimed Old Town in every city that has one—art galleries, bookstores, dance clubs, and Italian eateries. The restaurant was called La Buca and it was more than adequate and even interesting, given its cavernous atmosphere, exuberant wait staff, and well-made risotto and house red.

I spent most of the meal thinking about Peggy. Not that I

believed there was any place to go with our relationship, not that I hoped to undermine her engagement; just that I needed to be sure she was truly gone and to know that the place she'd ended up was at least a safe haven. Plus, she'd asked me to drop by, so that's what I would do. I asked the maître d' how to get there and was on my way before weighing the advisability of the foray for even an instant.

As instructed, I timed my arrival for nine. By the time I neared her neighborhood I was light-headed with anxiety and sweaty with anticipation. I wanted to see this guy, this Ted, the guy she was going to marry, the guy she'd linked with when she'd known she could have come back to me with no questions asked and no demands beyond proximity. I wanted to see him and take his measure and tell myself he wasn't my equal in any respect that mattered. I wanted it to be crystal clear that Peggy was making a mistake she would regret for the rest of her life, which would make her an eternal match with me.

I wanted more than I deserved.

The neighborhood was called Capitol Hill and its main street was Broadway, a commercial strip inhabited by elaborately garbed gays and extensively pierced punkers and a healthy supply of mind-altered transients. Peggy lived on the north end, on Thirteenth Avenue East between Aloha and Prospect near an open space called Volunteer Park.

The street was quiet and self-possessed. The house was large and well landscaped, its mock classical design featuring high white columns supporting a double-decked porch, glistening white doors, and large leaded windows beneath a cornice and an architrave and similar motifs from the past. It was a handsome and mature and reliable structure, much like its owner, I suspected; everything that I was not. I parked far enough down the block to remain incognito and waited for Ted and the dog. He appeared at nine sharp, as his fiancée had predicted.

The dog was an unprepossessing black Lab. His owner was tall and fit and clean-shaven, with thinning gray hair and an aquiline nose and a glint in his eyes indicative of purpose and commitment but not a whit of humor. His stride was brisk, his posture martial, his clothes—cords and sport shirt and windbreaker—casual but crisp, as if they'd never known a spot of sweat or suffered to the extent of a wrinkle. The man looked on the outing as a forced march and the dog was tugged back on track the minute he wandered toward shrubbery. The dog abandoned his ambitions sooner than he should have.

He was wrapped pretty tight, this Evans guy, tighter than I would have guessed for a good match with the Peggy Nettleton who had worked for me. But there are times when security and sobriety and dependability look a whole lot better than their opposites, and those times become frequent as your years sneak up on fifty. When Ted and his dog disappeared in the direction of the park, I got out of the car and stretched.

The house seemed even larger than before, the neighborhood even more elegant. Somewhere in the distance, the dog barked and was chastised. A car passed me at a crawl—a Mercedes the size of Michigan. I got back in the car and closed the door.

Peggy had asked me to come see her, and I wanted to do her bidding, but right at that moment I couldn't. Although part of me wanted to examine the fine lines of her life to see if they had anything in common with the one she had lived before, much more of me couldn't bring myself to confront such a contrast to my station. What did I have that could eclipse the endowments of a guy like Ted? Why did I think Peggy was the kind of woman who could be on the brink of a vow to cherish him unto death, then run off with the first idiot who offered an option? What could I promise that she hadn't already turned down?

When I got back to the motel, I called her office and left an apology on her voice mail. The voice mail didn't seem mollified.

"If we're going to do it, let's do it," she asserts with more bravado than she possesses.

"Let's start with the basics. Where were you born?"

"West Seattle."

"How old are you?"

"Twenty-four."

"Brothers or sisters?"

"Brother; twenty-two."

"What does he do?"

"He's a . . . journalist."

"You seemed to hesitate."

"I almost made a snide remark but I changed my mind."

"You and your brother don't get along?"

"No."

"Why not?"

"Ask him."

"I'm asking you."

"He thinks I'm spoiled and egotistic. I think he's sadistic and unfeeling."

"What does he think of your work?"

"I doubt that he's ever seen it."

"How about your parents?"

"What about them?"

"Are they alive?"

"In the biological sense."

"You seem to have a lot of hostility toward your family, Ms. Evans."

"That's what families are for, aren't they? If you don't know that, you don't watch enough daytime TV."

"What problems has your family caused you?"

"Mommy and Daddy divorced when I was twelve. I spent the next three years living in the garage and smoking as much pot as I could find, which was quite a bit in those days. What else do you need to know?"

"How are those relationships now?"

"With my parents? What difference does it make?"

"Please answer the question."

"My mom and I get along as long as we don't talk about where I've been or where I'm going. My father and I got along until he brought some mother superior home for dinner and she took it as an invitation to move in."

"That sounds a little Freudian."

"It's a lot Freudian. Which makes me part of a noble tradition of daughters who've been screwed by their daddies."

"You don't mean literally, I hope."

"What difference does it make? Figuratively hurts just as much."

¤   ¤   ¤

AS A CONSEQUENCE of my amative turmoil, I slept late: when I opened my eyes it was 9 A.M. Maybe it was the neutral surroundings, far removed from the city where I had collected animosities the way others collect painted plates. Or maybe it was because my relationship with Peggy had reached some sort of closure—she had gone to another man and was content with her choice; I was just here to cement her future. Or maybe the glimmer I'd gotten of Ted Evans's oddly intimate involvement with his daughter allowed me to wonder if Peggy's newfound love was flawed and I still had a chance with her. Whatever the reason, I'd slept the sleep of the sweet and didn't regain my faculties until I'd downed three pancakes and four cups of coffee in the restaurant that adjoined the motel.

The first item on my agenda was to talk with Nina's mother, to see if her daughter had been in touch of late, but my plans got changed in a hurry. When I got back from breakfast, two men were waiting in my room.

One was tall and slim and detached, one short and stocky and self-absorbed. The tall one had wispy brown hair that flew haphazardly about his head and a scar at the crest of an eyebrow. The short one had a pelt of black hair that was cut to the nub and a bit of a lisp when he talked. The tall one was Gary Cooper; the short one was Bob Hoskins. The tall one looked only at me; the short one was quickly seduced by his reflections in the motel mirrors.

"One of us has the wrong room," I said to get it started.

"Are you Tanner?" the short one asked, as gruff as a nurse at a physical.

"Sure am. You must be the limo service."

"Never mind who we are. What we want to know is who the fuck are you and what are you doing in Seattle?"

"I'm in a bit of a hurry. If you've got a questionnaire, I'll fill it out later."

The tall one pulled out a leather wallet and flipped it to reveal a shield. "I'm Detective Molson; that's Detective Nudge. Seattle P.D. This is an official call."

"Glad to hear it." I looked at the open door. "I'd like to report a breaking and entering."

"Who are you, Tanner?" Nudge demanded heavily. "Besides a guy with bad taste and a smart mouth?"

"That about covers it."

"I mean what the fuck are you doing nosing around in Gary Richter's business?"

"I was in the market for a passport photo."

Nudge's already dark face turned almost black and the muscles in his arms seemed to double in size. "Passport, my ass. Answer the fucking question."

When I spoke I spoke to Molson. "My name is John Marshall Tanner. I'm a licensed private investigator from San Francisco. I'm here on business."

"Yeah?" Nudge grumbled as Molson made no move toward comment. "What kind of business?"

"I'm looking for someone."

"Who?"

"I won't tell you that, but I will tell you it's not Gary Richter."

Nudge started to say something else but Molson held up a hand that stopped him. "We've been in two places in the last twelve hours—one last night and one this morning. The minute we start asking about Richter, we hear you beat us to it. We'd like to know why."

I opted for modified limited candor. "I thought he might know the whereabouts of the person I'm looking for."

"Did he?"

"I don't know; I never caught up to him. If you find him first, tell him I'd still like to talk to him."

My request didn't make a dent. "What's the connection between Richter and the guy you're after?"

I answered Molson's question with a question. "What's happened to Richter?"

"What makes you think something happened to him?"

"Because all of a sudden this has the smell of a homicide."

Nudge got back in the game. "Yeah? What kind of smell is that?"

I smiled. "Your cologne doesn't come close to covering it up." I looked at Molson. "Is Richter dead?"

The tall man made do with a brief nod. "They found him late last night."

"Where?"

"That's confidential at this point. Where were you between eight and midnight?"

I looked around the room, then remembered the mission to Capitol Hill. "Nowhere I can prove."

Nudge barely muffled a chortle. "Let's take him down to the building, Hal. Show him the facilities. Get some tips on interrogation techniques from the big bad boy from Frisco."

Molson didn't even look at him. "You the one who tossed Richter's place?" he asked me.

I shook my head. "It was that way when I got there."

"But you got inside?"

"No comment."

"Take anything?"

"I know better than that." The stone in my pocket was a sharply chiseled lie.

"Got any idea what they were looking for? Or who might have wanted rid of him?"

I had at least three ideas; two of them were named Evans and one was about to be. "I wasn't looking for Richter except as a lead," I said instead. "I've only been here a day and a half and I never laid eyes on the guy. If he was in the kind of fix that could get him killed, I didn't know what it was."

Nudge was crafting yet another pedestrian curse when the telephone rang. I looked at the cops. When they didn't do anything to stop me, I picked it up.

"Marsh? It's Peggy."

"Hi."

"Where were you last night?"

"I got tied up. I left a message at your office."

"I thought I saw your car."

"Must have been someone else."

"Oh. Well, I still need to see you."

"Good. Me, too."

"Can we meet for lunch?"

"I think so. Where?"

"There's a . . . you sound funny. Are you all right?"

"Fine and dandy."

"Are you sure?"

"Yep."

"I . . . Is there someone with you?"

"Yep."

"Oh. Is it . . . are you in trouble?"

"Not at the moment."

"Is it the police? Are you being questioned about something?"

"Yep."

"Oh no. Has something happened to Nina? If it has, you have to tell me."

"Nothing like that. Not that I know of."

"Thank God. Well. I guess we should wait till later to talk. Are you sure you can make lunch?"

"I'm not sure but I'll try."

"There's a Greek restaurant at University and Forty-seventh. Costas. I'll meet you there at twelve-thirty."

"Okay."

She paused. "If you don't show, shall I assume you've been arrested?"

"It's probably a good idea."

"I'll get a lawyer to stand by. Don't do anything dumb on my account. Please, Marsh?"

I told her I wouldn't and hung up. Molson was smiling when I looked at him.

"Client?"

"Friend."

"Sounded female."

"Was female."

"You move fast in a day and a half."

"Friend from the old days."

Molson nodded. "They're the best kind."

"Let's take him down to Third Avenue, Hal," Nudge said again in the midst of the sociology. "He's dancing us around, making us look like jerks."

Molson kept his eyes on mine. "You've got no privilege in this state," he said to me.

"Not in any state, that I know of."

"I could get you in front of a grand jury and give you immunity and make you talk or do time for contempt."

"Yeah, but it would take you a month to do it."

He shook his head once. "I've done it in less than a week. In the meantime, we could jam you up pretty good."

"No question."

"But we still wouldn't have what we want."

"Nope."

"So why don't we make it easy on both of us?"

I smiled. "I'm listening."

"How long you been a PI?"

"Fifteen years."

"You must know some guys on the force down there."

"My best friend is Detective Lieutenant Charles Sleet. You can reach him at the Central Station, but have him call you back, don't let them put you on hold."

"Why not?"

"He doesn't spend much time at his desk."

"He'll vouch for you? This Sleet?"

"He will if he knows it's serious. If he doesn't, he'll claim I'm a louse and a deadbeat."

"Why would he do that?"

"We play cards. I usually owe him money. I usually also owe him a favor. Sometimes I don't pay debts in a timely fashion."

Molson thought it over while Nudge seethed and glowered when he wasn't preening and flexing at the mirror, doing amazing things with his neck.

"Here's the deal," Molson said finally. "If you check out with Frisco, we'll leave you be unless you're in deeper than it looks. In return, two things. One, you come across anything about who might have had it in for Richter, you give it to us."

I nodded. "What's number two?"

"You tell me, right now, without names, what kind of job you're on."

I decided I owed him that much. "I'm looking for a woman who's on the run from her family. No evidence of foul play, probably a runaway, but they want her back. Or at least to know where she is and that she's all right."

"And the connection with Richter?"

"You look around in his place?"

He nodded. "Nice stuff, Some of it. Some of it not so nice."

"The woman I'm looking for used to pose for him."

"Shit," Nudge swore. "Woman'd do that's nothing but a whore. Folks ought to leave her be—good riddance to bad rubbish." He looked at his partner and pleaded. "Let's take him down, Hal. Come on. He's a major asshole."

Molson's smile was as lazy as Louisiana. "That's okay, Burt. So are we."

CHAPTER 12

"Is that it?"

"No. Now we get into abstractions."

"Like what?"

"Like, first of all, why do you do what you do?"

"You mean for a living or in general?"

"For a living."

"You're serious, I suppose."

"You may be assured that everything I do is serious."

"You need to lighten up, you know that?"

"I lighten up on my own time, not Mr. Lattimore's."

"Whoops."

"As you say."

"Don't worry, I won't tell anyone."

"Thank you."

"So who is this Lattimore guy? The name's familiar, but I don't—"

"You have no need for that information at this time. And you should certainly not take anything I've said to suggest that Mr. Lattimore has anything whatsoever to do with—"

"Computers, right? He's that computer guy."

"As I said, you have no reason to suppose Mr. Lattimore has anything to do with why we're here. Now. What is your answer? Why do you do what you do?"

"I do what I do because I like it. And respect it. And because I'm goddamned good at it."

"Have you ever posed for sex magazines?"

"No."

"Ever been a stripper or a prostitute?"

"No. Not that I think there's anything immoral about those activities. Not that I wouldn't do them if that's what it took to eat, for example. Or to buy ballet tickets."

"Have you ever had sex for money?"

"Not unless Caesar salad has become coin of the realm."

"You take off your clothes for a living. Your business is allowing people to make images of your body and sell them."

"That's one way to put it. A Puritan way, for example."

"You don't regard such conduct as immoral?"

"I regard it as exquisite."

"You don't find it embarrassing?"

"I found it embarrassing for ten seconds the first time I got naked in front of a Leica. After I heard the shutter start clicking, I wasn't nervous, I was ecstatic. And then I got on with the job."

"And what is the job, exactly?"

"To give the guy behind the camera what he wants. No. To give the guy behind the camera more than he wants. My job is to make him better than he is, sort of like I did with you twenty minutes ago."

"How do you mean, better?"

"Someone like you starts a shoot with a vision. A theme. Something you're trying to say with light and color and line and shadow. By the time you're done, if you're working with me, that is, you realize that your vision was far too narrow, your theme too mundane, your goal too unexceptional. I take you places you've never been; I make it impossible for you to be ordinary; I submit to the process more completely than anyone you've ever worked with. I become your equal as an artist, and together we create things that have never existed before."

"Really?"

"Really. Of course the ultimate beneficiary is the consumer of the product. Hear that, Mr. Lattimore?"

"Please don't make further mention of that name. Who is that consumer likely to be, by the way? What audience do you want to see your work? Who do you want to own it?"

"It doesn't matter."

"Surely that's not true. Surely you want people of intelligence and sophistication to—"

"Anyone can appreciate what I do. Anyone can be excited by it, awed by it, changed by it. As far as ownership goes, they don't own me. No one owns me. They just own what I did, what I was, what I wanted to be on such and such a date and time and instant. The moment the camera is put away, that date and time are history. The next time I'm someone else."

"So you're never really you when you're working?"

"I'm always *really* me. But I'm never really me for longer than one five-hundredth of a second."

¤　　　¤　　　¤

ON THE WAY TO LUNCH, I drove past Richter's apartment to see if there was any police activity I could kibitz with, but if there was anything official happening I couldn't see it from the street. I did see the guy who had squealed on me, though. He was sweeping the veranda in front of his place and looking as furtive as a peeping Tom. When he saw me watching from the curb, he dropped his broom and scurried inside, doubtlessly to cry wolf again.

Peggy was waiting at the restaurant when I got there. She wore a dark blue suit and an expression that was barely tamed. Her eyes were too bulbous, her hands too flighty—I hadn't seen her that apprehensive since the creep down the hall was toying with her over the telephone.

The restaurant's attire was far less kinetic—posters of Greece and cans of olive oil. "You weren't arrested, were you?" Peggy asked as I sat across the table from her.

"Nope, thanks to a decent cop named Molson. If his partner'd had his way, I'd be lying my guts out in an interrogation room."

"Lying about what? Why are they after you?"

The waitress floated over as I was about to ease my way into an answer. Peggy ordered the Greek salad and a cappuccino. I ordered a gyro sandwich and plain coffee.

"Do you know how Nina is earning her living these days?" I asked when the waitress was back in the kitchen.

Peggy hesitated. "I'm not sure."

"She's a model. She poses for photographs. Nude photographs."

Peggy closed her eyes. "Are you saying she's some sort of porn queen?"

"No," I said quickly. "I haven't seen any sign of that at this point, although I'll need to check it out if she doesn't turn up. What Nina was about was art. Her friends say she was serious about it."

Peggy shrugged to show her unconcern. "Nina was a nude model. So what? It's not illegal, is it? What does that have to do with the police coming to question you? And how did they know who you were in the first place?"

"Nina was doing some work with a photographer named Gary Richter. Ever hear of him?"

Peggy shook her head.

"This Richter guy was legitimate—showed stuff in good galleries, taught at a photography school, even made a living at it. He wasn't sleaze, at least not entirely."

"But what does he have to do with the police?"

I waited till a customer moved out of earshot. "Gary Richter was found dead last night. Murdered, apparently."

"My God." Peggy's hand flew to her mouth and her eyes exploded like popcorn. "What made the police think *you* knew anything about it?"

"I went looking for Richter yesterday, as a way to get a line on Nina. I talked to his next-door neighbor and I talked to the people at the photography school and I left the motel card with them so they could let me know if Richter showed up. The cops talked to the same people after the body was found. They wanted to know why I was hunting for the guy, naturally enough, and thanks to the cards they knew where to go for the answers."

Peggy leaned toward me and grasped my hand. "What did you tell them?"

I met her look with difficulty. "I told them I was looking for a missing person and I thought Richter might have some information I could use."

Peggy released my hand and slumped back in her chair. "So you told them about us." Her voice was as flat as the table; the pronoun she employed didn't encompass me.

I was irritated by her reaction, all the more so because of the little arrowhead that was smoldering in my trouser pocket. Most people who demand secrecy are guilty of something or know someone who is, which made me wonder what Peggy was hiding. Then I wondered why I didn't pack my bags and go home and leave the lovebirds to enjoy this particular premarital adventure on their own.

"I didn't tell them about you, Peggy," I said, more harshly than I planned to. "I didn't give them any names, not yours or Ted's or Nina's. But I had to give them something—there's no privilege for PIs, not unless attorney work product is involved, which it isn't in this case. You know all this from when you worked for me. Going to jail for contempt didn't seem the best way to go in this situation."

I looked at her until she looked back. She fumbled with her napkin and used it to dab her eyes. "I'm sorry, Marsh. I didn't mean you hadn't been . . . I didn't mean you should have gone to jail for me. It's just that Ted will be upset when he hears about this."

"You keep saying that, so I guess it must be true. But maybe being upset is something he'll have to live with."

She shook her head. "If he finds out you've gotten us involved in a *murder* case, I don't know what he—"

"Come on, Peggy," I interrupted roughly. "Cut me some slack here. *I* didn't get you involved in this; *Nina* got you involved in this."

Peggy folded her hands and bowed her head with contrition. "I know. I know. I'm sorry, I just—"

"It doesn't matter, anyway. The cops will get to Ted without my help—lots of people know Nina was modeling for Richter, plus her prints will be all over his apartment since that's where he did his work. If she was like everyone else I've talked to, she didn't like the guy much. There's enough motive around for getting rid of Gary Richter to keep the cops busy for months unless they come up with some physical evidence. Sooner or later, they'll work their way to Nina, and when they can't find her they'll come to Ted."

"Maybe they *will* find her. Maybe they'll take care of the problem for us."

"Maybe," I said. "And maybe the problem will get worse, the way it does in most murder cases."

"How?" she asked abstractedly, then leaned forward again. "You don't think Nina was *involved* in this, surely. I mean, she's high-strung, and willful, but she's not crazy. Or violent. She has no need to be—she handles men quite easily in my observation. If she wanted something from this Richter person, she could have gotten it without resorting to murder."

I backed away from her gaze. "I broke into Richter's apartment. His place had been searched. I can't be sure, but it looked to me like one of the reasons for the search was to remove all traces of Nina—pictures, contracts, letters, whatever. There's all kinds of stuff about his other models there, but not a scrap about Nina."

Peggy looked like a bird poised to fly around its cage till it found an exit, or die from exhaustion if it didn't. "There are all kinds of explanations for that. It doesn't mean Nina went there and . . . oh my God."

She was so distraught I was afraid she was going to swoon. "Surely he wouldn't . . ."

"What? Talk to me, Peggy."

In response to my question she leaned over and picked her purse off the adjacent chair and set it on the table in front of her. The purse was the size of a suitcase. She opened it slowly, then put her hand inside, as though fishing for a clog in a drain. After a moment of fumbling, she extracted a manila envelope and put it on the table in front of her. Her face was a stew of emotion—fear, bravado, shame, and candor.

"What's this?"

She took a breath and let it out. "I didn't tell the truth before. About not knowing what Nina did for a living." She paused and closed her eyes. "I feel like I did when we were in that park and I was trying to lure that awful man out of the bushes so you could—"

"Don't think about it," I interrupted harshly. "That's over. He's long gone. It has nothing to do with this."

"It has something to do with me, Marsh. With what kind of person I am. With not being able to keep myself from getting involved with men who . . ."

She lost the strength to continue and the pending indictment evaporated. "Men who what?" I didn't like myself for asking the question.

Her eyes were damp and fractured. "I haven't known Ted very long," she said, her voice scratchy and unstable. "I only moved in with him last Christmas. It's been . . . difficult, in some ways. I haven't lived with a man for twenty years. I haven't had to decide whether I want to marry someone for even longer. I mean, you and I never got to that point before . . . well, let's just say that what with Nina's disappearance, and with seeing you again, I got anxious and confused and I did something I'm not proud of."

"What?"

"I got nosy."

"How do you mean?"

"I decided I needed to know Ted better. To see if he had any secrets; to learn if he was hiding anything from me."

"To see if anything weird was going on between him and his daughter."

She blinked and sighed. "All right. Maybe that was part of it. So yesterday I started poking around. It's a big house. We have a maid. There are places I've hardly been in yet. Like the guest room. Like his study."

"So you decided to explore." I tried to take the edge off. "It's not a felony, I don't think. Maybe a misdemeanor."

"It's worse than that. It's betrayal."

"Nonsense, you were just cleaning house. What kind of treasure did you find?"

She gestured toward the envelope, then touched it with the tip of her finger and slid it toward me. "I found those."

I debated what to do without wanting to do anything. "Does this have anything to do with why I'm here? Because if it doesn't, I don't think I—"

She shoved the envelope another inch. I picked it up and extracted its contents.

"Shit."

I took a second look, turned them over to see if anything was on the back, then put them back in the envelope.

They were photographs, of course, formal nudes of Nina Evans posed not in the studied exploitation of the shots at Erospace but in artful explorations of the expressive potential of the female form. They were, I guessed, something that Nina was proud of.

"Where did you get these?" I asked.

"Ted's file cabinet. Bottom drawer. Underneath some business stuff."

"Where did they come from, do you know?"

Peggy shook her head. I looked at the envelope for evidence of mailing, but it was blank. "Richter's name is stamped on the back of the pictures," I said.

"I know." Peggy bowed in despair. "What do they mean, Marsh?"

"I don't know," I lied.

I didn't know, but I had a hunch. It was possible that Nina had sent the pictures to her father, as evidence of her life and work, but a more likely explanation was less benign—that Ted had learned of his daughter's work with Richter and had gone to his studio, demanded that he surrender the prints and negatives of Nina, and killed Richter in a rage when he refused to hand them over, then removed the pictures from the scene to eliminate her as a suspect. The best proof of the theory was the piece of pointed stone in my pocket.

"How would Ted have reacted to these?" I asked.

"That depends."

"On what?"

"On where they came from. If Nina gave them to him, he would have been overjoyed. But if he came on them himself, in a gallery or a magazine of some sort, he'd be incensed."

"Why? They're clearly art under most definitions of the term."

"Ted wouldn't see it that way. He'd see them as smut unless Nina told him they weren't."

"Why?" I asked again.

"Because he idolizes her. He wants to protect her from the evil in the world. He wouldn't see Richter as an artist, he'd see him as a pimp taking advantage of his daughter. Plus, he'd see her behavior as casting aspersions on him as a father, as proof that he hadn't done a good job. Ted doesn't like to be criticized. He doesn't like being considered a failure."

When I considered the eventualities, none of them were pleasant. "These pictures could be evidence, Peggy."

"I know."

"I'd better keep them." I put them in my briefcase, knowing how foolish I was being but unable to be otherwise. "If the cops ever ask you about them, deny you saw them. If it comes down to it, I can claim I searched your house and found them myself."

"But how can you claim you—?"

"We'll worry about that when the time comes. I need to talk to Ted."

"Why?"

"You know why. The pictures suggest he might have been the one who tossed Richter's place. If he did, he probably left traces. He could be in big trouble."

Her cheeks flamed red and her hands made fists. "I worked for you for nine years. Don't you think I *know* that? I knew that the minute you told me that this Richter person was dead."

At that moment, a woman swept to the table from out of nowhere and grabbed Peggy by the arm. "Peggy, darling. How *are* you?"

"I'm fine, Clarissa."

"You don't look fine, you look exhausted. First thing to do after you and Ted get married is quit that silly job. It's not as if you'll need the money, after all."

"I'll think about it. Thank you for your concern."

Clarissa was not so easily dismissed. "Missed you at the club Tuesday night. Marsha was saying the two of you had been to the most divine new restaurant in Madrona. I can't *wait* to go. Maybe you and Ted could join us this weekend?"

"Maybe. I'll have to check."

At this point, the woman looked at me, wriggled her nose, then paused to make room for an introduction. When one wasn't forthcoming, she frowned, then patted Peggy on the arm, then gave her a second chance to make amends, then bid her a brisk good-bye and swept across the room to rejoin her luncheon companion. When I looked back at Peggy, she was crying.

"What's wrong?"

"You know what's wrong. I have to go back to work and pretend that nothing's happened, then go home and make a cocktail for a man who might be a murderer instead of the thoughtful and generous man I'm planning to marry in a month."

"What do you want me to do?"

"I don't know. Keep looking for Nina, I guess. But promise me one thing."

"What?"

"That you won't leave Seattle until this is cleared up. That you won't make me wonder if—"

I grabbed her hand. "All the planes that Boeing's ever built couldn't fly me away."

"Promise?"

"Promise."

She lifted my hand and kissed it, somewhere near the ring finger.

CHAPTER 13

"Nina?"

"Huh? Who's this?"

"This is Chris. Congratulations."

"Huh? What time is it?"

"Nine A.M."

"It better not be. Congratulations for what?"

"You won."

"Won what?"

"You're the one we selected."

"Is this some sort of game show? Have I died and come back as Vanna White?"

"This is Chris Wellington. What's the matter? You sound drugged or something."

"I'm not drugged, I'm tired. This was my night of the week to sleep and you fucked me up in the middle of it. The video guy, right?"

"Right. I'm calling to tell you that you've been selected as the primary model for the DigiArt project."

"I feel more like I'm part of a sleep-deprivation experiment. So I won, huh? What'd I win?"

"A place in our digital art program. You'll be part of a historic advance in the visual arts." He pauses for breath. "We need to talk about it. In the meantime, you go on payroll as of eight o'clock this morning."

"You better not be jacking me around about this."

"I'm not. Can we get together this afternoon?"

"My place or yours?"

"Mine. The DigiArt offices. Three o'clock. In the meantime, I suggest you start packing."

"What?"

"Pack your stuff. We're going to move you to a condo in Madison Park. We want you installed in your new quarters by tomorrow night."

"Oh. Right. The new pad. This is still top secret, right?"

"Absolutely."

"Does DigiArt have anything to do with Gary Richter?"

"No."

"Good."

"You'll be ready to move tomorrow?"

"Ready and willing. I just have to drop off some stuff with a friend of mine first."

¤   ¤   ¤

THE OFFICES OF *SALMON SAYS* occupied an unremarkable brick building on Northlake Avenue opposite something called Ivar's Salmon House and Fish Bar, just west of the I-5 overpass. The door to the office said ENTER.

Three desks; two tables; four computers; six file cabinets. Alternative cartoons on the walls, grunge guitars in the air, psychedelic lighting overhead thanks to multicolored strips of neon stuck haphazardly to the ceiling in a pattern reminiscent of pickup sticks. Stacks of old newspapers; piles of empty Coke cases; jumbles of books and magazines with names like *The Stranger* and *The Rocket*. And no people. Not a single soul as far as I could tell, even though the door stood wide open.

I knocked on the only unoccupied surface I could find. Still no people. I looked in the Day-Glo yellow john. Still none. If I hadn't been an honest man, I could have made off with five thousand bucks' worth of electronics.

I was starting to think something in the nature of a neutron bomb had occurred in the past hour when a young man came through the door in a hurry. He wore cutoff khakis, black high-top tennis shoes sans socks, and a T-shirt that read Seattle Rain Festival—October through June. His hair was gathered in a pony-tail; his left nostril sported a silver loop; his wrist was wrapped with a black leather band and a watch the size of a silver dollar.

He looked at me and I looked at him. "I don't suppose you're Jeff Evans," I said.

"Sorry." He looked around. "You the only one here?"

"As far as I know."

"Please tell me you broke in."

I looked at the open door. "Sorry."

"Jesus." He looked at his watch. "Latte time. We're lucky we still have the furniture. I'm Brian Lux, by the way."

"Marsh Tanner."

"What do you want with Jeff?"

"Just talk."

"You a friend?"

"Of the family."

He thought about it, then shrugged. "Good luck."

"When I called, someone said they thought he'd be in around ten."

"That's as good a number as any."

He went to a desk and sat down. I asked if he was a reporter.

"The masthead says I'm the publisher."

"Does that mean you own the paper?"

"The bank and some rich guy own most of it. I own just enough to give myself a job."

"What kind of guy is Jeff?"

Lux flipped on a monitor and typed several strokes. What they brought out of memory didn't seem to please him. "I'm not the one to ask."

"Why not?"

"Jeff and I have some problems."

"Personal?"

"Philosophical."

"You mean like ontology and cosmology?"

"I mean like the nature of editorial responsibility."

"What's Jeff irresponsible about?"

"Human behavior."

"Is that all?"

He matched my grin. "Jeff's mission in life is to convince people that sex without pain is like cake without ice cream."

"You mean one makes the other lots better."

"Exactly."

"Sounds sadistic."

"That's putting it mildly. Two weeks ago he claimed the most exquisite form of foreplay is for lovers to pierce each other's body with needles prior to sex. The week before that he was recommending branding."

"Sounds dangerous."

"What it is is recklessness. And I won't stand for it. Jeff takes a pledge to clear his stuff with me or I take him off the masthead."

The door opened at my back. "Speak of the devil," Brian Lux said as he looked over my shoulder.

The young man in the doorway was sour and impatient. "Devil, my ass," he spat. "Where's Crowell?"

"Latte land, apparently."

Jeff Evans hurled himself into a chair, put his unlaced black boots on the corner of a desk, and leaned back. His hair was short and blond and bristly, his eyes blue and hyperkinetic, his cheeks hollow to the point of emaciation. He was either addicted to drugs or his natural energies consumed flesh faster than his metabolism could generate it. My guess was the latter.

The boots were thick-soled and high-topped and scuffed to the quick at the toe. Weathered Levi's and a plaid flannel shirt and wide red suspenders completed the impression that he'd just come down from the woods after clear-cutting a few thousand acres.

"Crowell's been hacking my stuff again," he declared heavily, the words aimed at Lux but the look aimed at me.

Lux wasn't fazed. "That must be why we call him an editor."

"He's making it soft. Making it beige. Making it dumb. Is that what you pay editors to do?"

Lux remained unflappable. "If that's what needs to be done."

"Well, I don't have to take it."

Their eyes met for the first time, about two feet in front of my chest. "No, you don't."

"You mean you'll call him off?"

"I mean you're not an indentured servant."

"That's for damned sure. *The Weekly*'s been after me for months."

"*The Weekly* has editors, too. A lot more than we do."

"They say they'll leave me alone."

"I said I'd leave you alone, too."

Jeff frowned uncertainly. "Yeah. You did. What happened?"

"*You* didn't leave you alone. You got crude and brutal and irrational. You used your position to initiate some sort of experiment in clinical psychology. You put a private agenda above the welfare of your readers."

"Bullshit. I've got the biggest readership on this pathetic fucking rag. I'm the only one who gets any mail besides the subscription department."

"No question. But your readership believes it's getting the truth; it believes it can trust you; it believes you care about them enough to give them straight information about their lives, and we believed that, too. When you write something that abuses that trust, such as trying to wean people away from normal, healthy sex, we edit it."

"Abuse of trust? How the fuck would *you* know an abuse of trust when you spend all day sucking Lattimore's cock?"

"The paper costs money, Jeff. I do what I have to do to assemble enough funds to put it out every week. That seems sort of an entry-level obligation for a publisher. And I'm not about to take lessons in personal ethics from someone who thinks people need to be encouraged to stick needles through other's cheeks."

"You may not need them from me, but you need them from someone. I seem to remember in your last editorial you jumped on board with the Seattle Commons crowd, people who want to turn half the city into Disneyland and piss on the wretches who lose jobs and homes in the process."

"The commons is part of an integrated master plan that will—"

Jeff leaped from his chair and confronted his boss with equal parts rage and physique. "Master plan, Brian? *Master-fucking-plan?* The last guy who had a master plan was Hitler."

Jeff Evans flashed Brian Lux a Nazi salute, then turned on his heel and left. I waved good-bye to Lux and hurried after my quarry. When I caught up to him he was about to climb into a 240Z whose once-black paint had been worn to a rusty red.

"Can I talk to you a minute?" I asked as he fished for his keys and adjusted his suspenders.

He looked me over, his chest heaving from the fury of his outburst and the pace of his exit. "I don't give private instruction," he sneered. "Spend a quarter and read the column."

I gave him a second to calm down. In the interim, he looked me over a second time and apparently saw something that piqued his interest.

"Hey. Is it true guys' dicks shrink when they get old? And women dry up so you can't do it without greasing the pole? When does that stuff start happening—I need to do a column on geriatric sex. Give our readers a peek at what's waiting out in senior land. You read anything on it? Come on, man; I need a resource person on this."

I waited for his brushfire of enthusiasm to die down. "I need to talk about your sister."

It took him a while to shift gears. "What'd she do, dump you? Don't feel bad about it. She's left a fucking *landfill* of guys in her wake."

"My problem isn't being dumped, my problem is I don't know where she is."

He shook his head impatiently. "That makes two of us. Try to be as happy about it as I am."

"When's the last time you saw her?"

"Weeks. Months. Years, in the spiritual sense."

"You don't have any sense that she's in some kind of trouble?"

"She's always in trouble."

"With what?"

"Drugs. Men. Money. Whatever. Nina's got problems; I got problems; all God's chillen got problems. It's sort of life's little cover charge."

"How about her mother?"

"Judy? What about her?"

"Does Nina keep in touch with her?"

He shrugged. "On and off. They fight. They make up. They fight again. Sort of like a family round-robin."

"What do they fight about?"

"For some reason Mom had trouble with the concept that her daughter was making a living letting some guy make postcards of her cunt. But hey, Judy still sees Nina as a Brownie and me as a Cub Scout. She was thrilled by my piece on nipple clips and cock rings, needless to say."

"Where does your mother live?"

"Mom? Phinney Ridge."

"Which is where?"

"By the zoo. Who are you, mister? You can't be from here if you don't know Phinney."

"I'm a friend of a friend of your sister's."

"Bullshit." He found his key and fitted it in the car door. "Not that it matters *who* the fuck you are; I've got no time for talk, I got to decide whether to walk out on this rag."

"Is the publisher as venal as you say?"

"Ah, Brian's all right. There are plenty of places worse than Lattimore to get funding. He could be tapping something *truly* nasty, like the NEA or the Washington fucking Arts Council."

CHAPTER 14

"Nice office," she observes, admiring the glass and the brass and the tile and the view of the bay and Olympics.

"Thank you."

"This is where you charm the customers, I suppose."

"Something like that."

"And impress them with your derring-do."

"Right again. Luckily it's not as hard as it was when we started, now that we have a track record."

"That nature of which you're about to explain."

"That's correct." He gestures toward a logo on the wall. "The company is called DigiArt."

"I gathered as much. There must be a dozen of those things between here and the front door."

"In the software trade, it doesn't pay to be shy."

"Not in my trade, either."

They smile jointly and he allows himself a chuckle. The laugh is cool and collected, like the rest of him. He is so different from Gary, she considers arranging a meeting, so Gary can see who and what she left him for. Then she remembers Mandy, and is all the more determined to disappear behind the digital wall that this handsome young man is offering to build for her.

¤   ¤   ¤

I FOUND MY WAY to Phinney Ridge though not without some doing—the road kept twisting and turning and telling me not to enter. The ridge really was a ridge, it turned out, the plateau a verdant swath that encompassed the Woodland Park Zoo, the flatlands below defining the neighborhood known as Ballard. The steep sides were striated with horizontal strings of homes that were clinging to the cliff by their fingernails in search of a spectacular view.

Judy Becker lived on Palatine Avenue, two blocks below Phinney Avenue near the corner of Sixty-second Street, in a bungalow blessed with a panoramic perspective—standing on the front stoop and looking back across the street, I could see the west flank of Seattle, the incision of the Ship Canal, the blue slab of Puget Sound, the tuft of Bainbridge Island, and, in the hazy distance, the jagged fence of mountaintops that rose out of the Olympic Peninsula.

The house was a gray stucco bungalow, single story, with a blue composition roof, a sloping front yard primarily devoted to shrubbery, and a deck atop the garage that extended toward the street from the portion of the house to the right of the front door. Clay pots and planter boxes sported a colorful variety of flowers, some of which were petunias and others of which were marigolds, the rest of which were beyond my store of botany. Four wooden chairs of Adirondack design were arranged in a convivial circle around a Plexiglas table; a barbecue bubble was charred from frequent use. An awning on wire runners could be pulled over the deck to shade it from sun or, more likely since this was Seattle, from the spray of winter drizzle.

The door opened before I had a chance to knock. "Are you here for the Stevenson dress?"

I shook my head. "I'm here for information."

"What kind of information?"

Her eyes narrowed and her lips pursed, creating grommets of

white stitches at the edges of her tanned complexion. She was handsome and with some effort could be more than that, but as if to stifle such tendencies she wore torn Levi's, a faded sweatshirt, and blue running shoes without the aid of socks. The front of her sweatshirt glistened with what I thought were sequins but turned out to be dozens of straight pins that made her shirt a coat of armor. Her hair was brown and streaked with gray and cinched in a ten-inch tail. Her eyes were suspicious; her hands were small and lively and cut and callused.

"I'm here about your daughter," I said into her lengthy assessment of my purpose.

"Nina?"

I nodded.

"What do you want with her?"

She seemed too sensible and self-possessed to be finessed. "I take it the police haven't been here yet."

She stiffened and stepped back. "Why would they be?"

"Because a man your daughter has been working with has turned up dead. Sooner or later they'll want to talk to her about it."

"I still don't—"

"He was murdered."

Her brow crumpled. "Murder? You can't be serious."

"I'm afraid I am."

"Well, I'm sure Nina knows nothing about it."

"That may be. But the police will want to question her nonetheless."

"If they need to talk to Nina, why would they bother me?"

"Because no one seems to know where she is. Do you?"

She started to answer, then stopped herself. "What do you have to do with it?"

"My name's Tanner. I'm a detective from San Francisco."

"Police?"

"Private."

She looked over my shoulder, her eyes sweeping the street for confederates. "Is this some sort of trick? Is one of Nina's friends making one of those home movies that make people look like morons because they aren't in on the joke?"

"This is no joke, Ms. Evans."

"I'm not Ms. Evans; I'm Ms. Becker. Judy Becker. And I still don't know what your interest is in Nina."

"I just want to find her."

"Why?"

"To confirm that she's all right so I can put people's minds at rest."

"What people are those?"

"I can't say. I'm sorry."

She crossed her arms above the straight pins. "Are you telling me my daughter committed murder?"

I shook my head. "I'm just saying the police will want to talk to her. And I'm saying she might be in danger herself."

Her eyes bulged with dismay. "Why? Danger from what?"

"I don't know yet. Have you seen Nina in the past month?"

"No."

"You're not worried about her?"

Her expression turned arch and defensive. "I learned long ago that worrying about Nina didn't make any difference—she did what she did and worrying never changed anything."

In the middle of her peculiar creed, I decided to do more digging. "Do you mind if I come in and talk for a minute? It would be to both our benefits if I could get a line on your daughter."

"I still don't see why. Is it because of this man who died? What man was it?"

I explained the connection between Nina and Gary Richter without describing the nature of the collaboration.

Judy Becker looked at me, then past me toward the distant mountains that wore a yarmulke of snow despite the heat of early summer, then up and down the silent street, then back at me again. She fiddled with the pins in her shirt as if the shiny slim devices were tiny transistors that contained important messages.

When she caught me watching the play of her fingers, she dropped her hands to her sides. "I sew," she explained with shyness. "That's what I do—make dresses. Mostly wedding dresses. I sell out of a shop in the market." She sighed. "Let's sit on the deck. The house is a mess when I'm working, which is pretty much always, thank the Lord."

"How much do you charge for a wedding dress?"

"Depends on fabric, style, amount of lace and beadwork involved, lots of things. I can make one for two hundred dollars and I can make one for five thousand. Do you have a daughter who's getting married?"

I shook my head. "Not now. Maybe someday." The acknowledgment seemed only slightly fraudulent. I was getting used to being a father, or whatever it was I was.

As my thoughts lingered over a little girl named Eleanor who was growing by leaps and bounds in a grandiose home in San Francisco, Judy Becker gestured toward one of the Adirondack chairs. I took a seat. She sat across from me and crossed her legs. Our glances met somewhere above the petunias. She was nervous, and irritated, and frightened of me or of some other aspect of her life, but it seemed not to occur to her that she had the right to order me off her property.

"I was talking to your son a while ago," I said before she summoned the courage to restrict me.

The reference seemed to alarm her. "Jeffrey? What about?"

"I was asking if he'd heard from his sister lately."

"What did he say?"

"That he hadn't."

She shook her head glumly. "They're not close."

"Why not?"

Her glance left my face and found new focus in a potted plant.

"No one in the family is close. We broke apart in a big bang and nothing ever put us back together. We lost our center of gravity; we're as scattered as the solar system." She shook her head. "I tried, believe me. But they won't even come to dinner."

"You're not in touch with Nina at all?"

Her eyes glistened momentarily, then dulled to a soup of resignation. "Sometimes I am. Sometimes we go places and have lunch and have the nicest time you could imagine, just the way you think you will when they're small and you dream of when they grow up. But other times we don't speak for months."

"Whose doing is that?"

"Hers. Naturally. I'm always glad to see Nina. She leads an interesting life. Rakehell at times, but interesting. It's hard when the only thing you've done in life is be a mother and your children keep secrets from you," she continued dolefully. "Of course I brought it on myself."

"How?"

"By making a bad marriage and a worse divorce. It changed them, even though they were so little you'd think they couldn't . . . but they absorbed it all, somehow; it got in their pores and their brain cells. The evil. The anger. They were different afterward, sour and mistrustful, even of each other. Dale and I were so hateful that our kids became better at it than we were."

I blinked at the sudden dissonance. "Who's Dale?"

"My husband. Ex-husband." Her look was pinched and pained.

I looked to the mountains to make sure they were still there. "I thought your ex-husband was Ted Evans."

She laughed dryly. "I've got more than one of them. Lucky me. Ted's my second ex-husband. Dale Crowder was my first."

"Dale Crowder is the father of Nina and Jeff?"

She nodded.

"Do they know it?"

She closed her eyes and rubbed them with her fingertips. "I . . . we . . . no. They don't."

"Why not?"

"Because I decided it would be better if they thought they came from a nice family like Ted's rather than a family without love or self-respect, a family full of meanness and intoxication."

"You mean Crowder."

She nodded. "He didn't deserve them. He never did anything but treat those babies like a rash he couldn't get rid of. Every time they'd make a sound, he'd light into them. One night I thought for sure he was going to strangle them, he got so mad when they wouldn't stop crying. And I was so young and ignorant, I didn't think I had the right to do anything about it."

"Sounds like a tough marriage."

Her voice became heated and rhetorical. "If you spent every night with a drunk and a sadist and a malcontent, how do you think you'd like it?"

"Not much. How old were the kids when you left Crowder?"

"Jeff was two; Nina was four. Jeff doesn't remember him at all. All Nina remembers is her father taking baths with her. She thinks it was Ted, but it wasn't." She started to add something, then stopped.

"Do you have any idea where Nina might be, Ms. Becker?"

She shook her head. "I've been trying to reach her for weeks. Her phone's been disconnected; she's moved out of her apartment; I don't know what else to do. Maybe you should talk to Ted." The name came crisp with resentment.

"He hasn't seen her, either. Do you know any reason why Nina might have wanted to drop out of sight?"

She turned my question back on me again. "Do you?"

"Not unless it's connected with Gary Richter somehow."

"The dead man." Her voice rose like a whistle in the wind. "Why are you here? Are you the police? You act like the police. I saw plenty of police when I was with Dale, let me tell you. At the end they were at the house every night, it seemed like—the neighbors had all they could take of his tirades. I had to bail Nina out a time or two as well, later on. Oh, I know plenty about the police, don't think I don't." Her words lingered like a stench in the still air.

"Why was Nina arrested?"

"Drugs. She never went to jail or anything, just juvenile probation. But I had to handle it. Ted was too busy and I wasn't about to hunt up Dale, so I'm the one who had to get her out. Men aren't worth a damn in an emergency, do you know that, Mr. Tanner?"

Our eyes faced off. I decided not to defend my gender, in part because I wasn't sure I was up to the task. "Has Nina been in trouble as an adult, Ms. Becker?"

She straightened her back and spoke with conviction. "Not once. She gave up drugs and running around and got herself together. I'm real proud of her, but I can't take credit for the change—the people at Roosevelt were wonderful with her. They saw to it she did her studies and went on to college. She was doing fine till she got obsessed with this modeling thing." She made it sound like an obsession with satanism.

"So you knew about that."

She nodded.

"Did it bother you?"

"Because she took her clothes off and let men take her picture? It's just life, isn't it? It's what men have always done, make pictures of naked women. The museums are full of them." Her voice dropped to a weary anticlimax. "Nina was always artistic."

"How about Dale? Was he proud of her?"

She blinked. "I haven't spoken to the man in twenty years. He doesn't have anything to do with me or Nina, either one."

"How about Ted? Was he upset with the modeling?"

She shrugged. "Dale was real sensual before he took to drink, but Ted was never at ease with the physical aspects of marriage.

Not that he was cold. Just that he was . . . proper. When Nina got old enough to see what she could do to him by running around without clothes on, she hardly got dressed anymore. I guess it's not surprising she gets naked for a living now."

I didn't know what to say so I stayed silent. After a moment, Judy Becker's face softened, then reassembled to reveal the comeliness that had made her attractive to such disparate personalities as her husbands seemed to possess.

"I hear Ted's getting married again," she said softly.

I nodded.

"I hope he'll be happy. I truly do. And I hope the woman knows what she's getting herself into."

"What is she getting herself into?"

The question snapped the benediction. "That's her problem, not mine."

"He didn't abuse you, did he?"

"Ted? Why would you think that? Ted's a kind, generous man."

I looked at the house and compared it with the mansion I'd seen on Capitol Hill. "He doesn't seem to have been too generous in the divorce settlement."

"I got all I wanted," she said stiffly. "He promised to give most of it to the kids when the time comes."

"What happened between you and Ted? Why didn't the marriage work out?"

"We were a mismatch from the start. He was rich and I was the child of his mother's maid. He was educated and I wasn't. He thought life was about money and I thought it was about love. Plus, he was shy. I was the first woman he made love to, so he thought he had to, you know, make an honest woman of me. He didn't realize that no one had been doing that for thirty years." She fell silent, her eyes depthless and unfocused, her breaths heavy with old air.

"Tell me more about Nina and Ted," I said.

Her eyes closed halfway, the way they do when the sun gets too bright or the pain gets too fierce. "I'm not saying any more about that. It's over and done with and no one's the worse for it, thank God."

Except it might only not be over—it might have led to Gary Richter's death at the hands of an emotionally outraged Ted Evans. "Did Ted fall in love with his stepdaughter?"

Her head jerked as if to deflect the question. "You'd have to ask *him* that."

"Was Nina in love with Ted?"

"Let's say she made out like she was."

"Why would she do that?"

"To punish me, was part of it. But mostly to explore her sexual powers. People think it doesn't happen, that young girls aren't that calculating about such things, but they are. Some of them. She had a new weapon so she decided to see what kind of damage it could do. It did a lot."

"Punish you for what? Leaving the man she thought was her father?"

"I think that was it. When you get down to it, it's all unconscious, don't you think? The bad things are down where we can't get at them, where we can't make them better but they can still make us miserable."

The indictment of our inner life split the soft breeze like a fin. I hoped Freud appreciated the testimonial. "Did Crowder ever find out his kids were going by Ted's name and calling him their father?"

"I don't see how. We all had Ted's name, we lived in a fancy house; I don't see how he'd make the connection. Plus, if he kept going the way he was, he's been dead for twenty years."

"Does Nina have any close friends, Ms. Becker?"

"Used to. She had so many boyfriends in high school I had to beat them off with a stick. She was sexually active at an early age—they could smell it on her, it seemed like. Whenever we went out of town she would have parties and the bed would look like . . . well. Let's just say she was popular."

"Has she stayed in touch with any of those boys?"

"Not that I know of."

"How about girlfriends?"

"She used to be tight as a tick with a girl named Roan. Her folks were hippies who lived in Wallingford. Used to follow the Dead every summer and leave Roan behind with us. They moved to Orcas and I lost track."

"I've met Roan; she doesn't know anything, either. Anyone else?"

"Not that I recall. Oh, there was a woman named Mandy she mentioned once. That's all I know, except I think something bad happened to her."

"What was it?"

"Nina didn't say. I think it had something to do with Jeff, some-how, but I don't know what. I guess I didn't want to know," she added glumly. "I was full of bad news as it was."

I handed Judy Becker a motel card and scrawled my name and room number on it. "Will you get in touch with me if you hear from Nina in the next few days?"

She took the card and nodded. Inside the house the phone rang and she muttered an apology and hurried in to answer it. I used the time to contemplate how a blunt and roughhewn woman like Judy Becker could have charmed a sophisticated man like Ted Evans. What I decided was that love was a vague and various concept and that no outsider can know the ways and means of someone else's heart.

When she came back she told me she had to deliver a gown to a customer. I thanked her for her time and turned to go, then remembered my job and turned back. "Can you tell me where your husband is these days?"

"Ted lives on Capitol Hill."

"I mean Dale."

She laughed bitterly. "After I threw him out, he was living in Youngstown, some shack at the end of Dakota Street. But if he's still there it'll be a miracle."

"Youngstown, Ohio?"

"Youngstown, Seattle. South of the West Seattle Freeway."

I thanked her and turned to go.

"I think it was the baths," she said suddenly. "Nina and the sex and the nakedness. I think it was because she and Dale used to take all those baths together when she was little. I didn't think so at the time, but now I think that was evil. I think that's when the wickedness got started."

CHAPTER 15

"There are two aspects to the DigiArt project," he says, crossing
his arms, leaning back in his chair, lecturing her like a school kid.
"The first, simply stated, is to exhibit electronically the finest
works of art in the world and make them available on our subscription system. To that end, our legal representatives are visit-
ing all the major art capitals acquiring licenses that allow us to
offer electronic reproductions of their collections—painting,
sculpture, tapestry, whatever—on a DigiArt CD-ROM. Within
two years, a DigiArt subscriber will be able, with the touch of a
button or verbal command, to sit in his den and surround himself
with the masterpieces of Leonardo, Raphael, and Tintoretto. Or,
for those of more modernist inclinations, Braque, De Kooning, and
Rothko."

She tries to remain blasé. "So you've got Mona Lisa on a computer. Who cares? The picture will be so fuzzy you can't tell her
from the Mario Brothers."

His smile is so condescending she wants to slap him. "We're not
talking conventional monitors, Ms. Evans; we're talking high-
definition, flat panel display screens that hang on a wall and
reproduce line and color with a fidelity far greater than anything
you've seen on a Trinitron."

"These things are really available?"

"Only prototypes at this point, of which DigiArt has several
dozen. A similar number are with Optical Inventions, their devel-

oper, in which we have a thirty percent ownership interest. Mr. Lattimore is on their board."

"Tell me about him. Just a little."

"You've heard of Bill Gates?"

"Like I've heard of the sun. Are you saying Lattimore is as rich as Bill Gates?"

"No, but he's not far enough back for it to matter to anyone but the IRS. Jensen Lattimore made his fortune creating a variety of unglamorous business software—accounting systems, inventory controls, receivables tracking—Lattiware, the company is called."

"Never heard of it."

"The apps are only of interest to business people. But they were quite successful and they made Mr. Lattimore a rich man. They also, after a time, left him quite bored."

"Good for him."

"Two years ago he left Lattiware and founded DigiArt."

She takes time to reorient herself. "I see what all this has to do with Da Vinci and Picasso," she says at last. "I just don't see what it has to do with me."

"Your participation will interface with the second aspect of the project. We will not only offer subscribers the works of accepted masters, we are also going to offer original works created by the finest video artists in the country expressly for our system, as an add-on to the basic subscription. This special selection of art work will be offered to subscribers who are willing, as serious collectors have been since the time of the Borgias, to pay a premium for orig-inality. They will own the one and only copy of the disk, to do with as they will, including exclusive enjoyment of the image."

"Only one person will see it?"

"If that's what the purchaser desires. It will be like acquiring a work on canvas—its fate will be determined not by its creator or distributor, but solely by its owner. If it ends up in the rumpus room, so be it."

"Where do I fit in?"

"We have dozens of people creating art with designs and graphics that take advantage of the properties inherent in digitization, of course. But it occurred to us that the classic subjects of the creative impulse over the centuries should be available to our subscribers as well—landscapes, still lifes, portraits—"

"And nudes."

"And nudes." He reaches into a drawer and withdraws a stapled sheaf of paper. "Take time to read this over. If you find the terms and conditions satisfactory, please sign at the red arrow."

"Shouldn't I take it to a lawyer?"

"That would not be possible. Not because we are trying to snooker you, but because we would no longer be able to maintain the confidentiality required at this stage of the project. But as you will see, the terms are clear and unambiguous. You agree to a six-month exclusive personal services arrangement with an option for six more months at our discretion, your time and talent to be entirely devoted to DigiArt in such manner as may be determined by the project director."

"Which is you."

"Which is me." He hands her the document. "Let me know if you have any questions."

She pushes the papers back toward him. "Not so fast, Mr. Director," she says with an unconcealed smirk. "You left something out."

"What's that?"

"You've seen mine, now I want to see yours. You and your friend Lattimore aren't the only ones with standards. Let's see some of this art you're so crazy about.

¤   ¤   ¤

SEATTLE'S YOUNGSTOWN SECTION is easier to describe than to get to. I took a wrong turn off the West Seattle Freeway and before I could get routed in the right direction I found myself in a maze of shipyards and container lots and railheads and other ventures allied with an active port. There's something exciting about a port—teeming ships, looming cranes, lurking railcars, inscrutable metal boxes bearing names like Hanjin and Matson and Hyundai—and in Seattle it is visible and vibrant even though much of it seems to be Korean. In San Francisco, the only place from which to view a port is Oakland.

I finally got headed in the right direction, leaving the boats at my back and climbing toward Dakota Street. I took a right off Delridge and followed Dakota to where it dead-ended, which was where Judy Becker had told me Dale Crowder was living. Since he wasn't in the phone book, my only option was a miracle.

The house was almost a hut—tiny and tin-roofed and barely visible through the thicket of brush and weeds that had overrun the narrow plot of ground on which it staked its claim. In the swale below the house, the blue-and-red buildings of Birmingham Steel added smoke to the afternoon air and answered a question—why did they call it Youngstown? From the length and strength of the rose and blackberry canes that crisscrossed the path to the door, no one had come calling in ages; of course, no one had come calling on me in ages, either. I eased my way through the brambles that guarded the stoop and banged on the door with my fist.

The woman who answered was sick or hungover or both: her moon face was crumpled with pain from a source that wasn't visible, like a pear that had started to spoil. She shaded her eyes from the light even though it wasn't all that bright out, squinting at the shadow I was casting across her life.

When she spoke, the words were swaddled with liquor and lethargy and a disinclination to commune with the outside world. " 'Guiding Light' starts in five minutes," she informed me without preamble, to set the parameters for discussion. "What'ya want?" Her floor-length shift billowed between us like a huge polyester pumpkin.

"I'm looking for Dale Crowder."

The lines in her face switched from horizontal to vertical, as though she were being etched from inside. "What's he done?"

"Nothing that I know of."

"That'd be a first," she grumbled, then laughed at a private joke, then cocked her head to listen to some dialogue that seemed to come from the TV. Someone was mad at someone else, accusing them of faithlessness, which meant it could be any episode from any soap in any year since 1950.

When the exchange ended and a commercial for Pampers came on, the woman rubbed her nose with the back of her hand, then inspected the viscous leavings of the exercise as though they might forecast her fortune. The reading didn't please her, so she hacked up something from her lungs and spit it out of spite.

"My name's Tanner," I said with the sunny cheer of a sportscaster. "Are you Mrs. Crowder?"

"Am not. Never will be. I'm Mabel."

"But you live here?"

"Where I live is none of your business. What is it you want?"

"As I said, I'm looking for Mr. Crowder. I was told this was his home."

"Is but he ain't here."

"Do you know where I can find him?"

"Probably down at the island, pretending he's looking for work. Half-hour of that, and he can head for the Juneau, which is what he wanted in the first place."

I was confused. "Juneau the city?"

"Juneau the bar, on Marginal Way. Dale gets thirsty this time of day. I've had garbage cans cleaner than the Juneau, but when Dale gets dry he'll drink out of a sock." She adjusted the shift around the swell of her pendulous breasts; the nipples that fell out of them were the diameter of dimes. "What's this about, anyway? He's not losing his benefits, is he?"

"What benefits are you referring to?"

"Disability. Dale's a hundred percent hurt."

"What kind of disability is it?"

"Back. Can't lift nothing heavier than a shot glass." She looked down at her bloated body as if to point me toward the source of the strain.

"If he's disabled, why's he looking for work?"

"He's not looking for work, he's *pretending* he's looking for work. That way the boys don't ride him; that way they don't know he's a cripp. Which he's not, he just pretends to be. For the check." She took a step back. "I hope you're not gummit."

There was a burst of terror in her eyes, as bright as lightning in a fishbowl. She'd told me more than she should have, but to her credit she decided to be brazen rather than apologetic. "Hey. Everyone's got to eat. Dale's had a hard life; he can't help it if he can't hold down a job."

"What's been so hard about it?"

"Women. That's what brought him down. Women take advantage of him. He's too damned good to them, is why."

The conversation was taking a surreal turn—the idea that Dale Crowder was burdened by benevolence was as absurd as my persistent mooning over Peggy. "I'm wondering if you've seen Dale's daughter lately," I asked, to keep contact with real life.

"What daughter is that?"

"Has he got more than one?"

"Claims to have several. Course he claims to know the mayor, too. Hell, he don't even know the mayor's a spade."

"I'm here about Nina," I said.

"The sexy one."

"So he knows her."

"Knows *of* her, anyways."

"Has he seen her lately?"

She shrugged without interest. "The brother was by, though; month or two ago."

"What was the reason for the visit?"

"Give Dale money, was part of it. He ain't been sober since."

"What was the money for?"

She shrugged, making everything beneath the shift bob like channel buoys. "Dale can't pay his bar bills on the disability, so he needs a supplement." She looked defensive, as though I'd contradicted her, but I hadn't moved an inch.

"Everybody needs a supplement," she went on. "Me, I got my Milanos. Don't eat a bag of Mints ever day, I don't feel chipper. Them Milanos perk me right up."

When I told her I knew what she meant, I wasn't entirely fibbing.

"Listen," she said, her eyes suddenly active, her face suddenly seamless. "I got to get back to the 'Light.' You leave your name and number, I'll tell Dale you was by."

"Did Jeff bring Dale money regularly?"

"Nope. Never seen him till a month ago, and ain't seen him since. Which I'm glad of. Dale's all of that family I can handle."

"Does Dale ever talk about Nina?"

"Only ever day."

"What does he say about her?"

"He says she's better-looking than Marilyn Monroe and Ann-Margret combined."

"Do you know if he and Nina ever—"

"If it ain't the devil himself," the woman interrupted, looking over my shoulder with a forced smile that bared a picket fence of rotted teeth and gave me a spray of beer breath. "Now don't he look like something the cat coughed up?"

The description was apt, even though it was uttered with something close to affection. Dale Crowder was as scruffy a human being as I had ever seen. His face was puffy and devoid of color but for the veins that laced his cheeks and nose. His eyes were bleary and languid smudges of soil. His lips were slack sacks sent occasionally atremble by the exhaust of his heaving chest. His clothing was a stained and torn ensemble of T-shirt and overalls and underwear; his posture was tilted and untenable.

He was drunk but not drunk enough to be oblivious—the conclave on his stoop disturbed him. "I told you not to let no one *in* here, woman. What you telling him about my business?"

"You *got* no business, you stinking old fart. The only business you got comes in the bottom of a bottle."

The insult didn't faze him. "I told you not to let no more people in here."

"He ain't in, is he? And he ain't *been* in. So take a poke at someone else 'fore I knock you down and sit on you. You ain't so drunk you can't remember last time I did it, either."

The purity of her riposte seemed to deflate him. "What's he want?" Crowder said as he shifted to retain his balance. I might as well have been in Cleveland.

"Don't know," she said with unconcern.

"Is he gummit?"

"Says not. Says he's looking for your dumpling."

"Nina?"

"That's right," I interjected heartily. "I wonder if you could tell me where she is."

His eyes wandered my way, though not in a straight line. "Why should I?"

"Because she might be in trouble and I might be able to get her out of it."

"What kind of trouble?"

"Police trouble."

"I knowed there was something wrong. She's in jail, right? That's where she went. What was it, drugs?"

"It's not that kind of trouble," I said.

"What kind is it?"

"Worse."

"What's worse than drugs?" he asked with odd sincerity. I think he really wanted to know.

As I was considering another line of questions, my silence made him nervous, the way men like him are always nervous when confronted by real or specious authority. "Who are you, the new stud?" he asked, his demeanor halfway between a bully and a sidekick.

"What stud are you referring to?"

"The one with the fancy car."

"I'm not him. What else do you know about him?"

"Nothing."

"She tell you his name?"

He shook his head and lost his balance again. "She don't talk to me. Don't even know me," he added mournfully. His sadness was so engulfing that I almost felt sorry for him, until I remembered the look on his ex-wife's face as she defined the contours of their marriage.

The orientation toward the past took the final puffs of wind from his bluster and without that ballast he drifted off center. He seemed to shrink in size and strength by half; the woman went to his side and held him upright by placing a beefy arm around his narrow waist. They looked like Ma and Pa Kettle.

Suddenly Crowder reached in his overalls and pulled out a picture and handed it to me. It was wrinkled and stained and smudged, but it was undoubtedly Nina Evans, nearly naked in front of a gray backdrop, wearing a silk scarf and a string of pearls and little else, as sensuous as a spread for *Vogue* by Avedon or Penn.

Crowder was grinning like a papa. "They don't believe she's mine," he said. "The boys at the Juneau think I got this out of some fuck book. But this ain't porn, is it, mister? This is art. Ain't it?"

I told him I thought it was.

"I'll be in the shed," Crowder tacked suddenly, and started down a path toward the rear of the house.

"Stay out there till you don't stink no more," the woman ordered heavily.

Crowder waved his fist and kept going. I started to follow but Mabel grabbed my arm. "He don't let no one back there."

"Why not?"

"Don't know."

"What's he do back there?"

"Mostly he thinks about what he used to have before he drank it all away." She looked down toward the steel mill, then at a ferry floating off in the distance. "Now all he's got is me. It ain't been enough to sober him up."

For the longest time she doesn't know what she is seeing. The screen is a blur of color and texture—shadow, then bright light; monochrome, then multicolored; flat, then puckered and creased and carved and twisted. Nothing registers and everything does. For an instant, she thinks she sees her subliminal self, there and gone in a flash, but decides she must be mistaken.

"How did you get it to go that fast?" she asks when the segment is finished.

"Get what?"

"The camera."

"The camera didn't move."

"Then you must be running the tape at fast-forward."

He looks at her triumphantly, as though it is the mistake he has predicted she would make. "There is no tape."

"Sure there is. There has to be. Videotape or film; that's all there is."

"Not anymore."

"What else?"

"When you were at the studio, did you notice the thing draped in white pima sitting on the tripod?"

"Yeah. So?"

"It's one of only four of its kind in the world."

"What is it?"

"A digital video camera. No film; no tape—the image goes straight to disk. You will be part of the first real-time, full-motion, binary imaging system in the history of the world. We've finally got the chips and accelerators and CPUs and MPEG compression technology and quad-speed CD-ROMs and the high-resolution display devices to do fully digital, 30 fps full-motion video. If this works anywhere near the way we envision, you're going to be a legend in your own time."

When she is sure he isn't kidding, she pulls the sheaf of paper toward her and begins to read the contract.

¤　　　¤　　　¤

ON THE WAY OUT OF YOUNGSTOWN I found a phone near the freeway and called the number Fiona had given me. She answered on the second ring.

"I'd like to talk to you about a few things," I said after she came on the line and I'd reminded her who I was.

Her voice was airy and abstract. "Have you found her yet?"

"No. That's what I want to talk to you about." I waited for her to say something about Richter's murder and was surprised when it didn't come up.

"I'm off to the gym in a few minutes," she said after a pause to consider my bona fides. "I could meet you there after my workout, it's on top of Queen Anne Hill. There's a little park nearby, we could go there afterward and chat. I'll bring coffee in a Thermos," she added, as though conversation without caffeine was unthinkable. We agreed to meet in an hour at Pro Robics.

I got there a little early, after some corn chowder and green salad at a café called the 5-Spot, which was better than its name implied. The gym occupied part of a larger building that housed everything from commercial offices to an Italian restaurant. The woman at the desk was young and cute and as tanned as a pomegranate. She was also friendly in the way that's depressing when you get to be my age, because it means they don't regard you as a conceivable complication should you misinterpret their kindness for chemistry.

I told her I was meeting Fiona. The woman told me the class had just finished and Fiona was probably in the shower. With a sparkle in her eye, she warned me that I'd have to take her word for it. Then she exactly estimated the state of my physical fitness by pointing to the couch by the TV as the place where I should park myself.

For the next five minutes a succession of sweaty bodies flowed past my post, coming from the StairMaster machines in the room to the left or the aerobics room to the right. Most of them were female, wearing Lycra shorts under jersey tops that were anchored to their torsos by thongs that would have been banned in Boston during most of my lifetime. I felt like a rake when I wasn't feeling as out of place as monk at a Pentecostal meeting.

A short time later, Fiona emerged from behind a swinging door, gym bag over her shoulder, wearing short shorts and heavy socks and a tank top that would have shown an extra ounce of fat if there had been one under there to show. She smiled and waved and went to the desk to retrieve her card from the clerk, then beckoned me to follow her outside—I hadn't been as relieved since the last time I got out of jail.

"Are you driving?" Fiona asked as she waited on the sidewalk outside.

I nodded. "That's the first black mark against your city, by the way. The stoplights."

"I know, I know; they last forever, even when there isn't any traffic, and they aren't coordinated. It takes hours to drive ten blocks."

"The lights are bad and the drivers are worse. Why did they make turn signals illegal up here?"

Fiona laughed. "At least they've stopped arresting people for jaywalking." She pointed. "There's a funny little place down that way called Bhy Kracke Park."

"Buy Crack Park? Anywhere near Random Shooting Plaza?"

"It's just pronounced that way; it's spelled differently." She patted her bag. "I've got some nice Kenyan," she said, and directed me to the park, which turned out to be a steeply terraced corner on the southeast edge of Queen Anne Hill with a panoramic view of the city. Mount Rainier looked on like a proud parent from beyond the spike of downtown, Lake Union and its floating homes lay low to the left, and the Northern Cascades were hints of winter in the distance.

We sat on a bench and sipped coffee. I told her the Kenyan was great without really meaning it, the way I say sourdough bread is great without really meaning it, either.

After some simultaneous sips, Fiona regarded me with a frown. "You're not really worried about her, are you? Nina's a cool head. She wouldn't do anything dumb."

"It doesn't take dumb to get in trouble these days. All it takes is a wrong turn."

She nodded thoughtfully. "In addition to those kind of hazards, once guys find out you take off your clothes for a living, they figure you'll be happy to do it for any gutbucket with the price of a beer." She took another hit of caffeine. "So what can I do for you, Mr. Tanner?"

"I wanted to ask some questions about the modeling business."

"What kind, figure or fashion?"

"Figure."

"What do you want to know about it?"

"For starters, how do you get into the field in the first place?"

"Lots of ways. You know a friend who knows an artist who needs a model who'll work cheap. You see a sign on the bulletin board at the local college that says the art department is looking for a subject for Life Drawing 101. Or you answer an ad in the paper for models, which can turn out to be anything from a rock video to a porn shoot."

"Are there agencies that handle that kind of thing?"

"Not figure work. Fashion, yes, but there's no money in figure work, so the agencies don't bother with it. Fashion work is pretty much limited to anorexics with attitude—five ten and size six— but figure models come in all types. I know one guy who refuses to use women who weigh less than two hundred pounds. Says he likes the volume."

"How much can someone earn at it?"

"Not much, even someone like Nina who works a lot."

"Why not?"

"It's not full-time, first of all. No matter how good you are, no one spends forty hours a week with their clothes off. Plus, at best it pays ten bucks an hour and usually not that unless it's for someone who's extremely successful or has a commission, and even then they can always get someone for less, so they figure why pay more. Most photographers think models are fungible. They're wrong, but they don't know it till the reviews come out, sometimes."

"Lots of times it gets personal, right? Artists and models have affairs all the time, don't they?"

"Sure. The environment sort of encourages it. Some of the relationships go on for years and sometimes the guy uses the girl till she lets him fuck her, then she's back on the street with a tin cup and he's out in the clubs recruiting a new one."

"I've been wondering if Nina hooked up with someone and the attraction was mutual and they pulled a Gauguin and ran off to Tahiti to make pictures together."

"It could happen. But not with Gary Richter. Everyone but *everyone* thought he was bile."

"How often did you work with Richter yourself?"

"Just once or twice a year. I didn't meet his requirements."

"In what way?"

"My daddy wasn't rich."

"What does that have to do with figure photography?"

"I'm not sure, but Gary liked to work with rich kids. He grew up in a rough patch in the Central District. I think he just liked knowing he could get debutantes to take off their clothes for him."

"Could he have been blackmailing the daddies to keep the pictures of their darlings private?"

She frowned. "I don't know. I never thought about it. Jesus."

"Do you know anyone besides Richter who Nina worked with to the extent of developing a romantic relationship?"

"No one on that scale. But I didn't know her all that well, so I'm not saying it didn't happen."

"So how about the steamy side of the business?" I asked when I'd drained my cup.

"You mean porn?"

I nodded.

"It's out there. I mean, if that's what you want, you can get it. Easy. Good money, too."

"How good?"

"Hundreds for still photos. More for work in the titty bars—tips are great if you give them what they want."

"Which is?"

"You touch them and they touch you. Couch dancing, they call it."

"I thought touching was illegal."

"Only if someone's watching."

"If you wanted to do porn work, how would you make the connection?"

"Just look for a job in the clubs. If you make a reputation dancing, sooner or later someone will come around and ask if you're interested in more rewarding forms of entertainment."

"By which they mean what?"

"Hard-core video; call girl work; you name it. Some of the so-called fine arts photographers peddle stuff to the smut rags when times get tough, too. That's the way most of us first get into print, unfortunately."

I raised a brow. "You?"

"*Gent* magazine, October '89, thanks to an asshole named Jamison. Quite a layout—lots of positive reader response. My mother was so very proud. I'm kidding," she added when she saw my face turn cockeyed.

"What dance clubs are the best?"

"The Lusty Lady downtown is run by a woman, so it's the cleanest—no grab ass or hustling drinks or anything. Look but don't touch—the girls are all behind glass. And then there's Victor Krakov."

"Who?"

"Victor Krakov. Runs a chain of dance clubs around the Sound, three of them here in the city. He owns half the bare tits in the state."

"Where can I find him?"

"Got an office out on Aurora—Aureole Entertainment Enterprises. Victor's always sniffing around for new women. No doubt he hit on Nina at some time or other."

"Does he have a reputation for violence?"

"There are rumors, but there always are in that business. Not murder, though; just batting the girls around a little when they ask for more money. But I don't know much about it."

"You never worked for him?"

She looked away. "No."

"Not even once?"

"Okay. Once. When I first came to town. I was broke and lonely so I danced at the Blitz Club for two weeks. Then I found a regular job and quit."

"Have any dealings with Krakov?"

"I just let him look at me to audition. Which was bad enough."
She snapped her fingers. "I just remembered. A couple of months
ago I heard some other guy was going around, fronting for a high-
class operation and offering big money for girls to work nude. I
never met him, but he was definitely making a pitch; at least two
of my friends told me about it. I figure he was fronting for one of
those executive titty bars that are all the rage now—you know, sex
for suits."

"Is there one here in town?"

"Not that I know of, but I'm sure there will be."

"What was the guy's name?"

"Chris something."

"What was the club called?"

"Don't remember. Sorry. But if you're asking if Nina was
hooked up with any of the slimeballs, I'd have to say no. She was
serious about her work. She saw herself as every inch the artist
that Cindy Sherman or Sally Mann is. Plus her old man had
money, so she'd never be hard up enough to go slumming."

I shifted gears. "Did Nina talk about her father much?"

"Some. I saw them at Ponti's one night, dressed to the nines. A
bit of a Butterfield 8–type thing, actually."

"Really?"

She shrugged. "It just looked funny."

Without really wanting to, I kept adding to my store of anec-
dotes about Ted Evans and his lovely daughter. "I take it you
haven't heard anything about Gary Richter lately."

She blinked. "No. Why should I?"

"Because he's dead."

She flinched as though I'd pinched her. "You're kidding."

"Nope. Murdered. It's in the papers. They found him floating
in the Ship Canal, near someplace called the Chittenden Locks."

"Jesus. Who said he was murdered?"

"The cops."

"You talked to them?"

"They talked to me. You looked like something came to mind when I said murder. Something or someone."

Her look became taut and distraught. "I was just thinking how many women I've heard say that they wished Gary Richter were dead."

When she finishes, she grabs the pen and starts to sign her name, then stops. "There's one thing that needs to be added."

"What's that?"

"I've had trouble with guys messing with my image. I mean literally. They've put things in the shot that weren't there, had me doing things I didn't do. I need to make sure this deal with DigiArt is straight—no tricks with the computer."

He smiles and shakes his head. "No can do."

"Why not?"

"Because that's the whole point. *Tricks with computers is what we do."*

¤   ¤   ¤

AURORA AVENUE TURNED OUT TO BE Highway 99, the major north-south road on the West Coast before Interstate 5 usurped it. Like most such thoroughfares, it had devolved into a string of faded motels featuring waterbeds and erotic movies, interspersed among an eclectic collection of establishments offering everything from auto parts to discount golf equipment with palm readings to spice up the mix. Of particular interest on this trip were a restaurant in the shape of twin teepees and a store doing business under the names of Chubby and Tubby.

The offices of Aureole Entertainment Enterprises occupied a nondescript building near the corner of Aurora and 135th Street.

The sign on the front was surprisingly muted and the interior was almost tasteful in the way doctors' offices are almost tasteful. The art on the walls was more bucolic than erotic and the nocturne on the sound system came by way of Poland, not Harlem.

The only person in sight was big and blonde and nearsighted; she squinted at me over the top of her computer the way jewelers squint at diamonds. "May I be of assistance?" The formal phrasing was at least as unnatural as her eyelashes.

Her hair and makeup were so theatrical it suggested she had been in the entertainment business herself not so long ago. Her dress was cut low in front, for reasons obvious from across the room. Her lips were as orange as a coxcomb; the fingernails that drummed the top of the monitor were dyed to match and double normal length. Only her eyes seemed dissonant—they were red-rimmed and raw despite her efforts to subdue them with wreaths of mascara.

"I'd like to see Mr. Krakov," I told her.

"I'm afraid that's not possible."

"Why not?"

"He's not here. Plus you don't have an appointment."

"How do you know?"

Her smile was more from pluck than mirth. The effort sabotaged her elocution. "'Cause Victor don't make appointments." She seemed buoyed by the success of her ambush.

I grinned to show I didn't hold it against her. "What if I said I was with the IRS?"

"I wouldn't believe it."

"Why not?"

"You got nice clothes. The field agents dress like car salesmen."

"You sound like you've had some experience."

She nodded somberly. "They were all over the place last year. Kept me humping for three months, dragging out files, digging out receipts, dusting off ledgers. They didn't find nothing, though—Victor's got a great accountant."

"Well, you're right about the clothes—I'm not IRS."

She grinned. "I knew it."

"If Victor's not here, where is he?"

Her breasts bobbed in aftershock to her shrug. "Could be lots of places. I can beep him if you want, but he mostly ignores it. Victor don't like phones—he likes face-to-face. He's a people person."

"Do you think he's at one of the clubs?"

"Maybe. Or maybe the studio."

"What kind of studio?"

"Where we shoot videos. We make great videos. Soft core only, though; not hard stuff." She started to say something else, then stopped and cocked her head. "Who are you, mister? Why all the questions? The city attorney isn't on another morality kick, is he?"

I shook my head. "My name's Tanner. What's yours?"

"I'm Lila."

"Well, Lila, let me tell you why I'm here. I own a string of clubs in the Central Valley in California. Seven of them, to be exact— Modesto, Salinas, Fresno, places like that. And what I want is to talk to your boss about sharing talent with me."

She squinted suspiciously. "How do you mean, sharing?"

"I send some of my girls up here; he sends some of his down there. Gives the customers something new and different to enjoy; gives the managers less headache than working with amateurs."

Lila frowned with uncertainty. "Sometimes the customers don't want new and different. Sometimes they like their favorites."

"Sounds like you speak from experience."

She straightened her spine, then propped her breasts atop the monitor. She wasn't flirting, she was resting—they must have been as heavy as mortar. "I danced for Victor for nine years," she said.

"How is he to work for?"

"Some girls didn't like him, but he was always nice to me so I was nice to him."

"You still dance?"

She glanced at the jut of her chest. "Naw. When I had my baby my assets sagged so Victor put me on office work. I don't make as much as I did with the tips, but I make enough for Marie and me to get by."

"Marie's your daughter?"

She nodded. "Two years old tomorrow. The terrible twos." Her expression turned beatific. "I can't wait. Sorry I can't help you, mister."

I hurried to salvage some treasure. "Maybe you still can. One of my girls has a friend who works for Victor or used to. Name's Nina Evans. If I could talk to her, I could get a better idea of how close our operations are—Victor's and mine, I mean—and see whether my plan is feasible. The problem is, Nina moved; the address I've got is no good."

Lila was shaking her head before I finished. "We don't give out the names of our dancers. Victor's real strict about that. There are some crawly people out there—one of them walked into a club down the street and shot one of the girls while she was onstage. Thank God it wasn't one of ours." She reddened. "Not that it wasn't terrible, anyway."

"I understand completely; I'm strict about privacy, too. Protect the talent—that's the most important thing. But, see, I already know her name. And I know where she used to live—Fifty-second and University—but they told me she moved a couple of months ago. So all I need is the new address."

She pursed her lips and leaned away from the monitor. "I don't know if I—"

"Tell you what. Check your records. You probably don't have the new address, either, so there's not even an issue. How about it?"

She thought it over, decided to make an exception, then punched some buttons on her keyboard. "What did you say her name was?"

"Nina Evans."

The machine beeped and clicked. "Sorry. She must not work for Victor. Either that or she changed her name. Lots of girls do that. They think it'll be a black mark on their record later on if someone finds out they used to dance. I don't know why— dancers do lots of good in the world. I'd hate to think what some of these guys would do if they couldn't at least *look* at some titty."

Her eyes grew misty and she dabbed them with a Kleenex.

"What's wrong?"

"Nothing."

"Are you feeling ill or something?"

"It's not me, it's one of the girls."

"Who?"

"Mandy."

There came that name again. "What's wrong with her?"

"She's gone back on skag."

"Heroin?"

Lila nodded. "She got clean and straightened out her life real good and then something must have happened because she went on the spike again. She'll probably OD just like all the others."

"What others?"

"The kids in Seattle dying from horse. It's as bad as the sixties, they say."

"You'd think they'd be smarter than that."

"They are smarter. But that doesn't mean they don't hurt. Smart don't kill pain, mister; smart makes it worse."

As a matter of fact, I agreed with her. "Do you get many college girls working for you, Lila?"

"Oh, yeah. Lots. They don't last long, as a rule—dancing's harder than it looks. But they come in all the time wanting a tryout."

"Would you have a record if someone tried out?"

"Not if we didn't hire her."

"Who gives the auditions?"

"Sometimes Victor; sometimes me."

I pulled out my picture of Nina. "Ever see her at the auditions?"

Lila looked at it and shook her head. "If she'd auditioned, we would have hired her."

I tried one last tack. "Ever hear of a guy named Richter? He's a—"

"Gary?" She brightened, then darkened in the next instant. "Sure. It's horrible what happened—you know about that, right?"

"Yeah. A real shame."

Lila dabbed at her eyes again. "I couldn't believe it. He was in here just last week, joking around like he does. He even brought me a double tall."

I was afraid to ask what that was. "What did Richter have to do with the clubs?"

"He took our publicity stills. He was good, too; the girls look better in the stills than in real life, some of them. Good for business, too."

"What do you do with the stills?"

"Lots of things. Sometimes we run ads in the paper. And we put them up in front of the clubs as a come-on, to let the guys know what's inside. And we pass out flyers once in a while. We use our own girls, too; not L.A. models like some of the places. We send stills to our special clients, too."

"What kind of special clients?"

"Businessmen, mostly. Or lawyers or doctors or anyone, really. They like to hire the girls for parties, sometimes. To spice them up. Sometimes to perform, but usually just to stand around and look nice. Mingle. You know."

"Does it ever amount to more than mingling?"

She met my look without flinching. "You mean prostitution? No. Oh, I'm not saying it never happened, but it didn't *have* to happen, if you get what I mean. It was strictly up to the girls. The thing was, though, if they slept with a guy, they couldn't bring him around the club. That's one of Victor's rules—he don't want the

dancers emotionally involved with the customers. Causes problems, Victor says. He's right, too. I had a guy climb on stage with
me once 'cause I wouldn't go party with him. Tried to tie me up
and carry me out to his Bronco."

I laughed because Lila was laughing, as though he'd only
tricked her with a joy buzzer. "I'm interested in those special
clients. I'd like to find out what the arrangement is in case I try to
start something like that down in Fresno. Do you have a list you
could give me?"

She shook her head briskly. "I couldn't do that. Not without
Victor's okay. That wouldn't be smart, I don't think."

"Why not?"

"You might try to take away the business, for one thing. The
special clients pay real good."

"How good?"

"I thought you weren't IRS."

I apologized for being a snoop. "Was Richter involved with the
special clients? Did they hire him to take pictures at parties, for
instance?"

Lila shook her head. "I don't think so. I heard him say something about Jensen once, but I never heard him talk about the
special clients."

"Who's Jensen?"

"One of the investors."

"So Victor doesn't own it all?"

"He got it started, but when no one would rent him space after
the city attorney started raving about decency, Victor needed
help to finance some real estate."

"For the clubs, you mean."

"Right. We own all our buildings now. That way we can keep
them real nice."

"Does anyone named Chris work for Victor?"

She shook her head.

"How can you be sure?"

"I make out the payroll."

"What's this Jensen do besides invest?"

"I don't know, but whatever it is, it makes him a lot of money. He gave me a diamond bracelet once, back when we were dating. Tennis bracelets, they call them. I still wear it sometimes."

"Did you and Jensen date for a long time?"

"Couple of months, is all. It wasn't serious, I knew that right off—man like that wouldn't want anyone like me around all the time. But he treated me nice and took me nice places and we had some fun. Mostly he liked to look at me. Naked, I mean. We hardly ever had sex. Never, actually."

Her voice was wistful and a trifle melancholy, as though his abstinence had been her personal failing.

CHAPTER 18

Compared to Gary's makeshift studio, with its Kmart floods and coffee-can spots and bedsheets hung as a backdrop, this is as elaborate as a movie set. Fresnels and carbon arcs and tungsten halogens and tweenies; honeycombs and grids and domes and discs; reflectors of all shapes and shades and surfaces. A green screen for background projections; a dolly on tracks. A Steadi-cam, two Betacams snug in metal cases, several handheld Canons and Panasonics, and a Kodak digital still camera that she knows is priced at over twenty grand. Banks of computers, both desktop and notebook, with God knew what monitoring inputs, so that everything is defined and numbered and labeled and stored, all for future editing. Most prominent of all, there is the pride and joy, sitting like the crown jewel in the middle of it all—the digital video camera, ghostly under its drape, mysterious in its capabilities. An elaborate electronic menagerie, all in wait for her.

Chris has asked if she minds technicians on the set. She told him she'd prefer just him at first, till she is fully focused, but that once they get into it she doesn't mind the others. He asked if she cared whether they were men or women. She said it didn't matter, but when the time comes she is disappointed to see that they are all female except for the lighting guy, who Chris has told her is a genius, a ponytailed jokster who plays his light board like a Steinway.

But that comes later. At first, it is just her and Chris, who is not armed with the new camera but only a small Panasonic, filming as he would film a parade. Basic lighting, basic background. Pose, then move, then pose, relaxed and easy and improvisational, like the acting exercises she'd done back when she thought she wanted to be a movie star.

Once in a while he murmurs instruction, but for the most part he leaves it up to her. Once or twice, before she is even fully into it, what she gives him makes him gasp.

They take a break and technicians and gofers swarm in. The digital camera is unwrapped, then they get down to business. It becomes ballet for the most part, with a dash of aerobics at the edges. She twirls, she glides, she slides, she stretches. She bends, she twists, she kneels, she curls. She kicks, she hops, she tiptoes, she crawls. It is slow and languid, then vigorous and sweaty. The hour is over before she wants it to be.

Do men feel like this? she wonders as she towels off. No. Men are just equipment. As trim and taut as they might become, as athletic as they might be, what they are is accessories. Wrenches and pipes and hammers, used to make nice things, at times, but at bottom only instruments. Not concepts or abstractions. Not beauty. Men are all and only plumbers. She smiles as she heads for the shower.

¤   ¤   ¤

BY THE TIME I WAS BACK in my car I realized what had started to nag at me, so I consulted the map, then drove south down Aurora until I could angle east on Green Lake. Twenty minutes later, I found a place to park on Roosevelt Way and entered the Erospace Gallery during normal hours.

The door was open, the lights were on, a small staff was on duty, and I was greeted with a smile by a tidy, officious woman wearing black tights, a leather miniskirt, and sandals that laced to the knee. On someone else, the outfit might have been erotic; on her, it was labored and slightly silly.

"I'm Fran Askwith, one of the proprietors," she said with the gravity of a royal proclamation, as if the prurient nature of her stock-in-trade would be legitimized by verbal decorum. "Are you interested in anything in particular?"

"Not really," I said as I wandered toward the wall where Gary Richter's work had been on display the day before. "Just getting a sense of what's available."

"We have some outstanding genitalia castings just in from L.A. Bronze and steel; male and female."

"I mostly collect photography," I said. "When I stopped by a few days ago, I was impressed by the work of a man named Richter. Then I saw in the paper he got murdered. I figured the market would jump when word got around—figured they'd make good investments on top of being decent erotica." I looked at the space on the wall. "But I don't see them."

Fran shook her head with what seemed to be genuine sorrow. "We decided to remove them from the exhibit."

"Why?"

"As a gesture of respect for Gary. We'll be mounting a retrospective of his work sometime later this year. He was one of our most important eroticists."

"So can I still buy the work?"

She shook her head. "I'm afraid not."

"Are you holding them back till the prices shoot up?"

She bristled at the insult. "Not at all. The work isn't available because they were all previously sold."

"Every one of them?"

"I'm afraid so."

"So that's what the little blue dots meant."

"Exactly."

"Who bought them? Maybe I can talk him into letting a few go."

"I'm afraid we don't give out that information."

"Why not?"

"Many of our collectors don't wish their interest in erotica to become public. It is not a point of favor in certain circles, as I'm sure you can appreciate."

"Then tell me this—was it someone off the street or an established collector?"

She thought it over. "I can safely say that those particular photographs will be part of the most extensive private collection of erotica in the entire Northwest."

"So who gets the money?"

"How do you mean?"

"Richter's share. Who gets it now that he's dead?"

She shook her head. "I'm not sure I know the answer to that. What difference does it make?"

"I figure his heirs will have lots of pictures to sell, don't you? Was he married?"

"I'm sure not."

"Does he have relatives?"

"I have no idea."

"Did he make a will?"

"I'd be surprised if he did—Gary was quite slipshod about both his personal affairs and his business arrangements. But I didn't know him nearly as well as your questions imply."

"How about the model in those pictures?"

"What about her?"

"It was Nina Evans, wasn't it?"

The question made her uneasy. "I . . . yes. I suppose there's no need to be coy about it. I take it you're familiar with her work."

I nodded. "She's a stunning physical specimen."

"Yes, she is."

"Do you have any other work in your inventory that features Ms. Evans? By Richter or others?"

"I believe that shoot with Gary was her only erotic session. She

mostly does art studies." Fran glanced at her watch. "Is there anything else I can show you? I have a bas-relief in the storeroom
from a Hindu temple near New Delhi—it's the most sensuous
thing I've ever seen."

"I wouldn't know what to do with it," I said. When I reached
the door, I indulged in a hunch. "Tell Mr. Jensen I'd like to talk
about the Richter pieces sometime."

"I don't know any Mr. Jensen. I'm sorry."

I was sorry, too. "How about a model named Mandy? I met her
at a party one night. Did Richter do any work with her?"

Fran shook her head firmly, to close off that question and any
like it. "That name is not familiar to me."

As I left the gallery, the doorbell tinkled at my back, accusing
me of child's play.

On the way back to my car, I had to wait for a light at Roosevelt and
Forty-seventh. As my mind oscillated between two-dimensional
images of Nina Evans and three-dimensional holograms of Peggy
Nettleton, someone joined my wait for a break in the traffic. At
first glance, it didn't seem to be anyone I knew. It seemed, in fact,
to be a particularly buffeted victim of life on the city streets. On
second glance, which was prompted by a low groan emitted
from somewhere near her viscera, I recognized the woman as
Roan.

She was clearly in pain and had curled at the waist to lessen its
sting. An eye was black, a cheek was swollen, a wrist was wrapped
with a rough-hewn bandage made from a torn piece of cheese-
cloth. One arm wrapped around her belly as though that would
keep things in place till she got where she was going.

When she started to cross the street, I put out a hand to stop
her. "Roan?"

She tried to resist and only relented when she saw who was
restraining her. "Oh. Hi."

"What happened?"

"Nothing." Her lips were barely supple enough to form the words.

"Did someone beat you up?"

She shook her head and winced from the effort.

"You act like you've cracked some ribs. You should see a doctor."

"That's where I'm headed."

"Why don't I go with you?"

"It's all right. I can manage."

"Who did this to you?"

"No one. I just fell." Her timid eyes made her answer inaccurate.

"What did they want? Were they looking for Nina?"

Roan shook her head. "They just wanted her stuff."

"What stuff?"

"The stuff she gave me to keep for her."

"What was it?"

"I don't know; I didn't look. She asked me not to, so I didn't."

Tears started to flow and the emission seemed to sap what was left of her strength. I grabbed her waist to support her.

"I tried not to tell them," she sobbed, "but they hurt me. The little guy would have *killed* me, I think; he was having *fun*. What would make a person that mean?" The question was as light and airy as a cloud of poison gas.

"Who was this guy?" I asked her.

"There were two of them. Older, like you. One was bald; the little one was Hispanic. I never saw them before. I hope I never see them again."

"What did it look like, this stuff of Nina's?"

"An envelope. One of those padded ones."

"How big?"

"Letter size. Maybe a little bigger."

"What was inside?"

"I told you I didn't look."

"What did it feel like? A book?"

She shook her head. "Papers, maybe."

"Photographs?"

"Maybe." Roan groaned again and twisted out of my grasp. "I got to get to the clinic before they close."

"Do you want me to come with you?" I asked again.

"No. Please don't."

I reached in my wallet and gave her a twenty. "Buy some food; buy some aspirin."

"Thanks."

Roan groaned with the effort to pocket the bill, then shuffled through a break in the traffic and disappeared down the block.

When I got back to the motel, there was a message from Peggy to call as soon as I got in. I poured myself a slug of scotch, indulged in some refreshed recollection of the times we had shared drinks at the end of a difficult day, then picked up the phone and did her bidding.

"Thank God you called," she began, her voice low and distressed and ulterior.

"What's happened?"

"They took Ted in for questioning."

"The police?"

"Yes."

"About Richter?"

"Yes. Apparently Ted did go to Richter's studio several days ago looking for Nina. He and Richter got in this shouting match and the guy next door came over to complain and at some point Ted told him his name. When the police were swarming all over after the body was discovered, this guy told them about the fight and the cops came to the office to question him. Whatever he said made them decide to take him downtown. Ted was scared to death. What should I do?"

"Get him a lawyer."

"I already did. Do you think he's in trouble, Marsh? Tell me the truth."

I decided not to tell her that was exactly what I thought. And maybe even what I hoped. "They're just covering the bases," I evaded.

"Are you sure? What about the pictures I found?"

"They won't know about the pictures unless one of us tells them. And even then, they just prove he was there, which they know already. Your man will be home for dinner. And after he gets there, I'm going to drop by for a chat."

"Why?"

"It's time we pooled our resources."

It took her a while to respond. "He won't like it, Marsh. He gets uptight whenever I mention you. He knows I still care about you. He's afraid I care too much."

My cheeks reddened and my chest tightened. If she'd been in the room, I'd have tried very hard to kiss her. Instead, I made do with logic.

"That seems less important at this point than finding Nina before the guy who killed Richter decides to do the same to her," I said, awash in self-righteousness.

"Do you really think that's likely?"

"I think Nina ran afoul of someone who's mad or jealous or afraid and wants to make sure she isn't a problem for him."

"But how could that have happened?"

What I thought was that it was because the guy has a fetish for erotica and wants to keep it a secret. What I said was that I didn't know.

"I'm coming over tonight," I said again.

"No. Not tonight. We're going out for dinner."

"Then when?"

"I don't know. Tomorrow, maybe."

"That's too late. What time will you get home?"

"Late, probably."

"Then I'll come by before you leave. Do you know anyone named Crowder, by the way?"

"No. Should I?"

The answer was yes, but I didn't say so. There were some things I wasn't ready for, either.

CHAPTER 19

It's as though she died and went to the penthouse—an entire apartment full of wonderful stuff, apparently just for her. For a moment of trepidation, she wonders what she will have to do to earn it. No one has ever paid her this well just for displaying her body.

There are things she's never had before, not since she'd left home at any rate, and sometimes even then. A poster bed, for example, draped in paisley like a caliph's. Matching sets of stoneware and stemware. Flowered sheets and scented soaps. Prints on the wall by an artist she's actually heard of. A food processor. A mini–espresso maker and pounds and pounds of Torrefazione to feed into it.

After a first quick inventory, she takes stock again, and then again, fingering objects, caressing fabrics, admiring artwork, disbelieving both the parts and the entirety. It is a palace on the lake, a view apartment with all the trimmings, a dream come true in the vale of Madison Park. The only thing missing is a telephone.

He will communicate solely by E-mail, he said, although at the time she didn't take him literally. Messages will come through the phone line and appear on her screen automatically, she just has to scroll to the end of the file to be certain she's gotten everything he wants her to have. She can talk back, but only to Chris and only to his office—the address is already lodged in a macro; she can summon it with a single stroke.

His salutation is still on the screen: "WELCOME TO YOUR NEW HOME. We've tried to provide everything you'll need—there is food and drink for five days and sundries for longer; there is a selection of casual clothing, some basic exercise equipment, and a variety of reading material and videos. If we've missed anything, let us know by way of the computer.

"You should not leave the apartment for any reason, or communicate with anyone but me. Work will begin in two days—prepare yourself accordingly. Chris."

Out one window is Lake Washington, blue and calm and reassuring. But out the other is a man, seated behind the wheel of a Cherokee, watching. It looks like the car she saw at Roan's, the one she feared was following her. The room is suddenly sinister. When she turns on a lamp, something about it makes the feeling intensify. She begins to tremble, and then to cry. She runs in the bedroom and hides beneath the quilted cover.

Seeking safety, she has found its opposite.

¤   ¤   ¤

THE BLITZ CLUB WAS only four blocks from the university campus, evidence that academics bubbled with as much repressed desire as the rest of us. The exterior was blue board and batten with windows obliterated by sheets of painted plywood that were plastered with examples of Gary Richter's soft-core accomplishments.

The door was lit by a naked red bulb directly overhead. Immediately inside, a bouncer collected a cover charge. The cover was five bucks; the bouncer was bored; the interior was as dark as an executioner's heart but for an array of filtered spotlights directed toward the stage and bar.

The stage ran the entire length of the room, along the wall to the west; the bar ran down the other side. In between were as many tiny tables and chairs as the narrow space would accommodate. At the far end was a door marked PRIVATE and another marked EMPLOYEES ONLY. There were three customers in the place. The music was loud and indecipherable.

As I made my way toward a bar stool, a woman wearing a short pink wrapper and red high heels came out of the door marked PRIVATE trailed by a young man with a red face and equally red suspenders that stretched like strapping tape over the swell of his flannel shirt. The woman in the wrapper disappeared inside the other door, scratching her hip as she went. The guy with the red suspenders joined a buddy at the bar and proclaimed the experience, "way cool." I slipped onto a stool and waited to be blessed with the bartender's attention.

She was toughly attractive and as bored as the bouncer. Her silicone breasts were impervious to the tight white leotard that enveloped them. Her hair had been blond from a bottle for so long it looked like a saffron scouring pad. A scar lifted her lip in a continual sneer; from the look in her eye she could have cut it on purpose, just to get men to back off.

I ordered a beer, then gestured toward the rear doors. "What goes on back there?"

"Couch dance. Want one?"

"What is it?"

"You sit on a couch, the girl dances for you. If you tip, she dances real close. And sometimes that's not all she does."

"How much?"

"Twenty plus tips."

"What do you get for a tip?"

"Whatever she thinks you deserve, as long as it stops short of touching."

"Her me or me her?"

She smiled. "Either way, cowboy. But you can rub her with your mind all you want."

"Too bad. I can do the mind stuff at home."

She shrugged. "A little visual stimulation never hurts, but the law's the law," she grinned, "when there's a cop on the premises. I can get April for you, if you're interested. She's a real flexible young lady."

I guessed the description applied more to her morals than to her spinal cord. I looked around. "Which is April?"

"She's back in the john—just got off shift. She's cute, you'll like her. Got enough meat to make it interesting, not like Linda up there."

Her look traveled to the stage, where a woman who was both naked and emaciated seemed grimly determined to make some part of her person vibrate. I looked back at the bartender. "How about you instead of April?"

She'd heard it before and then some. "Free drinks are against policy, so bullshit won't get you anything but air. And what you see is all you get; I gave up dancing when my implants started shifting. You want April or no?"

"I hear Mandy's pretty good."

Her eyes rolled like a vaudevillian's. "Mandy. Jesus. Don't mention that bitch again. I mean it."

"What's wrong with Mandy?"

She started to frame a hot retort but asked a question instead. "Who are you, pal?"

"A customer. What else would I be?"

"Vice. DEA. IRS. They all come by for a peek. But that's all they get, is a peek, 'cause we run a clean ship. If you're looking for something else, you're wasting your time up here. Be better off down in Pierce County."

"I don't think Pierce County has what I'm looking for."

"Which is?"

"A peek at Mandy."

"Well, we don't got that, either. Mandy don't work here no more."

"Why not?"

"She broke a rule."

"Which rule?"

She slung her bar rag at the sink. "The rule against too many questions. We got other girls, mister; new ones every hour. You don't like the selection, move on down the road."

"If I wanted to find Mandy, where would I go?"

"Regrade, probably."

"What's regrade?"

"The Denny Regrade, north of downtown and south of Denny Way. Used to be a hill till they graded it out way back when."

"Why does Mandy hang out there?"

"That's where white folks find dope. Cobain made his last connection in the Regrade, so they say. Me, I could give a shit—I still get high on Engelbert Humperdinck."

I laughed. "What kind of dope does Mandy use?"

"Same as all the grungers—heroin."

"I thought heroin went out with the sixties."

"It's back big time. Lots of rockers ride that horse all the way up the stairway around here."

"You mean they died of it."

"That's what I mean."

"You got an address for Mandy?"

"I got nothing at all for Mandy. Or you, either, unless you want another beer."

It was time to shift gears. "How about Victor?"

Her eyes narrowed. "Victor who?"

"Krakov."

"What about him?"

"He coming in today?"

"Why would he come in?"

"He owns the place; I thought he might keep tabs on his investment."

She shrugged. "He might. What of it?"

"I'd like to talk to him."

"What about?"

"Business."

"Victor don't talk about business; Victor just *does* business."

"He'll talk when he hears Jensen sent me."

"Who?"

"Jensen."

"Lattimore?"

Bingo. "Yeah. Lattimore. Tell Victor I'm here about Jensen Lattimore."

"Victor's not here; I told you."

"I thought he might be behind that other door."

"Well, he's not."

"Then I'll wait."

The bartender shrugged once more, then strolled to the CD player behind the bar. A moment later, the air was rent not by Nirvana but by Mozart. Behind me, a girl in a micronic thong bikini came out, wrapped herself around a pole at center stage, and proceeded to slither and snake her way up and down its brassy length to the strains of a flute quartet. The combination worked better than it should have.

The delicate mood didn't last. As the customers down front began to get restless, the bartender pressed a remote and the music switched to something with rhythms of the subtlety of pile driving. The dancer doffed her bikini and abandoned the pole and gave the customers what they wanted, which was an intimate view of her privates.

I must have been rapt myself, because when the song finally ended, I discovered that a man was sitting on the stool beside me. He was burly and ruddy, with hair tied in back in a ponytail, one ear that was missing a lobe, and lips as fat as night crawlers and as red as old lipstick. His eyebrows were as white and straight as lines of coke.

The bartender brought him a shot glass full of something

brown. "Hear Lattimore sent you," he grumbled, with gravel and evil in his voice, then tossed back the shot in a gulp.

"He's worried about some of your girls."

"Why?"

"He heard things."

"Like what?"

"Like too many of them are turning out to be junkies."

"Yeah? Like who?"

"Like Mandy."

"I told him Mandy don't work here no more."

"Or they run off like Nina."

"Who?"

"Nina Evans."

"Don't know her."

"She was one of Richter's models."

"Not for the club. I only use the dancers."

"Speaking of which, Jensen wonders whether you know anything about it."

"About what?"

"Richter's murder."

"Why would I know anything about that?"

"Jensen figured there might be word on the street about it."

"Tell him not this street." The big man drained a second drink. "And then you tell him I took him on as a silent partner, but this don't sound silent, this sounds noisy as hell. You tell him if I want some geek telling me how to do my business, I'll get someone who knows more about running skin than Jensen Lattimore."

Victor got off his stool and left the bar. The bartender gestured at the stage. "Sally'll dance for you if you want."

"To Mozart?"

"Who?"

I slid off my stool and headed back to the john, then found a phone and used it. "Hello?" said the voice, as faint as the strains of Pearl Jam that were leaping at me from the stage, but not so faint I didn't recognize the voice as Fran's, the manager of Erospace.

"This is Rufus Kline," I said, my tongue lolling somewhere near my cheek. "I work for Lattimore."

"What's with you DigiArt guys—you got more turnover than IBM. Tell him it's in the mail."

"What is?"

"The income statement."

"That must be someone else's department. I'm calling about the photographs."

"What . . . oh, the Richter prints. What about them?"

"I wonder when we can expect delivery."

"Whenever you want. You want them in Issaquah like last time?"

"Yeah."

"I can take them out there tomorrow night."

"Good. I'll let you know what time. It may be late."

"No problem. You still interested in anything else by Richter we can get our hands on?"

"Absolutely," I said, then went back to the bar. "I think I'll take you up on that specialty number," I said when the bartender drifted my way.

"That'll be twenty up front."

I slipped her the requisite bill.

"Which one you want?"

I gestured toward the stage. "How long's Sally been working here?"

"Long enough to know what to do with her booty. What difference does it make?"

"I want someone experienced."

"She's been here two years. Anything got on your mind, she's heard worse."

"I'll take her."

"Good choice. Go on back and I'll send her your way after she finishes her set. You want the bikini or lingerie?"

"Lingerie. And the Mozart."

"You got it if we got any."

The bartender resumed tending the bar and I went through the door marked PRIVATE. The interior was even more depressing than the barroom—greasy shag carpet, hideous plastic paneling, understuffed tweed couch, cheap boom box, and black velvet art of tigers and panthers stuck on the walls for some class.

When Sally came in she was panting. She had a towel draped over her neck and down her breasts and a piece of lingerie in her hand.

"Tough set?" I asked.

"They're all tough when you're on the rag. What's your name?"

"Calvin."

"I'm Sally. What type of entertainment you interested in?"

"Oral."

"Sorry. I don't know what you heard, but we don't do head tricks, not in the club, at least."

"I'm not talking sex, I'm talking conversation."

She frowned in disgust. "We don't do that, either."

"What do you do?"

"Dance. Sit on your lap if you make it worth my while. Rub up your johnson if you're generous. Put on this teddy if you like romance better than reality."

"I just want some information."

"About what? Heath care reform?"

"About Victor's special clients."

Her eyes flicked toward the corner of the room, which meant we were being miked and probably videotaped as well. "I don't know what you're talking about," she said flatly.

"I'm talking about the rich men Victor services with his girls. I'm talking about Jensen Lattimore, in particular."

"Don't know the man."

"You ought to—he owns the place."

She shrugged. "So?"

"I'm wondering if you ever had trouble with him."

"What kind of trouble?"

"Rough stuff—violence, kinky sex, sadism."

"That's not trouble; that's expertise."

I lowered my voice. "And I was wondering if you knew about Mandy."

She hesitated, then put her hands on her hips and adopted a menacing pose. "If you're not going to tip, I got to leave."

"I'll tip," I said, and got out another twenty. "If you make it worth my while."

She went to the boom box and punched a button; Madonna started singing about self-respect; apparently Sally didn't find it ironic.

When the music was sufficiently loud to preclude conversation, she started to dance, writhing and bobbing in time to the music, a curiously catatonic smile on her face as she gyrated six inches from my knees. The towel and the lingerie soon mated on the floor.

But I had misinterpreted her intentions. The next time she bent toward me and shimmied, she whispered without moving her lips. "They monitor this place," she said.

I nodded.

She waited until her dance offered another chance to whisper. In the meantime, I enjoyed the play of her hips and the smell of her sweat. "I never did special clients," she said as she thrust her pelvis at my chin.

"Did Mandy?"

"Yeah."

"Did Nina Evans?"

She shrugged.

"What happened to Mandy?"

"Junkie."

"Why?"

"Something happened."

"What?"

"Don't know."

"Where can I find her?"

"Second and Pike. Late."

"That's where she lives?"

"That's where she hooks."

CHAPTER 20

As much as she wants to revel in seclusion, she feels stifled within a week. Stifled and isolated; it is solitary confinement, basically, despite the three occasions Chris has picked her up and taken her out on a shoot, seeing that she earns her keep. But she is definitely under wraps—no phone, no radio, no newspaper. Somehow, the only TV reception is from cable channels like Lifetime and A&E, not network affiliates like KOMO and KING. Why is this happening?

Over the years she has become a news junkie and feels edgy without a daily dose, so she begins to scheme and plot. Her first foray is to stroll casually out the door and head for the Red Apple market, with the intent of buying a newspaper, but the guy in the Cherokee tags along, and when she enters the store he enters after her. It is spooky and surreal, even though he says nothing and does not acknowledge her presence. She makes do with a box of Tampax and a quart of nonfat yogurt.

She visits the neighbors, in hopes of sharing their newspaper or their Newsweek, but for some reason the neighbors are never home. On the way back from a shoot, she asks Chris to stop at a variety store—he picks a Fred Meyer. In the guise of buying an irrelevance, she intends to steal a radio and take it back to the condo, but when she sees the elaborate detection devices at the register, she knows her ruse will be exposed. Then God knows what would happen.

The answer comes while she is doing her laundry. As she is transferring her whites to the dryer, she hears the tremulous

*strains of "Chances Are." Her mother had played the Mathis
album ad nauseam, as though it restored her soul or her virginity
or something. She enjoys the song to its conclusion before she realizes that it suggests a solution to her problem. As the call letters of
KBSG echo through the basement caverns, she trails the sound to
its source, which turns out to be the furnace room.*

*The maintenance man is, by definition, a man, so she closes the
deal within minutes. She gets a half-hour with his radio on Tues-
days and Thursdays and he gets a Full Sail Ale as often as she can
manage it. He believes he's gotten the better of the deal and she is
happy for him to think so. Meanwhile, she covets the radio like a
narcotic.*

*The fifth time she tunes in, she learns of the death of Gary
Richter. She exults, then despairs; her paranoia returns full-blown.
But subsequently comes the framework of a plan.*

¤   ¤   ¤

AFTER I LEFT THE BLITZ CLUB I found a phone and punched in
the only 800 number I know by heart.

Clay Oerter is a stockbroker. Not my broker, since I don't have
anything to broker, but he's a good guy and on top of that I've
given him lots of coin in the form of poker chips over the years, for
which he gives me some corporate lowdown from time to time.

"DigiArt," I said when he came on the line.

He didn't ask why, he just punched some buttons. "Nothing
on it."

"It's in Seattle, if that helps."

"It doesn't."

"What does it mean when you don't have anything?"

"It means it's private and not San Francisco."

"You know anyone in Seattle in the broker business?"

"Is that where you are?"

"Yep."

"Is it true it rains every day?"

"Not a drop since I hit town."

"So how is it otherwise?"

"A lot like the city, except the neighborhoods are better."

"You mean they have yards and trees."

"Lots of each," I confirmed.

"Sounds nice."

"Is nice."

"You're not going to move up there, are you?"

"I'm too poor to move."

"Good. One of our guys went up there a couple of years back. His kid was into alternative rock and went to Seattle to join a band call Bung, and the old man tagged along."

"How did it work out?"

"Bung couldn't find a bass player, so the kid's the broker now and the old man is a drummer in an oldies band on weekends. Plays 'Louie Louie' four times a night."

"That sounds like a good definition of hell."

Clay laughed and gave me the name and number of his buddy and said he'd call and clear me.

The friend's name was Gil Driller. I called him from a phone booth near the Pike Place Market.

"Clay says you're a detective," Driller said after I introduced myself and my connection.

"Sad but true."

"Into something juicy?"

"Not yet. But sometimes the juice only starts to flow after I leave town."

"Must be stressful work."

"No more than being responsible for the life savings of widows and orphans."

He laughed, though not robustly. "How's Clay doing these days?"

"Doing great at poker. Don't know about stocks and bonds."

"How about that wife of his?"

"I don't know the woman and Clay never talks about her."

"That's funny. He talked about her all the time at the office."

"Probably I just didn't notice."

He laughed. "Probably you're just being discreet. Clay says to give you what I've got on DigiArt, but I'm afraid I don't have much."

"If you've got anything it'll be an improvement."

"Good. Well, DigiArt is a start-up, about two years old. Still private; CEO is a computer guy named Wellington. No major financing that we know of—hard for these information highway guys to find venture capital up in this part of the country. There's money here, but it's cautious money; hell, the whole town is cautious. But if they get something hot, they'll come up with the cash to come to market. Cable and Howse or Olympic Venture Partners will back them till it's time to go public."

"Any chance Ted Evans has money in DigiArt?"

"Possible, but Ted's more into real estate than high tech. You heard something along those lines?"

"Not a thing. What's Evans's reputation around town?"

"Good. Conservative, but good. No major killings, no major disasters. Commercial real estate in West Seattle and the east side, some Boeing satellites down by White City, a little maritime stuff in Tacoma. No computer ties that I know about."

"What's DigiArt's niche?" I asked. "What are they shooting for that Microsoft or someone isn't doing already?"

"Some kind of art service, as I understand it."

"What's that mean, exactly?"

"You've got interior decorators for residences, and design consultants that supply paintings and sculpture for the company headquarters. Well, DigiArt wants to replace all that with software. The art of the world piped through the PC, for your viewing enjoyment any time of the day or night. They're acquiring electronic rights to most of the world's major collections."

"How close are they getting to having something to sell?"

"No idea."

"What does Jensen Lattimore have to do with it?"

Driller paused. When he spoke, his voice was throaty and non-committal. "Nothing that I know of."

"Who is he, anyway?"

"Why?"

"His name keeps popping up."

"In what connection?"

Without knowing why, I decided to be cautious. "In a confidential connection."

Driller paused long enough to boil an egg. "Sorry," he said finally. "I can't discuss that particular individual at this point in time."

He was off the line ten seconds later, while I was still wondering why everyone tiptoed around the name Jensen Lattimore.

The DigiArt offices were three blocks south of the market across from a place that sold furniture. They were impressively impersonal and carefully unrevealing. This is a substantial business, the decor declared, without quite declaring what that business was.

I waited in the outer office for someone to join me, certain that my presence was being monitored. Finally a woman emerged from the back and asked how she could help me. She was exactly as handsome as the offices.

"I'd like to speak to the CEO. Mr. Wellington," I added, just to show I was dealing from strength.

"May I ask your name?"

"Tanner. Marsh Tanner." I bowed at the waist. "And may I ask yours?"

She was all business. "Maxine. You are representing what company?"

"Tanner and Associates."

"What is the nature of your business, Mr. Tanner?"

"Why don't we wait on that till I meet with Mr. Wellington?"

She crossed her arms. "Until I know the nature of your enterprise in detail, there's not much chance of that happening."

"Women," I said.

Her look marched from haughty to puzzled. "Is that an editorial?"

I shook my head. "It's a job description."

"Women?"

I nodded.

"What aspect of . . . *women* . . . do you work with?"

"The obvious aspect."

"I'm afraid I'm not sure what that means."

My smile said I was as tolerant of ignorance as a math teacher. "Your boss has been scouring the city for attractive women. I'm here to tell him that if that's what he wants, I'm the guy he needs to talk to."

"And why is that?"

"Because I represent a lot of them."

"Women?"

"Women."

"In what capacity?"

"In a capacity that your boss can use to his advantage, if and when we cut a deal. Now I'm about to walk out that door, Maxine, because you've been a trifle chilly toward me. I know it's your job to keep out the riffraff, but if I were you I wouldn't let the responsibility for letting me go fall entirely on your shoulders."

Her lip curled like a Pringle. "But I don't believe you. That you're some sort of modeling agent, I mean. You look more like a boxing promoter."

I smiled with what I hoped was celestial serenity. "Does it *matter* what you believe, Maxine? In the greater scheme of things?"

The rhetoric did the trick; she wilted like leaf lettuce. "I . . . perhaps not in this instance. Wait one moment."

She turned on her heel and marched through the rear door. I

used her absence to try to find something to indicate what DigiArt might be up to, but nothing turned up that was more intriguing than a Windows menu on a computer screen.

A moment later a man emerged from the back and gazed at me with equanimity. He was simply but memorably dressed, with boyish good looks and an artistic flair that extended from his white huaraches and black canvas slacks to the billowy peasant's shirt that was tied at his waist with a drawstring. His eyes were shiny and black; his hair was as slick as a seal's.

"I'm sorry you've wasted a visit," he began easily. "You are apparently under the impression that I'm recruiting women for one of our projects. But I'm afraid it's not true."

"It was true a few weeks ago."

When he shrugged, the cloth in his shirt fluttered like feathers. "Perhaps. But in any event, the search has ended."

"Because you found your girl."

"Precisely."

I waited till I had his eye. "Her name is Nina Evans."

It nudged him off balance. Not far off—his only reactions were to blink and rub his nose—but far enough. "What makes you think that?"

"Because I know you talked to her. And if you talked to her, you hired her."

"How do you know she was qualified for what we had in mind?"

I smiled. "I've seen her work. She's qualified for what *anyone* has in mind."

He frowned at my occupation of his turf. "Even assuming you're right, what of it?"

"Not much. I just need to talk to her about something."

"I'm afraid I can't help you."

"Because you don't know where she is or because your boss is keeping her under wraps."

He was too elaborately uninterested. "What boss would that be?"

"Jensen Lattimore."

Wellington's countenance darkened by three shades and a twitch emerged below his left eye. "Who says Jensen Lattimore has any connection to DigiArt?"

"I do." I smiled. "And since you're trying to keep it secret, you'll want to know my price for keeping quiet. My price is the whereabouts of Nina Evans."

His eyes traveled the room. "I can't tell you that. I'm sorry."

"The last guy who took pictures of Nina ended up dead. Doesn't that worry you a tad?"

His face reddened. "Don't be ridiculous."

"What do you know about a girl named Mandy who used to model for Gary Richter and dance for Victor Krakov?"

"Nothing." He glanced at Maxine. Maxine walked to the door and stood ready to usher me out. "I'm afraid I have business to attend to. It's been nice meeting you, Mr. Tanner," Wellington said smoothly.

I didn't budge. "What will happen if I plant a story in the local paper disclosing the connection between Lattimore and DigiArt and speculating about what you guys are up to? Maybe implying that it's some new form of pornography service, like some of the sicker stuff that keeps showing up on the Internet? How would the boss feel about that?"

Wellington sighed. A sweat stain blossomed beneath the billow of his shirt. "We wouldn't want you to do anything of that nature. Obviously."

"Then tell me where Nina is."

"Why do you want to know?"

"So I can put some people's minds at rest."

"I'm sorry, but I'm afraid I can't give you that information."

"I can take this to the cops, you know."

"Why would they be interested?"

"Because Nina might know something about Richter's murder.

They'll wonder what your connection with Richter is, too, I imagine, especially when they learn you stole his best model from him."

"Nonsense."

"You don't look like a bad guy, Wellington. But all of a sudden you look like a worried guy. I wonder why that is."

He left it to Maxine to dispose of me.

CHAPTER 21

Despite the melodramatics of her isolation, life with DigiArt has been benign. Although she is supposedly on call twenty-four hours a day, in reality her contact with Chris Wellington has been minimal. They have worked together twice a week for six weeks: six sessions, two in the studio and four at various points outside, including one in the Seattle Art Museum and one in the Japanese Tea Garden at sunset when the light was so thick and viscid it made her cry. They had used the venues after hours, had the places entirely to themselves as far as she could tell, which let her cavort among Pollocks and Picassos and rub up against weeping willows and mossy stones, all to her heart's content.

She wonders who pulled the strings. Not Chris, that's for sure. Chris barely has the ego necessary for the job at hand. He is far too deferential, too accommodating, too nice to claw his way to the top of the heap, even in the fledgling world of digital art. The contrast to Gary Richter couldn't have been more dramatic. Or more appealing.

She gets up from the chair on the deck and goes into the kitchen to refill her wineglass with Chardonnay. Nice. Nice and free and plentiful. It is becoming more difficult to stay angry and alert, to connect her current situation with the obscenities she unearthed at Gary's place and gave to Roan to keep for her, to flesh out the framework of her plan. To tell the truth, if she could just keep Gary's murder off her mind, and remember Mandy only from the old days, she would be somewhere close to happy.

Suddenly the light in the kitchen goes out and the stereo falls silent in mid-wail by Michael Bolton. As she is walking to the kitchen to see if she can find a fuse box, there is a knock at the door. A caller is sufficiently unusual to be alarming. She looks through the peephole but sees nothing. She hooks the chain and asks who it is.

"Chris," he says softly, appearing like a rubber ghost in the fish-eye of the peephole. "Can I come in?" He grins timidly. "I've got goodies."

She hears something different in his voice, an absence of formality, a presence of emotion, in contrast to his work persona. She wonders what he's up to and unhooks the chain to find out.

"Hi," he says as she opens the door.

"Hi."

"Is this all right?"

"Sure." She decides to put him at ease. "What's in the bag?"

"Strawberries and shortcake."

"Yummy."

"I remembered you like them."

"I do, but if you want milk we'd better eat fast. My electricity just went out."

He nods. "The whole building is dark. Must be a transformer somewhere. They'll fix it in a minute, probably."

She leans against the wall. "I'm having wine on the deck. Want some?"

"Sure."

"Might as well—you paid for it."

She goes to the kitchen and fills a second goblet and returns to the foyer and presents it to him. He toasts her silently, then follows her out to the deck.

"I thought you wanted me to lose weight," she says impishly. "Now you bring dessert. Which is it?"

"You could gain a pound or two."

"Where would you like me to gain it?"

His smile is oddly bashful. "I don't think you can choose, can you?"

"I usually gain in the hips. Then thighs. Then belly. Then breasts. Unfortunately, I reduce in reverse order."

"Sounds like you've made a study of it."

"My body is my only asset. I figured I should pay as much attention to it as other people do to their stock portfolios."

He examines her through the dusky twilight. "I wouldn't say it's your only asset."

"Oh yeah? What else is there?"

"Your mind, for one thing. I'm really enjoying working with you. You're quite funny, sometimes. And you have excellent aesthetic sense."

"You're funny, too."

"But I don't always mean to be."

She smiles to show she finds his artlessness charming, then finishes her wine and glances at the interior of the apartment. "So why are you here, Mr. Wellington?"

"I thought we could spend some time together away from the office, so to speak."

"What kind of time?"

He reddens. "Quality time, I suppose."

"Does the definition of quality have anything to do with sex?"

His writhe of embarrassment tips the director's chair. "Only if you want it to."

"Even if I want it to, we'd need to talk about a few things first."

"What things?"

"We have to talk about lamps. And then we have to talk about getting me a little something I can carry in my purse for protection."

¤ ¤ ¤

I CAUGHT AN EARLY DINNER at a place called the Two Bells Tavern, which served as good a burger as I'd had in years, then wandered back to the motel on a cushion of Pilsner Urquel. When I got to the room I called Peggy, even though it was before the appointed time.

"Yes?"

"It's Marsh."

"I asked you not . . . is anything wrong?"

"Nothing that wasn't wrong at lunch. I'm coming over."

"But we—"

"I need to talk to Ted. Have the cops released him?"

"Yes, but—"

"Is he home?"

"Yes."

"I'll be there in twenty minutes. If you think it's going to get messy, you can go to the party alone and he'll join you when we've finished." I hung up before she could dish up another excuse.

The Evans house loomed even larger than on my previous visit, gleaming in the summer evening like the palace of some minor king. It wasn't irrelevant, that house, not as much to the issue at hand as to the decision of its mistress to leave me.

As the years have passed, and the titans of industry and lions of literature and icons of sport have become my peers and younger, I've had trouble rationalizing my lack of financial attainment. Many of my friends, like Clay Oerter, are well-to-do. Some of my clients have been wealthy by any measure of the term. Almost everyone I know, including Charley the cop, earns more than I do in the average year.

I have plenty of proof of poverty. My car is ten years old and the seat fabric has worn to the foam. My house isn't a house, it's an apartment. My music still comes off vinyl and tape; my TV is a thirteen-inch RCA; I don't own a computer or microwave or a toaster that matches the current dimensions of bread. I don't own a stock or a bond; I have no interest in pension or profit-sharing arrangements; I possess no precious metals other than a dozen silver dollars I won one time in Reno. I do have a valuable painting, but it's something I'll never sell. The self-employment tax is killing me.

At bottom, my net worth, exclusive of personal possessions, totals thirty thousand dollars. In financial terms, my life has been a joke, quite simply, and more and more financial terms seem to be the only terms that matter. At one time or another, I have feared that every woman I've cared for would leave me for someone with money. More often than not, they have done just that.

I shook my head and laughed at my flight of fancy. The contours of Peggy's decision to leave me warped beneath tons of self-pity, I walked to the porch and rang the bell. My heart was thumping, my hands and forehead were wet with sweat, my brain whirred with the effort to mount some snappy sayings that would impress all concerned with my wit. When Peggy opened the door, she looked even worse than I felt.

"Hi," she said.

"Hi."

"This isn't nice of you, you know."

"This isn't a nice situation."

She closed her eyes and sighed. Her hair fell in a wave that always returned to its starting place. Her dress was an equally soft jersey, of the precise tint of her hair and eyes. It was probably Armani or one of those guys. It probably cost more than my car.

When she spoke again, the words trembled a bit; it wasn't cool enough for the cause to be climatological. "Now that you're here, you might as well come inside," she said.

"Does he know I'm coming?"

She nodded. "He went to the store for some liquor—we were out of scotch."

"He didn't need to do that."

"He thought he did."

She made room for me to pass and I entered Mr. Evans's impressive domain. His fiancée led me to the living room at the pace of a forced march.

The room was expensively and expertly decorated, mostly in mission style, the deep tones of burgundy and slate mixed with plenty of plaids and stripes to add to the sense of substance. The art on the wall was Native American—masks, blankets, sand paintings, headdresses. The rugs on the floor were in the same vein, as were the pots on the shelves and the baskets in the breakfront. It was a man's room, not a woman's, but I'd bet Ted had already promised that Peggy could redecorate once they had plighted their troth.

I sat on a leather wing chair and Peggy sat on the brown leather couch. She had dressed for the occasion as though it were a benefit ball—I resisted the urge to suggest that she kick off her heels and get comfortable the way she used to when she worked for me. But comfort wasn't on the agenda.

I made the requisite survey of the room. "Nice."

"Thank you. Ted has good taste."

"In women as well."

She blushed and was angry. "Please, don't."

I shrugged away my goof. "How did Ted fare with the cops?"

"I guess okay. He explained why he went to see that Richter man, and they seemed to take his word that it was nothing more than an argument."

"What made him go down there?"

"I . . . maybe he should tell you himself."

"Maybe so."

We zigged and zagged, our thoughts and glances dancing out of reach of each other in a game of emotional tag of the sort you play in junior high school. It occurred to me that middle age might mean that from then on you go backward, both physically and psychologically.

I decided to wait for Peggy to set the next direction. "I tried to convince him to just let her go," she said after a minute.

"How do you mean?"

"To get on with his life—our lives—and let Nina do what she will when she wants to do it."

"What if she can't?"

Peggy looked at me. "If she's been kidnapped or something, you mean?"

"I'm not sure what I mean. But if you think her disappearance is because of some grudge against you, I'm not sure you're right."

"Then what is the reason?"

"I don't know."

I started to say something about Jensen Lattimore, but the front door opened onto my question and someone came into the room. He was wearing his walk-the-dog outfit and carrying a brown paper bag; his eyes gleamed with equal parts interest and aggression.

I stood up. We smiled and nodded. We stuck out our hands. We stepped forward so we could shake.

"Marsh Tanner."

"Ted Evans. I've heard a lot about you over the past couple of years."

"I've heard a lot about you over the past couple of weeks."

He held up a paper bag. "Peggy says you're a scotch drinker. Ballantine's."

"Fine."

"Back in a flash."

Ted toted the booze to the kitchen. Peggy smiled tightly. I sat back down in the chair. "He's nervous," she said.

"So am I."

She smiled. "So am I."

We sort of laughed.

"Who would have thought we'd meet in a situation like this?" she mused softly.

"Like what?"

"Like . . ." She waved her hand, as if to encompass the universe. "This."

"I always thought your getting married was a pretty likely possibility, actually."

"But I always thought I'd be marrying you."

I glanced toward the kitchen, not knowing whether I was happy or sad that Ted was nowhere in evidence. In the nether reaches of my mind, I heard Peggy whisper an apology.

A minute later Ted was back, bearing drinks on a silver tray. Mine was at least a double, with three clear cubes of ice. I never know how rich people keep them clear like that. "I hope it's all right. The ice."

"It's fine."

He handed Peggy what looked like a gin and tonic, then picked up a glass that contained what looked like sun tea but was probably bourbon. "Cheers." Peggy and I raised our glasses and repeated the word.

I drank enough to matter, then raised my glass again. "Here's to your future happiness. As Mr. and Mrs. Evans. Or Nettleton-Evans. Or Peggy and Ted, or whatever you're going to call yourselves."

"Thank you," they said, exchanging thankful looks, grateful to have it out on the table. As we drank to their connubial future, I didn't even cross my fingers.

Ted sat next to Peggy on the couch. Peggy looked at each of us in turn, then stood up. "I think it's time for a bachelor party," she said, and hurried to another part of the house or maybe off to the dinner engagement. Her drink lingered on the coffee table, a sweaty token of her affection.

"Well," Ted said.

I asked a question I'd asked of Peggy. "How'd it go with the cops?"

"All right, I guess. I didn't say much—my attorney advised me not to—so they're not very happy with me."

"Cops aren't happy with anything short of a full confession."

"Yes, well, I don't have anything to confess."

I smiled. "I wish I could say the same."

"But you . . . oh. I see. Yes. Well, we're none of us perfect, of course, but I don't really think they expected I'd had anything to do with Richter's death." He looked around the room. "I mean, after all . . ."

I nodded my agreement: "After all" is the best defense there is. "Are the police going to be looking for Nina?"

"They said so, but I'm not sure what that means."

"Neither am I, beyond some sort of all-points bulletin. Do they have a motive for the murder?"

"Not that they disclosed." Ted took a swig from his drink. "Have you learned anything at all, Mr. Tanner? Where do you think she is?"

"I think she's hiding from whoever killed Gary Richter."

His eyes widened and he leaned toward us. "Who do you think it was?"

"I think it was connected with Richter's work. Someone who became obsessed with Nina's modeling, maybe. Someone who wanted her for himself or maybe wanted to keep her from exposing herself to the world the way she was doing. Someone who saw himself as her savior, or maybe the opposite."

"You make it sound so . . . biblical."

"Murder gets biblical pretty fast. So does sex if you let it."

"So we're looking for some religious nut?"

"Maybe. Some sort of fanatic, anyway."

"You sound like you know his name."

I shook my head. "I don't. Do you?"

He blinked twice. "No. Of course not. How would I?"

"I thought maybe Dale Crowder might fit the bill."

His glass stopped halfway to his lips. He rose off the couch, looked at the direction in which Peggy had disappeared, then sagged back into his seat. "Does she know what you know? About all that?"

I shook my head.

"Does she have to?"

"Not unless it's relevant. Is it?"

"I don't have the faintest idea. Crowder's a worthless sot who's been out of our lives for years. I doubt he could have summoned the effort to attack Richter even if he wanted to." Ted's voice turned misty. "I tried my best to replace him, to be everything he wasn't in their lives. I thought I did a good job. Till this."

I wasn't moved to dispute him. "If Crowder found out how Nina was earning her living, do you think he might have gone gunning for Richter?"

"Maybe."

"The same way you might have."

He met my look with his best effort. "Except I didn't."

"You tossed his place."

"Tossed?"

"Searched."

"No, I didn't."

"You didn't remove all traces of Nina from Gary Richter's apartment?"

"How could I?"

"Then where are Richter's copies of the pictures in the Erospace exhibit?"

His surprise seemed real. "What Erospace exhibit?"

"The pictures of Nina with the flags and the knife and the slogans, on the wall of the Erospace Gallery of erotic art."

He rubbed his face with his hand. "My God."

"Did Richter try to blackmail you with those pictures?"

"No. I had no contact with him whatever except when I went there to ask about Nina."

"You knew he was working with her."

"Yes."

"How?"

"She told me."

"And sent you pictures?"

"Yes."

"Why?"

"Why what?"

"Why did she send you pictures?"

"Because she was proud of them. She wanted me to see her work."

"What did you think of it?"

"I was . . . amazed."

"And?"

"And impressed."

"And excited."

He reddened. "What are you implying?"

"I'm not implying anything. I'm asking you what your relationship was with Nina."

His pupils shrank to the size of pinpoints. "I don't know what you want me to say."

I didn't, either. "Were you in love with her?"

His hands made fists that lay like clamshells at his waist. "No. How dare you suggest that we . . . No."

"Was she in love with you?"

"Of course not. I'm her father."

"No, you're not."

"I'm the same thing as."

"That didn't stop Woody and Soon-yi. Maybe things went too far and Nina began to feel guilty about your relationship. Maybe she's hiding from you."

His face turned the color of the wing chair. "That didn't happen. I won't have you implying it did. What do you think I am?"

"I don't know. What are you?"

He wiped his brow. "I'm a worried father. And a man who's very much in love with Peggy Nettleton, which is a fact that seems to make you want to savage me."

"This isn't savagery, this is interrogation. Savagery is when I hit you with something."

He stood up. "If it wasn't for Peggy, I wouldn't stand for this."

I stood beside him. "If it wasn't for Peggy, I wouldn't be doing it. Do you carry Indian arrowheads on your person?"

"What?"

"Arrowheads. I hear you collect them. Do you carry one around with you?"

He nodded. "As a charm. Why?"

"Show me."

He hesitated until he saw my smile. Then he reached in his pocket and produced a small brown stone, notched and pointed like the one in my pocket. I wished it was back where it came from. "What do you have to do with Victor Krakov?" I asked.

"Never heard of the man."

"How about Jensen Lattimore?"

"He used to invite me to parties and approach me for financing from time to time. What about him?"

"Did you give money to him?"

"No."

"Why not?"

"Because I'm not technical enough to evaluate his businesses."

"Do you know a company called DigiArt?"

"No. Why?"

"Has Lattimore ever met Nina?"

"Not that I know of. Where are you going with this? Do you

know something that suggests Lattimore is involved in Nina's disappearance?"

I shook my head. "I'm just surfing."

"Well, Jensen Lattimore doesn't need to do anything weird with women. He can buy anything he wants and then some."

"In my experience, rich guys tend to be turned on the most by things they can't have."

"Like Nina, you mean?"

"Maybe. Or maybe they fell in love and Nina ran off to Majorca with him."

Ted shook his head. "Nina doesn't fall in love, I don't think. She dates, she has relationships, but they never seem to have much to do with love."

"What do they have to do with?"

His eyes lost focus. "Making men do and say things they shouldn't. Making them want what they can't have."

He was so obviously talking about himself that he didn't try to hide it. I asked him a question other than the obvious. "Why does she do it?"

"I don't know. I'm not very good at the Freudian stuff."

"I think you need to convince me you didn't sleep with her."

He walked toward the wall, then turned back. "I didn't. That's not what she wanted. What she wanted was for me to want to."

"Did you?"

"Of course. In some sense. But I never would have. I'm not a libertine, Mr. Tanner. At most I was a lonely, needful man."

"Lonely, needful men do stupid things all the time. I've made a living getting them out of trouble."

He looked at me. "Then get me out of this."

"The marriage?"

"Of course not. The problem with Nina. Get her back so Peggy and I can get on with our lives."

Silence engulfed us. There wasn't anywhere else I wanted to

go, another question I wanted to ask. Suddenly Ted put a hand on my shoulder. "I do love her, you know."

"Peggy?"

He nodded. "I know you and she were close. I know she admires you a great deal. And I know you will want to continue your friendship now that you are back in touch with her. I just want you to know that it's all right with me."

"Thank you."

"You are welcome in this home at any time. And you are welcome to attend the wedding if you wish."

"Probably not. But thanks, anyway."

"I understand. And I will also understand if you decide to leave this mess with Nina for us to work out ourselves. There's no need for you to—"

"I tend to see things through, as a rule," I interrupted. "Keeps the night sweats short of flood stage."

He blinked and looked for Peggy. "Of course. Well, if I can help, I will, but I've told you all I can. I don't really know where else to turn." His voice became oracular. "I'm beginning to be afraid something unspeakable has happened."

"Don't project, Mr. Evans; you'll drive yourself crazy. Just wait for it to happen. The good news is, it always does."

"Not always, surely."

"You can make book on it."

CHAPTER 22

"Who picked out the furniture for this place?" she asks.

"Who did what?"

"The lamps. Who picked them?"

"Why? What does it matter?"

"Humor me, Wellington. The boss man did, right? Jensen Lattimore picked them out himself."

"I believe he did. Yes. He or his decorator. Why?"

"I saw them in another apartment that he decorated much like this one. I like his taste; I like his money. I want to meet him. How soon can you make it happen?"

"I'm not sure that's in the cards."

"It has to be, or this little party doesn't get off the ground and I don't go to work tomorrow. You have to promise to tell Lattimore I want to meet him. ASAP. Okay?"

"I'll tell him, but I can't promise anything else."

"Oh, I think he'll see me. I think he's had that in mind all along, don't you, Christopher? Now what was it you came by for? I think you'd better remind me."

He puts down his wineglass and takes her hand. "Promise you won't say anything about this? It'll be all over for me if you do. I'm the one who cut the power off."

"Say anything to whom?"

"Anybody."

"Lattimore, you mean."

"To anybody."

She nods. Without resistance, she goes where he wants to take her.

¤　　¤　　¤

SECOND AND PIKE WAS one of those infarcts that inhibit the heart of most cities, a twilight zone with its own morphology, psychology, and mythology, all of it pathogenic. It's a place where laws aren't enforced, where morality is a memory, where common sense is as rare as good teeth. I got there just before midnight.

The light was an odd mix of moonlight and some new form of streetlamp that made it seem as if we were swimming in urine, which we might as well have been from the smell of it. The stores at street level and the offices in the towers above them were all closed but for a girlie show down the block. The traffic was sparse but what there was was menacing—boom boxes filling the air with war chants, tinted windows making even parking seem nefarious, golden wheel covers and plate brackets making the occupation of the occupants seem questionable and excessive. Although there was no obvious reason for it, and indeed plenty of reason for the opposite, the people who milled like Herefords on the corner seemed charged with industry and large with self-importance.

"Need a bag, man?"

He was toothless and ragged, his yellow eyes floating on a boiling oil of chemical intoxication, his black hands as active as moths in bright light.

"Not now," I said with bored connivance.

"Pure China, man."

"That's what they all say."

"Yeah, but mine is clean."

"Flea powder, more like it."

"No, man. My Aunt Hazel is fly. Ask anyone."

"Later."

"Be sold out later."

"I'll take my chances."

He muttered an oath and hopped off. "We can do a deal if you put me next to Mandy," I called after him in afterthought, but the name didn't slow him down.

Jitters was replaced by a woman, tall and languid and anorexic, dressed in a black leotard top and a leopard skirt slit up the side to her waist. "Looking to party, handsome?" Her voice was contralto and contrived; her eyes touched on everything but me. I wasn't even sure she was a woman.

"I've already got a date."

"Yeah? With who?"

"Mandy."

"Shit. Mandy can't do nothing for you."

"Why not?"

"She a channel swimmer, man. Strung out tight as trip wire."

"Strung out on what?"

"Dog food, man."

"Heroin?"

"Rock, too. Murder one, baby."

"She make her connection down here?"

"Here, there, everywhere. Not hard to feed the monkey in Seattle."

"She usually come around about now?"

"Don't matter—I do you as good. I may lack some necessaries in the tit department, but my pussy can walk and talk and tickle your chin."

I laughed because I thought I was supposed to. "I'll keep it in mind."

"You got a car? Do you for ten in the car. Take it clear to my belly, man, and you got the piece that can twiddle my tonsils. I can tell." She reached out and rubbed my crotch.

I stepped back. "Maybe next time."

"You go with Mandy, won't be no next time."

"Why not?"

"She a rock star, man. Fucks for bucks for the mainline."

"I owe her money," I said. "I need to get it to her."

She held out a hand. "Give it to me. I get it to her."

I smiled. "I'd take it to her place in the Regrade, but I forget the address."

"Don't know about no Regrade," she said, looking past me for a hotter prospect. "Mandy nothing but a nun, man. No head, no ass, no nothing you can't get from your old lady. I give you a pro job and there ain't nothing not on the menu."

Her recital was halfhearted; by the time she'd finished her pitch she had her sights on someone else. When I turned to see who my replacement was, I looked into the anxious eyes of Nina Evans's brother.

He wasn't looking at me, he was looking up the street, in the direction of the Regrade. As if on cue, down the walk came Mandy, at least a close enough approximation of a picture on the wall at the Blitz Club for me to make that assumption.

She was tall and thin and blonde, dressed in a baby-doll dress that barely covered her butt, with bows at the shoulders and lace at the neck. Her hair was pulled back with a blue barrette. Her tights were white but had holes at the knees and a stain at the thigh. She was sucking a lollipop and trying to look twelve. She was doing a good job of it until you got to her eyes, which jumped on and off the denizens of the corner with a frenzy born of withdrawal.

Her wits and reflexes were so scattered she could hardly stay on the sidewalk. By the time I got within ten yards of her, she had started to cry without bothering to hide it. Her lollipop fell to the ground and shattered, which meant it wasn't candy anymore, it was trash.

I started to say something but Jeff beat me to it. I couldn't hear what he told her, but when she heard his voice she brightened, then ran to his side and linked her arm with his. She asked him something, he answered; she got angry and twisted away. He said something else, then took her arm, then pointed. Ten yards from the end of his finger was the once-black 240Z.

After another whispered exchange, Jeff led Mandy to the car, helped her inside, then climbed behind the wheel and drove away. The tortuous Seattle stoplights worked in my favor this time, because the one at the corner of Union and Second held them long enough for me to get back to my car and follow them.

I kept my distance as the Z turned up University and left on Third and headed north through the high-rise handmaidens to the city's power structure. When we got to Wall Street Jeff turned right, drove a block, turned left, then right, and pulled to a stop in front of a brick building that bore the name the Palms. I assumed it was meant to be sarcastic.

Jeff and Mandy held a huddled conversation, then he got out of the car and went to the passenger side and helped her to the sidewalk. She seemed on the brink of breakdown as he led her toward the building. They got in without using a key, which was another bad sign, among many. Moments later, a light went on in the unit front left, second floor.

I decided to wait and see if I could get Mandy all to myself. An hour later, the light in the apartment went off and Jeff Evans trotted out the front door, climbed into the Z, and zoomed off. I retraced his steps, which was far too easy to do.

The air inside the building smelled like smoke and rubbing alcohol. When I got upstairs, I knocked on the door three times but got no answer except for the music leaking out, an angst-ridden strain of a postmodern dirge that lamented everything in life but misery.

I tried the door. The knob was warm in my hand, as firm and slick as a young woman's breast in midsummer. Since it was obvious I could do so, I opened the door and stepped inside.

The interior was dark and fetid, smelling of rancid foods and sweaty clothing and the fluids that gush from fevered flesh. The only light came through the front window, which was the only one not masked with black plastic. Evidence of another being on the premises came in the form of an ugly, fractious sound, the sound of farm animals and lawn mower engines. I edged toward its source. Mandy was naked on the bed, wearing only the diaphanous light from the moon, snoring like a long-haul trucker on a layover at Little America. Her baby-doll outfit was a wad of desperation next to the tattered pillow.

I felt her pulse—on the low end of normal but steady. Since she seemed sufficiently deep in sleep to allow me to look around, I turned on a lamp and began to search the place without knowing what I was searching for.

Mandy's surname was Lorenzen—that came courtesy of the junk mail sprinkled over the room like salt. And the rumors were true—Mandy was a junkie. Her works were spread like condiments across the dinette in the tiny kitchen—syringe, spoon, swabs, lighter; the rubber rope that tied off her vein guarded the rest of the works like an adder. Although there were no drugs in sight, the temperature of the spoon suggested she'd shot up in the past hour—I wondered if Jeff had shared the hit or only supplied the dust. In any event, their little pas de drug suggested that Ted Evans needed to worry less about Nina and more about his son.

When I returned to the body on the bed the scabs and bruises of intravenous drug use scowled at me, not from their usual nest at the hinge of the inner arm, but from down at her feet and ankles. The tattoo at her pubis didn't begin to dilute the carnage.

The only other evidence in plain view suggested Mandy's calling. There was a gross of condoms in a box by her bed, along with two tubes of KY jelly and a jar of Vaseline, plus a pan and sponge for washing off beforehand, some vinegar douche for afterward, and a collection of lingerie and leather appointments for those who like their sex with some theatrics. The indications weren't decisively commercial until you included the credit card register on the table by the bed. Since nothing was telling me not to, I decided to dig deeper.

The clothes in the closet were soft and shear and redolent of sweat and cheap perfume. The skirts were short, the tops tight, the pants torn in provocative places. A couple of the spandex numbers would have served her well on the stage at the Blitz Club; a couple of the leather numbers would have hauled in plenty of johns on the corner of Second and Pike. None of it was clean and none of it looked comfortable.

There were exceptions to the tawdry thrust of most of her wardrobe, however. Way in the back, so you wouldn't see them without trying, were a couple of cocktail dresses and a strapless blue ball gown with sequins that shimmered even in the light of a forty-watt bulb. The labels were Klein and Karan and Kamali, which made them a reach for a whore, at least for a whore with a habit. The dresses must have been from an earlier life, before Mandy's had started to fracture. I still hadn't found a reason for the fissure.

Part of an answer came from the bookshelf, which was less a shelf than a couple of cardboard boxes stacked on top of each other and stuffed with tattered paperbacks. The contents were on a more elevated plane than I expected—novels by Smiley and Oates and Kingsolver; feminism by Steinem and Paglia and Woolf; politics by Phillips and Ehrenreich and Woodward; poetry by Graham and Jong and Sexton. All of which was a clue to what she thought. The clue to who she was was in the yearbooks.

There were three of them, all from the Chadwick School, for the years '88, '89, and '90. I picked one up and leafed through it. The introduction announced that Chadwick was a private school located on Capitol Hill, co-ed, grades 6–12, with a campus that looked more Ivy League than Pac Ten. The pictures were in both color and black and white, the binding was real leather, the paper stock was heavyweight and glossy—a class production, including the work by the school photographer, who was identified in the acknowledgments as Gary Richter.

When I looked in an index, Mandy Lorenzen was listed twice. Both were group shots—one of the entire sophomore class, the other of the Poetry Club. The '89 volume had six listings, in which she moved from timid and unremarkable to lovely and spirited, as evidenced by her election to the student council. Her senior year she was all over the place, on one occasion dressed in the sparkling blue gown as a member of the Chadwick Queen's Court.

There was another Lorenzen in the index, too—someone named Todd, who looked enough like Mandy to be her younger brother. No timidity about Todd—his freshman picture snapped outside the Blue Moon Tavern as he posed with a pint of ale even though he couldn't have been more than fourteen. As an after-thought I looked up Jeff Evans. He was there, too, a year behind Mandy, a member of the literary magazine, the Jazz Club, and the school newspaper. When I looked for Nina Evans, I didn't find her.

A few years ago, Mandy Lorenzen had been happy and healthy, intelligent and attractive, with a limitless life that would stretch well into the twenty-first century. Now she was a whore and a junkie and a wastrel—if she'd escaped HIV it would be a miracle; if she lived to see the millennium I'd be surprised. The only thing I knew of that might have caused that slide was her association with Krakov and Richter.

I looked for evidence—pictures, correspondence, something that linked her to those men and established what they'd done to her—but I came up empty. I'd pretty much run out of options when Mandy groaned, rolled over, and fell to the floor with a thud. She swore and spat, tried and failed to extract herself from the sheets that wound around her like kudzu, then flopped to her back in frustration. A pearl of drool rolled down her chin; a scab at her ankle started to bleed. One leg and one breast were free of cover, one incisor was missing from her mouth, one eye was bruised beneath its socket. Her breath smelled like death from toxic substances; the tattooed mons was back under cover.

I tugged on the sheet until it unloosed her body, then draped it across her. She tossed my gesture aside with anger. Her breasts sloshed down her sides, her belly swelled and heaved like the bellies on starving children, her lips formed words unlinked to wit or context.

"Who're you?" she managed finally.

"Tanner."

"'Pointment?"

"No."

"Money?"

"Yes."

She nodded with gravity fit for a wake. "You want it down here or up there?" Her eyes were black vats of disinterest.

"I'm not here for sex, Mandy."

That I knew her name excited her. "Did Jeff send you? Where is he? Did he score more white?"

"Does Jeff do dope with you, Mandy?"

"Jeff? Nah. Jeff's an angel. Gets me good shit. Almost as good to me as Todd. Poor Todd," she added, then rolled to her side and looked at me with what she thought was allure but was much closer to odium. "You're here to fuck me, right, mister? Can we do it now? I got to go to the bathroom pretty soon." She struggled to get up to the bed.

I put out a hand to keep her where she was. Her skin was cold and clammy, chilled by inner winds. "Where's your brother, Mandy?"

"Todd?"

"Yes."

"Todd's dead."

"How?"

"Car."

"A wreck?"

"Accident, they said. *Not* an accident."

"Murder?"

She shook her head with the first vigor of our acquaintance-ship. "Suicide."

"Why?"

"Todd did what Daddy wanted. I'm trying, too." Her eyes strayed to the works on the table; the sight of the syringe made her shudder.

"Why did Todd commit suicide?"

"Daddy wanted him to."

"Why?"

"Said Todd was bad."

"Why was he bad?"

"Wasn't. But Daddy thought he was."

"Why?"

"The picture."

"What picture?"

"The one . . ." She uttered a mournful groan, then curled into a fetal sphere. "If we're not going to ball, get out."

"What did you do for Victor Krakov, Mandy?"

"Danced for him."

"That's all?"

"Fucked him."

"Did he turn you on to dope?"

She shook her head. "Wants me to kick. Everyone wants me to kick. Everyone but Daddy."

"How about Gary Richter? Did you model for him?"

"Sure."

"What else?"

"Fucked him, too."

"Did he photograph it?"

"Sure."

"Where's his darkroom? Do you know?"

She shook her head.

"What's your relationship with Jeff Evans?"

"I fuck him, too. I maybe even love him. Hey." Her eyes brightened briefly, like a coin half-buried in mud. "I fuck everyone, don't I? Maybe Daddy's right."

"About what?"

"Maybe I even fucked Todd."

Because she intends to use him, make him betray his principles, enlist him as an unwitting accessory to her plan, she grants him a limited lease of her most prized possession. He uses it gingerly, kindly if not deftly, with a reverence she appreciates and is used to. He is sufficiently earnest and so unabashedly needy that her own desires steam to the surface from the cave in which they have slumbered in the weeks of her confinement, so that by the final mounting she is as ardent as he. They buck toward release in a gruffly elegant gymnastic, become swift and sweaty and simultaneous, and vocalize the onset of climax in sync with the poundings of orgasm. They become equally and pleasantly spent.

Condom disposed of, she reminds him of her insistence that he arrange for a meeting with Lattimore. Giddy in the aftermath, already angling for a reprise, he agrees to do what he can. As she nibbles at his ear, she suggests that what he can do is show him her art.

¤　　　¤　　　¤

I HELPED MANDY ONTO THE BED, made sure her pump and bellows were functioning within normal ranges, then left money on the dresser to compensate for her time, although a tuna sandwich and some chicken soup would have been a preferable currency. After a check of her pulse at her lissome throat, I left her to the dungeon she had constructed for herself with a lot of aid from Gary Richter and more than a little shove from Daddy.

I got to bed by two, to sleep by four, and was roused at eight by the telephone out of a dreamscape that looked a lot like East Oakland.

"Hi," she said.

"Hi."

"Ted said you guys had a good talk."

"So we did."

"He said he liked you."

"Same here."

"Really?"

"Really."

"I'm glad. He said he invited you to the wedding but you turned him down."

"Right on both counts."

"Why won't you come?"

"I'm cutting back on self-abuse."

"It won't be that bad. Will it?"

"I don't think I need to find out."

"He said he also told you that he hoped we would keep in touch."

That was a little strong but it seemed pointless to quibble. "Right."

"I hope we will, too. We will, won't we?"

"Sure."

"You don't sound convinced."

"At this point, the only thing I'm convinced of is that my prostate's going bad."

"What do you . . . oh. You're still in bed. You haven't . . . sorry." She giggled. "Should I hang up or shall we take time out?"

"Time out."

I was back in ninety seconds. "Did you do anything interesting last night?" she asked as I crawled back under the covers.

"Picked up a woman at Second and Pike."

"No."

"Yes."

"But that's where . . . why on earth would you do something like that?"

"The woman's name is Mandy Lorenzen. Know her?"

"I've heard the name from Nina, I think. If she's the woman I'm thinking of, her father was president of one of the big banks till it merged with someone or other. What's this Lorenzen woman got to do with anything?"

"She and Nina were friends. They both modeled for Richter. I think he may have exploited Mandy Lorenzen the way he was trying to exploit Nina, and somehow it destroyed her life. Plus, she seems to be Jeff's girlfriend."

"What Jeff? *Ted's* Jeff?"

"Right. Do you know where he lives?"

"I've never been there, but from what I understand he lives in a warehouse. There should be an address in . . . yes. Warsaw Street. That's down in Georgetown, I think. Near Boeing Field." She gave me a number.

"Any place else he hangs out?"

"Ted and I met him for breakfast at the Stoneway Café once. That's not far from the *Salmon* offices. And I met him for coffee at a place called the Road Runner a couple of times, back when I thought having intimate little talks with Ted's children was the way to win them over." Her laugh was mordant. "Other than that, I don't know." She paused. "Is Jeff in love with this Mandy woman?"

"Looks like it."

"What kind of girl is she? I'm almost afraid to ask, given where you met her."

"She's got problems," I said, cheerily imprecise, "but don't we all." I told Peggy I'd call her that night, then headed for the Stoneway Café.

It was less mannered than the Last Exit on Brooklyn, just a

workingman's café featuring coffee, not espresso; fried foods, not tofu; dense starches, not croissants and crepes. Fine so far, except Jeff Evans wasn't there and hadn't been for days.

The Road Runner turned out to be part coffeehouse and part comic book emporium on the corner of Fortieth and Bagley. The coffee came in gaily decorated ceramic cups and the comics came with titles like *Hate* and *Hellblazer* and *Evil Ernie*. I only relaxed when I spotted *Veronica*. Jeff had just left, as it turned out, headed who knew where. Seattle people seem to respect each other's privacy even more than does the café society in San Francisco, which has rather strict mores on the subject itself. Or maybe they were just unfriendly.

The paper was nearby, so I stopped in to ask for Jeff. The only person there told me he hadn't been in and wasn't expected. When I asked if she knew where he might be, she named the places I'd just been, then shrugged and said, "The Rubber Tree, maybe?" When I asked where it was, she told me it was up near the Wallingford Center. When I asked how to get there, she gave me cogent directions.

I found the Wallingford Center easily enough, but when I asked a couple of people where to find the Rubber Tree, they seemed inordinately amused by the question. The second guy pointed me toward Burke Avenue, and slapped me on the back as I headed that way. When I arrived, the mysteries were solved. The Rubber Tree wasn't a restaurant and it didn't sell plants: the Rubber Tree sold rubbers.

Prophylactics. Hundreds of them, in all sizes and shapes, colors and flavors, compounds and curvatures, unfurled for the world to evaluate like hard sausage swinging from the ceiling in a North Beach deli. If your eyesight was less than perfect, you could pretend you were in a balloon shop, but if you were 20/20, those flaccid tubes of latex could only be one thing. I was as embarrassed as I'd been the first time I'd bought one.

The guy at the desk near the door had hair to his waist and a ring in his lip. I asked if Jeff Evans was in.

"No one by that name works here."

"I didn't ask if he worked here, I asked if he *was* here."

"Yeah."

"Yeah what?"

"He was here."

"When?"

"Yesterday. And the day before that."

"How about today?"

"That, too."

"He here now?"

He rolled his eyes. "Do you see him?"

"No. Do you?"

He shook his head then looked past me. "You in the market for protection?"

"I sell it; I don't buy it."

"Yeah? What line? Trojan? Lifestyle? What?"

"This line," I said, and moved my jacket enough to show him the butt of my gun.

The game ended right there; he held up his hands in surrender. "Hey. You got no problem with me, pal. Make love not war—that's what the Tree is about."

"Let's hit the highlights. Jeff was here but he left."

"Right."

"Say where he was going?"

"Home."

"He still live on Warsaw?"

"Yep. Look out for the dog."

"What kind?"

"The kind with teeth. Name of Codpiece."

I started to go, then stopped. "What's Jeff do here, anyway? Does he own the place?"

"Naw, Jeff just hangs out. He likes to talk sex. For his column, you know? People come in for a condom, it tends to be on their mind."

"But only men, right? Given the product?"

"Hell, no; most of the regulars are women. They like stock on hand—women don't trust men to do *shit* anymore; one of them makes her old man wear three at a time. Plus now we've got condoms for women. Inside, you know? Guy doesn't even know it's there."

I left before he could make sex sound even more like book-keeping.

The warehouse was the only one of its kind in the area. It occu-pied a lot on Warsaw near the corner of Carleton Avenue, across the street from the Georgetown Gospel Chapel, which was cele-brating its Fiftieth Jubilee. A faded sign said the place had once housed a bakery, but what it housed now was people in need of cheap rent.

The interior had been inexpertly subdivided with low-grade plywood and cast-off Sheetrock. The doors cut into the unfin-ished walls bore handwritten numbers of personal significance—in keeping with his profession, Jeff's was number 30. His neighbor was 7.141; the guy down the hall was 666.

When I banged on the door a dog growled from the other side. "Easy, Codpiece," I said, mostly as an excuse to use the word.

"What the fuck you want?"

"I need to talk for a minute."

"I don't talk; I write."

I lowered my voice. "You also provide controlled substances to a woman in the Regrade."

The only response came from the rumbling curse of the dog and the cough of a nearby truck as it pulled away from the curb.

A head emerged from the doorway, tousled, disgusted, and irate. "What the fuck are you doing, banging around out there?" he challenged before I was even in focus. "I just got to bed, god-dammit."

"I'm Tanner. We met yesterday at the paper."

He didn't remember. "Then you've already had your audience. If there's a problem, write a letter to the editor."

"I don't have a problem; Mandy has a problem."

Sleep fled his eyes and he was as wary as a coach at a press conference. "Mandy who?"

"Mandy Lorenzen. The woman you picked up at Second and Pike at midnight last night. The woman you left on the nod after she shot up the goodies you bought her."

"What the hell are you trying to . . . ?" He seemed too dispirited, or maybe too scared, to continue. "I suppose you'll rag me till we do this."

"Count on it."

"Come on in, but don't expect, like, hospitality. The coffee's gone and I'm not making more—that shit costs a fortune all of a sudden. Fucking frost in Brazil or something."

"I can live without coffee or hospitality, either one."

"Yeah? Most people around here can't."

He led me to his digs, which were more barren than furnished, more nihilistic than cheerful, more industrial than residential. We sat across from each other on similar stiff chairs, chess players in the Gobi Desert. "So what's this shit about Mandy?" he asked.

I didn't quite answer the question. "Have the cops caught up to you yet?"

He was puzzled. "About Mandy?"

"About Richter."

He swore. "Yeah. They caught up to me."

"What did you tell them?"

"I told them my ignorance was as boundless as my contempt for the man."

"Could you tell them something else if you were so inclined?"

"What's that mean?"

"I mean do you know anything about Richter's murder?"

He leaned back and looked at me intently, as though to scan the contours of my brain. "What's this have to do with Mandy?"

"I know you and she have a relationship and I know you give her drugs."

His eyes narrowed and he aped my speech pattern. "What are you inclined to do about it?"

"Nothing, if you tell me what you know about Richter. What I need is—"

He held up a hand. "Back up a minute. Why are you ass deep in my life all of a sudden?"

"The woman your dad's about to marry?"

"Peggy? What about her?"

"She used to work for me."

"So?"

"I used to be in love with her."

"When?"

"Six years ago."

He examined me once more. "When else?"

"Whenever. Which is why I'm trying to help her out."

He frowned. "You sure that's what you're doing? Or are you trying to fuck her up?"

"Sure I'm sure," I said, then matched his grin. "I think."

"That's cool," he said, and seemed to mean it. He lit a cigarette and relaxed. Maybe he knew enough about sex to write a column; what he didn't know enough about was cancer.

"I need to find your sister so Peggy can get married on schedule," I said.

"I told you before—I don't know where she is."

"But you know Mandy. And you know why what happened to her happened to her."

"What do you mean, happened?"

"I mean why she went from a beautiful young model to an addict and a prostitute within the space of a year."

"What difference does it make why it happened?"

"Because Nina was a model, too. Now she's disappeared. Something similar may be happening to her."

He looked beyond me at the window, a cocky, complicated young man with a lot of smarts and a lot of guts and a big need to seem on top of the world. But underneath, he was still a kid with a girlfriend and a sister, both of whom were in need of a hero, neither of whom he could figure out how to rescue.

He got up, walked behind a freestanding screen to what I assumed was a bedroom, then returned with something in his hand. "This is what happened to Mandy." He waited while I examined it.

It was a photograph, folded, wrinkled, stained, and chipped, of a couple engaged in sexual intercourse. They were young, from the look of their trim taut bodies, and they seemed engaged in a mutually eager exercise. They were Mandy Lorenzen and her brother, Todd, their faces clean and clear and unmistakable, their copulation thrilling to behold until you remembered their degree of consanguinity.

I turned it over. On the back was a message, scrawled with felt-tip pen and fury: "You are no longer my children, you are something foul and evil—I will do everything I can to destroy you as you have tried to destroy me by your godless deeds." It could only have been written by a father.

I returned the photo to Jeff. "How did you get this?"

"Mandy carried it in her purse. She kept taking it out and looking at it before she shot up. She wouldn't show me, so I took it. When I saw what it was, I didn't give it back."

"What does she say about it?"

"She says it didn't happen."

"It looks like it happened."

Jeff stood and loomed over me. "Don't you *get* it yet, detective? *Nothing* is real. Not anymore. Every image is any lie they want to make it; whoever owns the digits makes the truth. The eyes are victims, man; you can't believe them, you can only close them down." His voice dropped to an agonized rasp. "Her old man didn't understand. I tried to tell him, but . . ."

"Who did this to her?"

"Richter."

"Why?"

"Blackmail."

"Of who?"

"Her old man."

"I've been to Richter's apartment. It didn't look like he had any blackmail money."

"He had other apartments."

"Where?"

Jeff went to the door and leaned against it. "You're from out of town, right?"

"Right."

"You're not technical, right?"

"All the tech I've got is my digital watch."

"You're tough, she says."

"Peggy?"

He nodded. "She told me about you, once. About some shit with this big deal consumer guy. She said you went after him even though he carried a lot of weight."

"That was my first case. A guy named Roland Nelson ran something called the Institute for Consumer Awareness. He wasn't all he was cracked up to be."

"So you're not afraid to take on the big guys."

"It's sort of an avocation."

He stood up. "Come on."

"Where we going?"

"Gas Works Park."

I followed him and Codpiece out the door. As we reached the street, a huge jet swooped too low for comfort, as though it wanted to land in the next block. A moment later, that's just what it did.

CHAPTER 24

"Where are we going?" she asks as they drive up Madison toward the freeway.

"His weekend cabin."

"This isn't the weekend."

"And it isn't a cabin."

"What is it?"

"An ego manifestation."

They cross the I-90 bridge in silence. When they zoom through Mercer Island and Bellevue without slowing down, she says, "Where is this joint, anyway?"

"The Issaquah suburbs."

"I didn't know Issaquah had suburbs."

"They're the best kind of suburbs—invisible."

They take the Issaquah exit and turn south, toward densely forested hills. The sun is setting to their right; the shadows spilling across the road could be bloodstains. "Was it hard to convince him to see me?" she asks within the cone of silence created by the engineers at Porsche.

"Not at all. He was about to suggest it himself."

"Why?"

"I showed him our last video."

"The one in the Japanese garden?"

"Newer."

"You mean it's one I haven't seen?"

"Not yet. But I'm sure you'll see it tonight."

"What makes you think so?"

"Because that's what he does."

That she is about to become fodder momentarily chills her. "What else does he do besides show skin flicks?" she asks innocuously.

"Use your imagination. I can't believe you want to go through with this," he adds after a moment, jealousy a husk around each word.

"It sounds like fun," she laughs teasingly, knowing he is hoping she will bow out, knowing he is miserable. "What's that supposed to mean?" she asks in the next moment.

"What?"

"That look."

"Nothing."

"Bullshit. You're pissed at me."

"No, I'm not."

"You're upset that I'm going to spend the evening with your boss."

"What if I am?"

"You don't need to be."

"The hell I don't. You don't know what he does to people."

"Are you talking violence?"

"He doesn't have to bludgeon people to get what he wants. He can just buy them."

"He can't buy me."

"Yes, he can."

"How do you know?"

"Because I thought the same thing about myself and he bought me in two hours. He owns every ounce of me now."

"No, he doesn't."

"I'm here, aren't I? Delivering you to him like some kind of Christmas fruitcake. And he'll devour you just as fast."

"Hey. It's no problem. Fruitcake lasts forever."

¤   ¤   ¤

OUR DESTINATION WASN'T the park itself, but a building just west of it. Jeff pointed with his finger as I drove past, toward a two-story building of no obvious functional bent, white stucco and blue trim and flat roof with parking for four out front. At the moment, the spaces were filled with police cars.

"Shit," Jeff muttered, and directed me to turn around in the driveway that served the Harbor Patrol, then to park in a lot that served a shipyard.

"What is that place?"

"Richter's lab."

"You're sure?"

"Sure I'm sure. I've been in there."

"When?"

"Two weeks ago."

"Was Richter with you?"

"Hell, no."

"How'd you find it?"

"I tailed him."

"Why?"

His eyes turned to ice and his jawline buckled. "Because when I found out what was going on with Mandy, I decided to shut him down."

"How did you go about it?"

"I broke in the place. When I saw what he had, I got ready."

"Ready for what?"

Jeff looked toward the graffiti that was smeared across the iron and steel remnants of the abandoned gas plant that occupied the adjacent park. The blatant vandalism seemed to fuel his already frothing ire. "Ready to destroy his inventory. And ready to castrate the son of a bitch."

"Because of Mandy?"

"And Nina."

"What did he do to Nina?"

"He made pictures of her I didn't like."

"The Erospace exhibit," I said.

He looked at me. "You saw it?"

"Yep."

"What'd you think?"

"Marginal art; juvenile politics."

"Yeah, well, what I thought was rape. Her and Mandy, both. Rape and slavery. The bastard used their bodies like he owned them. Then he traded their flesh for cash."

He was gripping the door handle so hard I was afraid he was going to tear it off and chew on it. I gave him a moment to cool. "I'm kind of surprised by your reaction," I said finally.

"Why?"

"I'm surprised you found Erospace offensive, given what you do in your column."

"Hey," he bristled. "My column's about sex. Daring sex and equal sex, both sides willing and able to take some risks and use some new nerve endings. I tell them how to do it safely and I tell them how to do it better by trying stuff that never occurred to them."

"How's that different from Richter?"

"A guy like Richter isn't about sex, he's about power. He's basically an assassin."

"Of what?"

"Dreams and desires. Women see his legitimate work and agree to pose for him and go into the studio thinking it's about ideas and ideals and art. Richter takes what they've brought to the table and turns it upside down and pisses on it."

"They agree to appear nude. They sign releases letting him use the work however he wants to."

Jeff's eyes sparked with the heat of his rhetoric. "They don't have the faintest *idea* what digital photography is capable of. They don't know that he can corrupt and destroy them with a couple of clicks of a mouse. They don't know what they're agreeing to."

"Maybe they do know it. Maybe they don't care."

He shook his head. "There's always been porn and there always should be, probably. There's nothing wrong with a hard-on, and there's nothing wrong with a woman tickling her cunt if that's the way she wants to earn her living. And some do. Feminists claim they don't believe it, but some women get a charge out of turning men on and some get off on demeaning them. But Richter takes it further. He makes Mandy sleep with her brother. He turns Nina into a fucking fascist. He makes a woman define herself in ways she's never *thought* of. With tools like Richter has, he doesn't *need* consent. A couple of candid snapshots and he's got all the raw material he needs." Jeff paused and wiped his eyes. "I have a hard time remembering he's dead."

"What kind of tools are you talking about?" I asked.

Jeff pointed toward the stucco building. "Tools like the ones in there."

"What are they?"

"Hardware and software, man. Multi-fucking-media."

He made the term obscene. "Tell me how they work. If you know," I added.

"Oh, I know. When I figured out what had been going on, I read up on it, then got some guys at the paper to show me how it works. When I got back inside, I was going to wipe the whole thing out."

"Why didn't you?"

"Richter fucking died on me; they put the lab off limits."

I gestured toward the building. "Tell me what's inside. How did he come up with that picture of Mandy and her brother?"

Jeff leaned against the car door and closed his eyes. When he spoke, his voice was tinged with awe, as though he were describing an alien civilization that had terrible tools of destruction and didn't appear to be friendly.

"First you need input," he said. "Input can come from a digital still camera, or, in a year or so, a digital video camera, too, although they only get you to a couple of million pixels, so definition isn't all that sharp. More commonly, it comes from film stock or a slide transparency or a printed photograph; that gets you to 18 million pixels. In Richter's case, the input was usually an Ektachrome negative from the medium format Hasselblad he used in his studio. That was the shot he had of Mandy. The shot of Todd he got from a school picture he took with his Nikon." Jeff chuckled dryly. "It's the only reason he took the job at the schools, the asshole, to get photos of rich kids. Raw materials," he added gloomily.

"We've got input," I said. "The input goes into what."

"A scanner. Richter used a Nikon LS-3500, but there are all kinds of them, with various degrees of sensitivity."

"The scanner does what?"

"The scanner turns the image into bytes—the ones and zeros that are the basis of all digital information. Once it's been digitized, you load the file into your computer, drag it into your software, and then you can do anything you want with it."

"What kind of software are we talking about?"

"Richter used Adobe's Photoshop, that's the most popular. Plus he had the Aldus Photostyler, Alias Eclipse, Kai's Power Tools, PhotoMorph, and Studio Pro. With those babies you can treat a photograph just like a piece of text—cut, paste, edit, combine, enlarge, reduce, colorize, color adjust, chrom plate, mezzotint, whatever. If you've got enough memory you can make Hillary Clinton look like Minnie Mouse."

"And you can mix one image with another image."

"Definitely. With *any* other image. That was Richter's specialty—take a woman who thinks she's posing for art studies, then put her in the computer and give her some slutty accessories. In

Mandy's case, the accessory was her brother," he added with a lethal undertone.

"What kind of hardware are we talking about?"

"Richter had lots of it, but he did most of his work on a Mac Quadra 950 with 200 megs of RAM and a Thunder Photobooster accelerator card."

"That's a lot of memory, right?"

"Yeah, but you need all you can get. He had a 1.2 gigabyte hard drive and a quad-speed CD-ROM drive, too. If you do anything of any degree of refinement, you're going to end up with a file of 20 megs, and photo files of 200 megs aren't unheard of."

"Okay," I said. "We've got input, and software, and hardware. What's next?"

"Output. Once you've got the image composed inside your computer, you can keep it there as video art or you can send it through something like the Kodak Premiere Workstation and turn it into a slide or a photographic negative—back to square one, in other words, only with a completely different image from the one you started out with. Usually a photo lab or service bureau does this part because the machines are so expensive—a hundred grand or more for something like a Superset Imaging Workstation. Richter used a Fire 1000 film recorder, which isn't as powerful as a Kodak but it will do the job for the type of stuff he put in Erospace. And sent to Mandy's father."

I leaned back in the car seat and looked at the dome light. It reminded me of what we used to think a spaceship looked like. "This is pretty scary, when you think of it."

Jeff nodded. "With the Pentium and Power PC chips online, and fuzzy logic compression calculations and high-end workstations, pretty soon you'll be able to turn a still photograph into a feature film and put Garbo and Gable back on the silver screen with brand-new scripts and no one can tell they've been dead for years. They're close to doing that already, if you've read about the work the Industrial Light and Magic and Digital Domain people did on movies like *Mask* and *Forrest Gump* and *Pagemaster*. We're at a point where a guy like Richter will be able to take a picture of Julia Roberts out of *People* magazine, put it through his imaging system, and come out the other end with an X-rated movie of her taking on the Supersonics starting five and show it on the PC in the bedroom. And then he can send it off to a few of his horny buddies to download off the Internet. Poor Julia won't know a thing about it unless he hires a hall and starts to sell tickets. And even then all she can do is sue him."

"And this is what happened to Mandy and Nina."

"Sure. With Nina, all he added was props—flag, knife, graffiti. With Mandy, he took the photo session shots of her and the school pictures of Todd, mixed them with some copulating nudes he probably got from some poor souls he hired off the street, then convinced old man Lorenzen that his little prides and joys were fucking each other's brains out. It's as sick as it gets, the bastard. I wish I'd killed him myself."

"So you didn't."

"No."

"Who did?"

"I thought that was where you came in."

Jeff fumed to silence. I tried to think of what the enterprise he'd just described might have meant in the larger sense. "What would you say Richter's system cost altogether?" I asked after a minute.

"A hundred grand, easy. Maybe twice that."

"Lots of money."

"So?"

"Where do you think he got it?"

"Blackmail."

"It's a chicken or egg problem, isn't it? He needed the images to do blackmail, but he needed the blackmail to fund the images."

"So maybe he had some backing."

"My thought exactly. Any idea who?"

Jeff hesitated, then shook his head. "You?"

"Nope," I said and left it there, even though both of us were lying.

I looked at the featureless building. "Why don't we go see what the cops are up to?" I got out of the car and waited for Jeff to join me. We walked across the street and loitered near the blue-and-white police vehicles until a familiar figure showed its face: Lieutenant Molson, followed by his sidekick Nudge, the Mutt and Jeff of Seattle homicide.

When he caught my eye, Molson strolled our way, as lanky and nonchalant as ever, his sport coat an inch too short in the arms, his slacks luffing like sailcloth around his skinny legs. Nudge was a bundle of hostility, dressed in warm-ups and cross-trainers, but he was more interested in a female technician in a white coat and short skirt than he was in me or Jeff Evans.

"Gentlemen." Molson's laconic opening contrasted with the bursts of activity by the tech staff at his back.

"What's going on?" I asked in all innocence.

"The fact that you're here suggests you already know."

"Richter's secret lab."

"Right."

"What are you going to do with the electronics?" Jeff asked with a surly grunt.

"Leave it here for now. Impound it as soon as we find someone who can show us how to run it." Molson's smile was slow as the clouds drifting eastward overhead. "If you're thinking about sneaking in and accessing some files, don't—the place will be under guard."

Jeff started to say something sarcastic but I grasped his arm to stop him. "Did you find anything on Nina Evans in there?" I asked Molson.

"No comment."

"What was it? Hard-core?"

"From what I saw, it was every kind of core you can think of."

"Are you talking still photographs or video?"

"Still."

"You didn't look at the files in the computer?"

"I told you we have to find someone who can run it."

"Any idea who was behind the porn setup?"

Something in Molson's eyes struck sparks. "Richter. Who else?"

"I thought someone might have been backing him."

"What makes you think so?"

I smiled. "Just a hunch."

"We don't put a lot of stock in hunches, Tanner. Particularly not California hunches."

I shrugged. "If I were you I'd look for evidence that this lab was tied into a blackmail scheme. And I'd consider the possibility that the beneficiary of the scam was someone other than Gary Richter."

"Would you happen to have a name for that someone?"

I shook my head. "Not at the moment."

"Well, I've got a name," Jeff spat angrily, his lust for vengeance overriding his common sense.

Molson didn't bat an eye. "I'd be happy to hear it."

"Victor Krakov," Jeff said. "I assume you know who he is."

Molson's grin displayed teeth as long and narrow as his torso. "We have a chat with Mr. Krakov once in a while."

"Well, next time maybe you'll do more than chat—maybe you can lock him up."

Molson's brow lifted. "For what?"

Jeff's words were bilious and belligerent. "Contributing to delinquency, pimping and pandering, blackmail, extortion, assault, battery, buggery, burglary, barratry—"

Molson smiled his undertaker's smile. "If you've got evidence of any of those things, we'd be happy to have it. And while we're talking it over, we'll show you the stack of letters we've gotten about your column, the ones that claim it's obscene and suggest you ought to be executed."

Jeff shook his head and stomped off toward the car.

I looked at Molson. "There's going to be some smutty stuff in those machines."

"Expect so."

"It'd be a civic contribution if it got lost."

"Probably."

"I don't suppose that decision is yours to make."

"And I wouldn't anyway, as long as it might be evidence in a homicide."

"What if I come up with the guy who killed him? What if you had plenty of evidence without introducing what's in those computers?"

"I don't get your point."

"Accidents have been known to happen. Even in evidence lockers."

He smiled. "*Especially* in evidence lockers."

"What if it was a quid pro quo? I give you what I get on the Richter killing; you give Jeff Evans access to Richter's computers for twenty minutes."

He was silent long enough for me to sweat. "I'd think about it," he said finally.

"That's all I can ask."

"That's more than you can ask," he said.

Chris is right—it isn't a cabin, it is a dozen cabins, attached to each other like freight cars, winding in and out of a grove of conifers. The windows in the center sections mimic the sheen of the adjacent lake. The rough wood of the siding and shingles complement the boughs and branches that sway in the breeze above them. It is a horizontal castle, a fortress as comfortable with its surroundings as a Kentucky log cabin is with a stand of oak and hickory.

As they pull into the circular drive and stop beneath the rough-hewn portico, she is more cowed than she expected to be. Anything can go on in there, she feels, without reason or restraint or sanction. For a moment, she fights for breath. Only when she recalls the roots of her mission does her sense of purpose reclaim her.

Chris regards her timidly. "Are you sure you want to do this?"

She opts to be blasé. "Sure as shootin'."

"If anything happens, I won't be around to protect you."

"Nothing will happen that I don't want to happen."

"I'm sorry you're so naive," he says with as much anger as he can muster. "And I'm sorry I'm too impotent to stop you." He is gripping the wheel with neon knuckles as she gets out of the car and goes to the door and rings the bell. At her back, the Porsche spins away in a cloud of exhaust and bark dust and frustration.

The door is opened by a small black-haired man of Latin ethnicity and paramilitary bearing. "You are Ms. Evans?" he asks with more hostility than deference.

She nods.

"Please come this way."

She follows him across the tile corridor and down a narrow hall and stops before a door with the logo of Lattiware carved in its grainy wood. When she is at his side, her escort knocks. Another man—bigger and more brutish—steps from the room into the corridor and trains an electric wand at her privates and her purse. When it points at her purse, it beeps.

The burly man extends his hand. "I need to look."

She speaks loudly enough to be heard by the person she assumes to be seated beyond the hand-carved door. "He won't like it if you do."

"Why not?"

"Because it will spoil the surprise."

"What surprise?"

"A toy I brought with me. An accessory, you might say."

"Accessory to what?"

She smiles. "To anything Mr. Lattimore might have in mind."

He isn't swayed. "I still need to look."

"If you do, I'll junk it."

"Why?"

"Because it won't be exciting anymore; it'll just be one more thing Mr. Lattimore has under control." She strikes a pose. "What you need to understand is that with me he gets astonishment."

A noise at his back makes the sentry reenter the room. Moments later he reappears. "He says it's okay. Even though it isn't," he adds as a final bleat of competence. Nonetheless, he steps aside.

Lattimore is sitting by the fire, in a chair that enfolds him like a clamshell. There are computers to his left and right and large black panels recessed into the cedar walls like the ones she has seen at DigiArt. The decor is men's club rustic—pine and oak and cowhide; bone and stone and planking. It is expensive but unimaginative, like the condo he designed for her, like the lab he designed for Gary.

He gets to his feet as she approaches. He is quite short, she is surprised to see, a trifle overweight, more than a trifle balding. A boyish crewcut makes him seem both guileless and malleable, but she knows he is far from either.

"Miss Evans." *He clasps his hands behind his back and inclines at his pudgy waist.* "We meet at last."

"So it seems, Mr. Lattimore."

"Call me Jensen."

"Call me Nina."

"Wonderful. Please sit down. It's always a pleasure to meet a professional as accomplished as yourself."

"Likewise," *she says.*

"I've enjoyed your work tremendously," *he continues as he takes a seat and crosses his stubby legs.* "It's the best of its kind I've seen."

"I'll take that as a compliment—I imagine you've seen a lot."

His chest swells like a robin's. "I have seen approximately ten thousand naked women over the past twenty years." *He reddens at his boast, then controls it.* "Not all of them live, of course. Most were featured in various forms of media." *His expression intensifies, as if he is about to make a point.* "You have the third-best body I have ever seen."

She tries not to laugh at the adolescent calculus. "Only third? Who are the first two?"

"First is a woman named Jill who appeared in Swank in 1982. Second is a woman who calls herself Sally Slide. She appeared in a stag film called Sally and the Spaceman *some years back.*"

"Sorry. Didn't catch it." *She crosses her legs and attracts the expected attention.* "I thought you were interested in art, Mr. Lattimore."

"I am, of course, but we're talking natural endowments, not finished product."

"Hardware, not software."

His grin is gleeful. "Precisely."

"Well, I'm pleased that you like my mainframe." She recrosses her legs and gives him a second glimpse. "What are you planning to do with it?"

Although her entendre is double, he assumes she refers to commerce, which no doubt explains his affluence. "We will be offering two varieties of software—one to DigiArt subscribers; the other to our special clients. The latter works will be put up for on-line auction in a manner to be determined, but one that is fair to all concerned."

"Who are these special clients you're talking about?"

"You'd be surprised," he says with pride, then quells an urge to boast. "They are people of proven interest in the arts, but I'm afraid I can't be more specific."

"Why not?"

"Some people think nakedness is by definition pornographic."

"Some wives, you mean."

"Wives can be a problem." He glances at the monitor to his left; it seems to be printing E-mail. He reads a message, nods, then looks at her with boyish candor. "Why did you request this meeting, Miss Evans?"

"I wanted to meet the boss." She displays an equal enthusiasm. "And to see what you've done with me."

"In the computer, you mean."

She nods.

"Why?"

"I'm interested in my fate as an artist."

"You regard yourself as an artist?"

"Of course. Don't you?"

"Oh yes. Definitely. You achieve effects that I've never seen anyone duplicate. After Christopher does his thing with Optical Effects and Elastic Reality, the results are spectacular. I believe you will become a legend among a select group of connoisseurs."

"Show me," she says firmly.

He hesitates, then nods. "Come with me. And by the way, what's this surprise you have in store for me?" He is as excited as a kid at Christmas.

"That comes later," she says, and gives him a teasing poke in the vicinity of his genitalia.

¤   ¤   ¤

WHEN I GOT BACK TO THE CAR, Jeff was nowhere in sight; I assumed he was on a bus heading back to the warehouse, plotting further vengeance on the man who had turned his girlfriend into a walking wasteland. I was plotting some vengeance myself, but my target was someone other than the person Jeff Evans had named as the culprit. To get the job done, I was going to need help.

I found a phone and called Fiona. When I asked if I could see her, she seemed agreeable but apathetic. I'd hoped Fiona might be an antidote to my unrequited urge toward Peggy, but obviously it wasn't going to happen, for reasons best left unprobed. I suppose it didn't matter, except in the reaches of the heart where rejection always leaves a blister.

She suggested I pick her up at the gym and give her a ride home after her workout. I said that would be fine. Which gave me two hours to kill. I used one on the telephone and the other on lunch.

My first call was to the corporate headquarters of DigiArt. When I asked to speak to Mr. Lattimore, I was told he wasn't on the premises. When I said I had a proposition to present to him, I was told to put it in writing and submit it to his attorney. I broke the connection and dialed another number.

"This is Marsh Tanner," I said after her hearty voice bounded down the line. "Remember? From Fresno. We talked about switching some of my talent with some of Victor's talent."

"I remember," Lila responded with caution. "Did you ever catch up with Victor?"

"I did, as a matter of fact. He's an interesting gentleman. But a bit . . . *conservative* for what I have in mind."

"Victor? *Conservative*? You must have got the wrong man."

"It was Victor, all right. I'm sure he's good with the bar scene, but I'm moving beyond that now, taking advantage of some new technologies. Why go to a smoky bar when you can bring a gorgeous woman into your home and have her do whatever you want her to do right before your eyes. And I do mean whatever."

Lila paused. "I guess I don't get it."

"You don't have to at this point. But if this thing takes off the way I think it will, I'm going to need a coordinator of the Northwest Region by the end of the year. You could fill that slot for me, Lila. I can tell you know your way around show business."

"Thank you."

"But first things first. What I need you to do right now is get me together with Jensen Lattimore."

"Why?"

"Because he's got the two things I need in a partner—money and vision. Between the two of us, we can revolutionize the skin trade."

Her tone turned dubious. "I don't think Victor would want me taking part in this. Sounds like he could end up on the short end of this thing."

"The beauty of it is, it won't matter. Not to you. You'll be a key member of my management team."

Her loyalty was gilt-edged. "I don't know. Victor's been good to me."

"I know he has, but Victor's not going to be hurt. There'll always be plenty of mouth breathers who like to whoop and holler and see real girls bumping and grinding with sweat dripping off their boobies. We'll leave the goat ropers for Victor. Lattimore and I will be going after the high-end users."

"Like his special clients, you mean?"

"Exactly. Do you happen to know a man named Ted Evans, by the way?"

"Sure. From way back."

"Is he one of the special clients?"

"Used to be, but I don't think he is anymore. Why?"

"I'm thinking of bringing him in on this, too. To make sure it's structured right on the corporate side. To make sure key people like yourself will be compensated appropriately—with bonuses and stock options."

"Stock options?" she trilled. "For me?"

"Absolutely."

"What exactly is it you want me to do?"

"Set me up a meet with Lattimore tonight. All I need is an hour of his time."

"To do what, exactly?"

"Explain my proposition."

"What if he doesn't want to hear it?"

"You'll have to convince him, Lila. Tell him I'm bringing a sample of a revolutionary approach to nudity."

I was so sure she would buy it, I was already planning my pitch to Fiona. But instead of buying, she turned thumbs down.

"It sounds real interesting, Mr. Tanner, but I think I better stick with Victor. He paid my maternity bills, you know? And he bought Marie a stuffed monkey and now it's her favorite toy. I don't like to go behind his back; I hope you won't ask me to again."

Lila hung up the phone with a bang; integrity tends to pop up where you least expect it. My next call was in the nature of corroboration, to buy myself some peace of mind.

I passed through several layers of resistance before I reached the right person. "My name is Tanner," I began when I got her. "I'm Chief Operating Officer of Eclectic Arts Incorporated of Palo Alto," I lied. "We're a subsidiary of Paramount Communications," I lied again. "I'm calling about electronic reproduction rights in the permanent collection of the museum. I'm told you're the person who handles that."

"That's true," she said. "What is it you wish to know about the rights?"

"I assume I'm not the first to make such an inquiry."

"No, you're not."

"I imagine Microsoft has beaten me to it."

"No comment."

"Presumably the rights you've already granted have not been exclusive."

"Of course not—we're a nonprofit entity."

"Good. For my part, let me assure you that we're both willing and able to pay what a license to a collection such as the one at the Seattle Art Museum would warrant."

"That's nice to hear."

"I do, however, need to get some idea of how many pieces of this pie have already been cut."

"Come again?"

"I need to know how many other systems will be offering the same base. Perhaps you can tell me how many licensees you've already struck deals with."

"Two."

"Who?"

"I don't believe I can say."

"I understand. Believe me. There is one company, however, that we seem to be bumping heads with in this area, and for our discussions to go forward I need to know if they're a player."

"I'm not sure I can—"

"There are personal animosities involved between the respective CEOs, and, well, I'm sure you understand. I'd hate to waste both of our times if this deal was out of the question from the get go."

"I certainly understand professional animosity," she said, with enough steel in her voice to let me wonder at the acidic content of office politics in the world of fine art.

"The company I'm referring to is DigiArt," I said easily.

"We have no deal with them."

"How about Lattiware?"

"No."

"Jensen Lattimore himself?"

"No."

"You're certain he's not behind any of the—"

"I'm certain," she confirmed coldly. "When can we expect to receive your proposal, Mr. Tanner?"

I gave her the date of my birthday and told her I'd be in touch.

Comforted by the fact that at least part of the DigiArt project was bogus, I swung by a video store to rent some hardware, then picked up Fiona outside Pro Robics. She directed me down Queen Anne Avenue, then right on Aloha, then left and right again, then told me to park wherever I could find a slot. The street was West Olympic, the building was the Irish Apartments; I followed her to a unit in back.

It was cozy and dark, with hardwood floors and a redone kitchen and grillwork on the windows to fend off the fiends. The inclinations of the occupant were obvious—the living room walls were covered with Imogen Cunningham; the kitchen walls were covered with Edward and Brett Weston; the bedroom walls were covered with Fiona. When I asked if I could go take a look, she gave me reluctant permission.

She came in a variety of packages, from expensively framed enlargements to Polaroids glued to poster board to snapshots stuck around the edges of the dresser mirror. The poses were various, from formal to casual, stylized to realistic, somber to smiling, indoors to out, nude to swimwear, sportswear to formal attire. Fiona in all her aspects, Fiona everywhere, Fiona flagrant and coy and ethereal and enticing.

When I got back to the kitchen I was smiling. "Nice portfolio."

"Thanks. Real or decaf?"

"Decaf."

"Sumatra all right?"

"Some of my best friends are Sumatrans."

She put the coffee in a metal filter. "Who did you want to be when you started modeling?" I asked as she waited for the water to heat.

"Cheryl Tiegs. She did fashion and TV, then got her own line of clothing and married a rich guy. Seemed like a perfect life."

"How far did you get with it?"

"Not far. I started to outgrow the mold by the time I was eighteen. I starved till I was anemic and anorexic, and worked out till I had shinsplints and stress fractures, and still couldn't keep down to a six. So I went on to other things."

"Figure work. With a pass at smut along the way."

She shrugged. "That's life." She finished with the foam and looked at me. "Why are you here?"

The bedroom display had rendered me foolish and fervid. I draped an arm across her shoulders. "Does there need to be a reason?"

She stepped away and lowered her eyes. "I think so."

I snatched my arm back to my side. My face was as hot as the coffee.

"I'm sorry," she said quickly. "I know I flirted with you yesterday, and you seem like a nice enough guy, but . . ." She shrugged. "I've screwed for a lot of reasons but there was always *something*. You know? I'm sorry," she repeated.

"Don't worry about it. It was dumb of me to think you'd be interested."

"You're upset."

"No, I'm not."

"Yes, you are. I led you on. I do that too much. I thought, well,

I don't know what I thought—that you were dangerous or some-thing. A Bad Boy. Someone I could brag about to my friends—a romp with the private eye. But when the chips are down, that doesn't seem to be enough."

"It shouldn't be."

"I'm glad you understand."

What I understood was that she'd been around beautiful bod-ies all her life and it was only natural that she couldn't force her-self to be interested in someone whose skin sagged and belly bulged and hair was speckled and sparse.

Fiona focused on the espresso machine for the next few min-utes, steaming the milk, pouring a second round of coffee, giving me a chance to regain self-respect. When she was finished she looked at me. "If you're going to be around, maybe we could go out once in a while. You know. See if something develops."

"Thanks, but if things go the way I think they will, I'm leaving town tomorrow."

She frowned. "What way is that?"

"I'm closing in on Nina. The key is a guy named Jensen Latti-more. Know him?"

"I've heard the name."

"Every beautiful woman in Seattle has heard his name. Did his people try to recruit you?"

"Yes, but I didn't play ball."

"That makes you perfect."

"For what?"

"Bait. I can't get to Lattimore except by offering what he craves."

"Which is what?"

I met her look and held it fast. "I've got a video camera in the car."

"So?"

"I was hoping you would make a movie that Lattimore can't

resist. One that will make sure he sees me when I tell him I'm your representative."

Her scowl was quick and damning. "I suppose you'll be the art director."

I shook my head. "I've got a tripod. Just set it up and do your thing. I'll be back about eight for the tape."

"Tell me why I should even *think* about this."

I said what I had to say to win her. "Because if you don't, Nina Evans may end up like Mandy Lorenzen."

She paused for so long I was sure she was going to send me packing. "I can't," she said, and started to cry.

"It's all right. I understand. You don't do that type of—"

"It's not that I don't want to, it's that I can't."

"What do you mean?"

"I can't be what he wants." With an angry jerk, she raised the hem of her shirt and showed me the scar on her belly. It was long and white and eerily phosphorescent, like the skin shed by a poisonous snake.

"Caesarean," she murmured softly. "Eight months ago. The baby was choking; they needed to get it out in a hurry to save it."

"Did they?"

She shook her head. "I hope you have better luck with Nina."

CHAPTER 26

"What is this place?" she asks, nervous for the first time as she is led into a chamber dark all around with dusky walls and charcoal furnishings and black vinyl flooring.

"The Reality Room."

"You mean *virtual* reality, don't you?"

"I mean what I say. This room contains the only life I wish to live. What happens in here is infinitely more engaging than anything outside." He giggles. "Forgive my intensity."

She gulps a gift of air. "What do I have to do?"

"Sit in that chair and keep your eyes open."

"I don't wear goggles or anything?"

"We're beyond such rudimentary instruments—this is an immersion chamber; the environment contains an image over 270 degrees of surface. Of course, a chamber like this is not optimal, either."

"Why not?"

"It's immobile—both the system and the user must be fixed for it to function. Resolution is less than ideal, also. Fortunately, that won't be a problem much longer."

"Why not?"

"The people at the Human Interface Technology Lab are working with Micro Vision to develop a retinal display that will be as mobile as a pair of eyeglasses."

"How would that work?"

"A small headset projects a laser image directly onto the retina.

The entire retina is occupied; there is no leakage. Reality is impenetrable; it follows you everywhere." He laughs at his joke so she does, too.

"This thing is ready now?"

"Not quite. But soon."

She looks around the room and experiences the zing of claustrophobia. "Where are you going to be during all this?"

He gestures with a finger. "In the command center, punching up the appropriate files. Ready?"

"I guess so."

"Good. The first sensation you will experience is absolute darkness. Unless you're a particularly adventuresome spelunker, it's not a condition one encounters often. But don't be alarmed."

"Easier said than done, I have a feeling."

Lattimore disappears and she wriggles toward comfort in the upholstered chair. When the lights go out she discovers he is right—there is no visible distinction between having her eyes open and closed. It is disorienting and a little fearsome; she subdues a surge toward panic by pressing a fingernail into her palm.

Time drifts. She begins to think it's a trick, that her plan has been divined and she has become imprisoned. Then comes a blast of light and roar of sound and she is surrounded.

By herself.

Her likeness is straightforward at first, posed in the various venues Chris selected for their shoots. The distinction is in clarity—she seems more real than real, her body more defined and dimensional than it appears even at home in her mirror. She is magnificent. She is overwhelming. She is omnipresent. She is also irritated that they have toyed with her so blatantly, but as the display progresses she begins to be transformed. She is fascinated, then amazed, then astounded. Within minutes, she is aware of nothing but her own evolution within a world she has neither visited nor heard about.

It begins subtly, her body lengthened, then shortened, widened, then narrowed, as though she has stumbled into the hall of mirrors, as though she has become a fluid. Colors cascade over and around and through her, reminiscent of the psychedelic light shows she has seen in sixties movies, to the accompaniment of acid rock. Then she is dissected like a frog, her legs, arms, and chest, and nose and ears and eyes become star players and take a solo turn, after which they multiply—suddenly she has six feet, four elbows, nine knees, a dozen breasts, a score of buttocks lined up like balls in a bowling alley. Then it becomes surreal.

Her parts are rearranged—nose in her navel, hands at her ears, eyes in her breasts, nipples on her knees. Then it turns bucolic. In the middle of a tranquil meadow, she emerges from the soil like a sunflower, as rarified as Primavera, a triumph of botany and biogenetics. Solitary on a beach, she is engulfed by a roiling sea, becomes as much a part of it as kelp. Supine on a bright white rock, she seems entirely unaware that a tiny red rose has blossomed from the black grass of her pubis. Splayed on black pavement like a murder victim, she is suddenly aloft, drifting on a cloud, the world an irrelevance below her, her business that of angels.

She then becomes a tree, her face lined and solemn within the trunk, her arms laced into the branches, her legs thick roots that plunge into the loamy soil in search of sustenance. Then she is a car, her smile a chrome amusement. Then a fish. Then a bird. Then she becomes commercial. She performs a runway show of fashion, her attire ranging from strapless gowns to sassy shorts to a variety of enticing lingerie even though she has never worn such items in her life. Each costume change is instantaneous.

As it threatens to become too much, an overdose of improvisation, the chamber is briefly black, then lights come on and Jensen Lattimore is by her side.

"Well?"

"Amazing."

"I thought you'd like it."

"What are you going to do with it?"

"Sell it."

"For how much?"

"Fifty bucks a disk, probably."

"How many customers are we talking about?"

"A million, maybe."

"So you'll make fifty million bucks off me."

"Gross. Yes."

She laughs. "Now let's see the good stuff."

"What do you mean?"

"You know what I mean. The private stock. The stuff you keep under the counter that goes to the highest bidder."

¤   ¤   ¤

THERE WAS A MESSAGE at the motel to call Chris Wellington. When I did, he asked if I could see him right away. I told him I had some business I was trying to set up for later that evening, but I would try to come by in the morning.

"If the business has to do with Jensen Lattimore," he said stiffly, "then you won't waste your time coming here first."

I was headed for the door when the phone rang. "How's it going?" Peggy asked, her voice faint and dejected.

"Okay. How's it going with you?"

"Not good."

"What's the problem?"

"I don't know. I'm getting to think I don't know Ted as well as I thought I did."

"This isn't a good environment to make that kind of decision," I said. "Emotions are too close to the surface. Wait till Nina is back in the fold and things have calmed down."

"When do you think that will be?"

"With luck, by tomorrow."

Her breath hissed like water about to boil. "What have you learned? Where is she?"

"I'm not sure I've learned anything; I'm just taking a flier in hopes of shaking something loose." I hesitated, then blurted what had been on my mind all afternoon. "I'm trying to do the same thing you did six years ago."

"What's that?"

"Use a woman for bait in hopes the bad guy will be lured into the trap."

She paused long enough to reprise that awful evening. "Well, I hope it works out better than last time."

"I'm not confident of it."

"Why not?"

"My bait's not as good."

She laughed a rueful chorus and told me to be careful. I told her that I'd gotten better at it since she'd seen me last.

I got to DigiArt in twenty minutes. Wellington was dressed in camouflage gear and his face was smeared with black grease-paint. He didn't give me time to ask why.

"I've done something dumb," he said even before I sat down. "You seem like the kind of guy who can get me out of it."

I shrugged. "I've had some experience along those lines."

"This particular brand of dumb put someone I care about in jeopardy."

"Are we talking about Nina Evans?"

He nodded, then invited me to sit down, so I did. He asked if I wanted some coffee and I declined. I asked if he had any liquor.

He shook his head. "I'd prefer you keep a clear head," he preached with a lump of self-righteousness.

"Why's that?"

"I'd like you to help me this evening."

I looked at his outfit. "Do what? Assault the post office?"

"Get Nina back from where I took her."

"Where's that?"

"Jensen Lattimore's cabin."

"The one in Issaquah?"

That slowed him down. "How'd you know about that?"

"Sources," I murmured, as though I had counterespionage at my disposal. "As a matter of fact, I was planning to pay Jensen a visit myself if I could figure a way to get in. How'd you find Nina?"

"I didn't need to find her; she's been with me all along."

"Where?"

"A condo in Madison Park."

"You were living together?"

He shook his head. "We were working together."

"On what?"

"A project for Mr. Lattimore."

"Maybe you'd better explain."

And he did—the exclusive arrangement, the condo, the secrecy, the video sessions, the breakthroughs that were behind it all, names like Electric Image and Silicon Studio that permitted tricks and capabilities with film and video even beyond those that Jeff Evans had told me about.

By the time he was finished, he had answered a lot of questions but not quite all of them. "If you cared about her, why did you take her to Lattimore?"

The twist in his face suggested he had already asked himself that and wasn't proud of his answer. "She asked me to. She said she wouldn't do any more work if I didn't. She said if I didn't take her she'd go on her own."

"Why'd she want to see him? I thought she didn't go along with the smutty side of the business."

"Curiosity, maybe. Or maybe she was going to try to reform him. Women do that, I've noticed," he concluded dispiritedly.

"Why are you worried that something bad is going to happen?"

His expression turned grim and fearful. "Because Jensen Latti-more is insane."

"Insane how?"

"He's obsessed by women. Not women as people; not even women as sex objects—I think he may be a virgin, in fact. But he's obsessed with women's bodies and by what can be done with the female form after you scan it into a computer. The naked woman is a metaphor for everything he believes that cyberspace can be."

"What does that mean?"

"Jensen grew up in an age when looking at naked women was wrong. Shameful. Immoral. I'm sure he got caught some time or another and was punished for his peeping. And I'm sure as an adolescent he got slapped for trying to go too far with girls he dated. Well, now he looks at naked women all day long."

"He just looks?"

"And manipulates. He gets off on controlling every square inch of their flesh, which he can do the minute he digitizes it. The images he creates are symbols of his ascendance over the forbid-den world of female flesh, of the obsolescence of old rules, of the reversal of roles. What he does is turn the tables. He makes women ashamed of posing the way he was made to be ashamed for looking at them back when he was shoplifting *Playboys*."

"Is he dangerous? Voyeurism isn't always violent; sometimes it's even a palliative."

"If he doesn't get what he wants, he can be."

"Has he harmed women in the past?"

"Usually he just threatens to embarrass them. Most of the time, that does the trick. But he's got some thugs on hand in case it doesn't."

"He used those methods to raise money, too, didn't he?"

Wellington nodded. "That's how he got started. Back when he was trying to get financing for Lattiware, he and Richter lured the daughters of several prominent men into his web. He paid most of his start-up costs with the checks their daddies wrote to keep pictures of their darlings from being leaked to the skin mags or the tabloid media. But what was originally a blackmailing tool soon became an obsession. He kept manipulating women long after his need for money evaporated."

"Did Lattimore kill Richter?"

Wellington shrugged. "I don't know. He might have, if Richter threatened to expose his scheme."

"But you don't have proof?"

"What I've got is this."

Wellington walked to what looked like a huge TV set with the name Silicon Graphics stamped on it, then flipped a button to turn it on. When the screen filled, he grabbed a mouse and clicked on some icons. Moments later, the screen darkened. Then the silhouette of a man emerged. Wellington walked to the wall and turned off the lights.

It was a trip into film noir, black and gray shapes moving through a wet, foggy city to the accompaniment of gloom and shadow and ambiguous doings initially indecipherable, then increasingly sinister. I didn't know the producer or screenwriter, but the director was Chris Wellington and the star was Gary Richter.

In the opening scenes, Richter was going leisurely about his business, wandering the Ave, drinking coffee at the Still Life, flirting with women, debating with men, returning to his apartment in Fremont when his evening amusements ran dry. There wasn't a sound track, and there wasn't much in the way of dramatic development, either, but as he approached the stairs to his studio, a villain emerged from the sculpture garden next to his home and shot Gary Richter in the back of the head.

After gunning down his victim, the killer dragged Richter's body to a car and began to stuff it in the trunk. As he was wrestling with the corpse, the killer's face was illuminated by the streetlight, almost as though he knew he was being filmed and wanted to steal the scene.

After the trunk banged shut and the car disappeared around a corner, Wellington turned on the lights.

"Who the hell was *that*?" I asked.

"Jensen Lattimore."

"Lattimore shot Richter?"

"That's what it says, doesn't it?"

"Who shot the film?"

"I did. Although shot isn't quite the word. I assembled it, more accurately."

I blinked. "You're saying this is fake."

"Does it matter?"

"Of course it matters."

"It depends on the purpose, doesn't it? If the purpose is to get to Lattimore and distract him while I search for Nina, then it's as real as it needs to be. Right?"

"It may be effective, but it's not real. Do you think Lattimore really killed him?"

"I don't know."

"Well, I don't think he did."

"Why not?"

"Because if he had, he would have done something more imaginative with the body than dump it in a canal."

Wellington shrugged. "Maybe so. But solving a murder isn't the issue at this point; getting Nina back safely is. I brought you in on this because I thought that's what you were trying to do. Now you're turning soft on me."

"The rough stuff only works in B movies," I said. "Tell me more about Lattimore."

"How do you mean?"

"How'd he get the way he is? Why does he go to such

extremes? In my experience, guys with lots of bucks don't find it hard to get dates."

Wellington shook his head. "For one thing, Jensen's impatient. He wants what he wants right now, he doesn't want to have to woo someone. For another, he's unattractive. As you could tell from the video, he's short and sort of odd-looking. He looks like Telly Savalas with hair, huge head on a pudgy body. And his personality is even worse than his physique—he's offensive without even meaning to be, and when he wants to be, which is most of the time, he's insufferable."

"How so?"

"He has no tact, no sophistication, no clue to basic psychology. He's blunt and gross and obvious; women have avoided him all his life. Worse, they've laughed at him. So what he wants is two things—he wants the most beautiful women in the world at his beck and call, and then he wants them humiliated. And he learned early on how to get them to cooperate in their own destruction."

"How? Money?"

He shook his head. "Film. People will do anything to be in the movies. Ever since he was a kid, Jensen was a film nut—he has a video library of more than two thousand titles; some legitimate, lots pornographic. Russ Meyer and D. W. Griffith are his heroes—Griffith because he pushed the technology beyond previous limits; Meyer because he filmed naked women when it was considered immoral to do so. Jensen decided to take that combination to a higher level and he found some men who would pay him to do it."

"The special clients."

"Right. Victor Krakov steers them his way."

"How does Krakov find them?"

"They're his customers. Businessmen who sneak away from the office to visit titty bars, lawyers who rent hard-core videos on weekends, doctors who buy rubber aids to spice up their sex lives. Krakov keeps track of every transaction just like Radio Shack keeps track when you buy batteries. Then he gives the names to Jensen and Jensen makes his pitch at the parties."

"Where do you come in?"

"What I thought I was was an artist, working with state-of-the-art computers to create a new form of imagery and even a new aesthetic. What I really was was a front man, making prim little video pieces at DigiArt while behind me, Gary Richter was turning out hard-core smut to pay for my indulgence."

"Why did you work for him? What did you need from Lattimore?"

Wellington reddened and looked away. "Money, naturally. Hardware costs a fortune. The stuff in this building—Indy work stations, editing machines, Keying systems, optical effects printers, scanners, enough memory to digitize *Gone with the Wind*—cost over two million dollars. Far beyond my ability to raise." His look turned sheepish. "I have artistic ambitions of my own."

I had an urge to jostle his rationale. "How many Mandy Lorenzens are running around out there?"

He recoiled as though I'd slapped him. "Not that many, if you mean women he destroyed. Most of the daddies paid up, so the obscenities never saw the light of day, and Jensen moved on to other victims. Lattimore kept that part of the bargain, at least. But Mandy was his favorite before Nina, and she wouldn't play ball so Jensen sent an obscenity to her father." The words turned brittle and arid. "He obliterated the whole family—the father forsook his kids and got bounced from the bank; the son committed suicide and Mandy might as well have."

"What's Lattimore want from Nina?"

"Jensen's got what he needs in terms of financing, so basically we're talking control and degradation. He's going to take the most beautiful woman he's ever seen and make her ashamed of who she is."

"Why pick Nina?"

His smile was paternal. "You don't know her, do you?"

I shook my head.

"If you did, you wouldn't ask."

"How do you mean?"

"She was born to be a model. She uses her body like a Stradivarius; she's truly a virtuoso. She literally assaults the camera—usurps it, controls it, dominates it. I'm just a lackey, rushing to keep up with her. She must have studied herself in the mirror for hours, because she knows exactly how to make herself look unique and enchanting, as dazzling and unpredictable as some new lifeform. It's the best work I've ever done," he added glumly, "and it's for a perverted purpose. To top it off, I just delivered my model into a den of iniquity."

I slapped him on the back. "Then I guess we'd better get her out."

I placed a call to Fran and arranged for a midnight delivery of Richter's Erospace photographs.

The lights go out; the world turns upside down. Good has become evil; art is obscenity—in the universe that envelopes her, she has become a slut and slattern. She asked for smut and has gotten it—as filth unfolds around her, she fights the urge to vomit.

Yet somehow it becomes magnetic. She is displayed in places she has never been—dark, depressing dungeons adrip with instruments of torture and humiliation. She is paired with a succession of strangers, huge men and tiny men, African men and Nordic men, men with organs the size of fists and forearms and men who turn out to be women when they ultimately disrobe. She is doing things she has never done, is manipulated in ways she has never imagined, is penetrated by objects of peculiar purpose, is debased repeatedly and beyond projection.

It is so foreign and fantastic, it becomes a philosophical abstraction; she begins to wonder how it was accomplished, and why. It is so horrifying and unnerving, so removed from the world of aesthetics and achievement she has fought so long to occupy, that she begins to laugh. Perhaps this is justice; perhaps nakedness is sinful after all and the film is her punishment, the inevitable embodiment of original sin.

As her laughter dies, the lights come on and Lattimore slips through an invisible door and stands before her like a pint-sized cyclops. "I'm glad you enjoyed it," he says, his smile a smarmy misinterpretation of her reaction.

At least she remembers her pose. "I can't believe it, Mr. Lattimore. You must be able to make anybody do anything. No one will know what's real and what isn't anymore."

"It's all real, Ms. Evans."

"But I didn't do those things."

His condescension is repulsive. "Not even in your dreams?"

She decides to simply smile.

He pushes the rhetoric further. "If you didn't do those things, who did?"

"You did them. You and your machines."

"Then that makes them real, does it not? As real as automobiles? As real as shoes?"

Lattimore gives her what he thinks is time to admire his sophistry, but she uses it to reassemble her intentions. As he whistles a toneless tune, she slides her hand to his thigh. "Those movies got me hot. I want to pose for you."

"Good."

"Is there a place we can go?"

He hesitates. "Of course."

He helps her to her feet and leads her out of the spooky chamber and down the hall to a room designed for just one purpose. It is an adolescent's vision of heaven—ceiling mirrors and satin sheets and lighting in the pink palette of a bordello—but the effect is more suffocating than sensual. The air is too falsely fragrant, the floor too thickly carpeted, the bedding too slickly scarlet, the theme too eager and unalloyed. It is so pathetic, she feels a sense of sympathy, but only momentarily. At the push of a button, the screens on the walls leap to life with nudes, women cavorting around the bed like participants in an erotic olympics.

When he starts to unbutton her blouse, she grasps his hands to stop him. "You first."

He reddens, as if it is the first time the issue has presented itself. "Maybe I should slip into something more comfortable."

"Maybe you should."

After he disappears into an anteroom, she places her purse on the bed and extracts her accessories. When he emerges minutes later, looking like a doll-sized gladiator in red silk jock and satin slippers, she picks up her camera and aims it.

The flash is blinding. His hands go to his eyes and he swears at her. Sightless, he staggers toward the wall and gropes for a switch. The ceiling lights go off, to be replaced by a dozen others, multi-colored strobes that animate and enliven the room. The music goes from soft to hard, a throbbing threnody of rock and roll that seems to mimic rutting.

"No more cameras, goddammit—I'll take care of the pyrotechnics."

As he squints into the light that shields her, she returns the camera to her purse and picks up her pistol and shoots him.

He is on the ground, rolling and moaning and clutching himself, as she rushes from the room. When there is one last door in the way of her freedom, the beefy guard steps from behind a post and grabs her and lifts her off the ground.

"You're going to wish you hadn't done that," he says, with what she sees is relish. "I told him when we saw you dogging Richter that you were trouble. I told him when we got the stuff you stashed with your skinny buddy that he'd better put a muzzle on you. I guess now I got to do it myself."

The arm around her throat squeezes until she gags.

¤　　　¤　　　¤

IT WAS AN HOUR BEFORE MIDNIGHT when we turned off the free-way and snaked through the foothills of Issaquah. The evening mist dampened the windshield with a rash of tiny blisters until the wipers swept it clear in a minor miracle of healing.

The rental car was quiet; Chris Wellington was intent on driving; I could easily have fallen asleep. "Where do you think he's got her?" I asked after we'd cleared the commercial cluster of the village.

"Pool house, probably. It's detached from the main building and it's got lots of little rooms to stick her in."

"So I go to the big house and you head for the pool."

"Right."

"Are you sure he'll see me?"

"I told him you have something on that disk that he absolutely has to be aware of."

I took the shiny CD-ROM out of my pocket and looked at it like an aborigine encountering a wristwatch. "What does he think this is?"

"Porn, probably. That's mostly what he does out here. The legitimate stuff goes on in the city."

"The disk comes from me? Not you?"

"Right. I made you sound like this big, tough guy from out of town who's the front man for an extortion scam."

"What do you think he'll do when he sees what it is?"

"Well, he'll know it's a fake, obviously, and he'll wonder who made it and why."

"Won't he know it came from you?"

"No. I dumbed down the technology so it's way short of leading edge. And even if he does figure it was me, it shouldn't matter at that point. This has to be in and out fast. Right?"

"Right. Will he be worried enough to distract him even though he knows it's fake?"

"Probably not for long. He's skated away from some sticky stuff over the years, including charges of fraud and extortion by women who haven't wanted to play his games. The complaints all evaporated once they got to city hall."

"He won't react at all?"

"Oh, he'll react. He'll be pissed that you thought you could fleece him."

"That I turned the tables, in other words."

"Right. And he'll want to punish you for it."

"What kind of security does he have out here?"

"Lots of weapons; just two men."

"Are they trained or just beefcake?"

"One's ex-FBI—a little Latino who got bounced for sexual harassment of a female agent a couple of years back. The other's a former Tacoma cop—he left the force to make money."

Wellington turned a corner and stopped the car. The light of a lonely streetlamp performed an alchemy by making the mist a spritz of gold.

"That's Lattimore's place down there," Wellington pointed. "We'll be under camera surveillance the minute we enter the gate. There's one thing you should be ready for," he added after a moment.

"What's that?"

"He's got this room. The Reality Room, he calls it. It's basically an isolation chamber in which everything you see and hear and smell comes from Lattimore's command and control consoles. He takes charge of your senses and turns them against you. The experience can be pretty mind-boggling."

"You've gone through it?"

"No, but I've seen people who have. They look like they've seen Satan, sometimes."

"Maybe they have," I said, remembering the hell that Mandy Lorenzen had descended to, remembering the shove that had put her there.

I looked around to make sure we were alone. "I guess this is where you get in the trunk."

Wellington nodded and climbed out of the car. A button on the key ring opened the lid. He gave me back the ignition key and took the rest of the ring into the trunk with him, to use to make his exit. As I closed the lid on his fetal curl, he wasn't as scared as he should have been. That's one of the virtues of amateurism.

I drove through the gate and followed the asphalt lane toward the house. Lattimore called the place "Lattitudes," the plaque on the gatepost told me; I wondered again at the origins and effects of a raging ego.

The house was more subtle than I expected, a dark log laid casually across the wooded landscape, a young boy's fort writ large. As I came to a stop under the portico, the massive door opened immediately. The man who came out to intercept me was huge and hostile and hyper-alert, so much so that I worried that this was some kind of trap, that Wellington remained in cahoots with Lattimore and had set me up for a fall.

He held the door as I got out of the car. His brows were as bristly as ropes and his hands as big as saucepans; his greeting lacked words of welcome. The quick once-over didn't include the trunk but it encompassed everything in sight including me. When I gave him my name and said I had an appointment, he was as interested as if I'd told him I was a Presbyterian.

When I was inside the house, he put out a hand to halt my progress so he could frisk me both manually and electronically. "What's that?" he asked about the object in my left hand.

"CD-ROM."

"For him?"

"Right."

"He knows what it is?"

"Only generically."

"Generically. Yeah. That's a good word for it." His disgust seemed directed at his boss' predilections more than at me and my slender alm.

"You're the ex-cop, right?" I asked.

"Yeah. Why?"

"Know anyone on the Frisco force?"

He shook his head. "Why would I?"

"No reason. Just making conversation."

"Well, make it go away."

He motioned for me to follow and I trailed him down a hall that seemed as long as the supercollider. When he stopped by an open door he pointed toward the innards of the room. "Wait there."

"How long will it be?"

"However long he wants it to be. Had a guy wait three days once. Slept in a chair; pissed in a plant. Never did do any business." He laughed and lumbered back the way we'd come.

I entered the designated holding cell and sat in a club chair to wait. The room was busy but impersonal, with nothing to suggest the mind of its owner. Lattimore had probably learned long ago to keep his mind out of sight of his guests. I wondered if Chris Wellington had managed to slip out of the car and into the pool house. The more I thought about it, the more I doubted that anything good could happen in the next hour. When I looked for a way out, I didn't see anything but the way in.

Twenty minutes later, Jensen Lattimore showed up. He arrived in a hurry, dropped into a chair across from mine, and inspected me with intensity, mouth open, eyes bugged, the way an anthropologist would inspect a potsherd. No name, no greeting, no pleasantries—just an open and unabashed assessment of my essence, as though my IQ were imprinted on my forehead and my neuroses were etched across my eyeballs.

He was dressed in fifties freshman chic—madras shirt, chino trousers, white socks, penny loafers. His hair was brush cut and his eyes were described by horn-rim glasses: that the fifties had become fashionable again was one of life's minor mysteries. The only dissent to his outfit was his left arm—it was bandaged from wrist to elbow in white gauze and wide adhesive that looked to have been freshly applied.

"You persuaded Chris that you've got something I need to see," he began, his eyes locked on me like radar, his words as rapid as a teletype. "He'd better be right."

I held up the disk.

"What's on it?"

I smiled. "Something you should see."

"Women?"

"Why don't we make it a surprise."

For some reason it was the wrong thing to say. "I've had enough surprises for one night," he said angrily, lifting his arm and inspecting the bandage. "What format?"

"What?"

"The disk. DOS, Unix, OS/2, System 7, what?"

Chris had briefed me. "System 7 point five. Power MAC platform."

"What application?"

"Something new."

"Who wrote the code?"

"I did."

"Bullshit. I could tell you weren't technical before you opened your mouth."

"How?"

"You blink too much and you hold that disk like a dog turd." He stood up, walked to the corner of the room, opened a recessed refrigerator, took out a piece of cold pizza, and took a big bite. "Cut to the chase. Is this some sort of garbage downloaded off the Internet? *Debbie Does Dallas* scanned onto disk? Beaver shots of your daughter? What?"

I expended the energy necessary to keep from stuffing the pizza in his ear. "I'd say this is more like *Blow Up*. And I'm pretty sure you're going to like it."

"Why?"

"Because you're the star."

"Star of what?"

"My movie."

"Another skin flick, I suppose." He shook his head. "You're like everyone else with a narrow bandwidth. You think I'm a pornographer when what I am is a redeemer."

I raised a brow. "Of women?"

"Of men, of course."

"How so?"

"Beautiful women are evil incarnate. They have wreaked more havoc than all the weapons of war in history."

"What kind of havoc are you talking about?"

His cheeks reddened and his eyes bulged with fervor. "I'm talking about the belittlement of the male that they feast upon; I'm talking about the humiliation that they traffic in; I'm talking about the teasing they employ in order to maximize the pain of the denial they invariably impose; and I'm talking about the mocking of normal desires that they find so titillating."

I suppressed a laugh. "And how do you go about saving the male animal from all this?"

"I bring to the surface the evil that lurks within them. I show such women in their true light by removing the veil of loveliness from the depravity that lies below it. Utilizing digital technology to reveal these truths is my most important contribution."

"To what? Your bank account?"

He put out a hand to silence me. "Much as I would like to expand on my liberation of the male animal, I don't have time. Assuming I have an interest in your database, what's it going to cost me to license it?"

"Why don't you look at it first? Then we'll talk."

Lattimore shrugged, then reached for the disk, then left the room at the pace he had entered it. After he was gone, I felt I should be doing something to protect myself from what was coming, but I didn't know what that would be.

When he returned to the room he had friends with him. They flanked him like praetorian guards, the burly ex-cop and the wiry ex-agent, poised to protect their charge from anything I could throw at him. For his part, Lattimore was an inch away from foaming at the mouth. His breath sizzled like steak on the grill, his eyes were as bright as bad bearings.

He waved the disk under my nose as if the ink on the label was wet. "You asshole. Who the hell do you think you are, coming in here with shit like this? Don't you know who I am?"

"You're a blackmailer and a pornographer and you murdered the guy who fronted for you. Unfortunately, when you bumped Richter off to keep him quiet, someone caught it on tape. Gives you a lot in common with the cops who pummeled Rodney King."

He waved the disk again. "Bullshit. This isn't off video stock, this is jury-rigged with stone age hardware and a half-assed piece of code—I'm embarrassed to have it in my home. Who the fuck packaged it?"

I shrugged. "What difference does it make?"

"I like to know who I'm dealing with."

"You're dealing with me."

"Bullshit; you're a stooge at best and a nuisance at worst. Where'd you get the disk?"

"I found it."

"Where?"

"Mailbox."

"Bullshit. Who else has seen this abortion?"

"No one."

"Not the cops?"

"Nope."

"How many copies are there?"

"Enough to keep me safe and sound."

Lattimore circled the room before he spoke again, his goons moving around him like satellite moons—it looked like a road production of *Grease*. But if I'd moved a muscle in my foot, they would have pounced on me.

"It's bogus, you know," Lattimore said finally.

"Is it?"

"Sure. I didn't kill Richter."

"Who did?"

"How should I know? He was into all kinds of sub-rosa stuff. Only part of it was mine."

"Whether you did it or not, if the cops get pointed in your direction they'll find plenty to perk them up. Cops love the hell out of porn—it confirms what they think about people, women especially. Probably be six months before they sort it out, and even if you skate on the murder charge, they'll find something else to hang you on. In the meantime, you'll be out of business."

He'd figured it out already, of course, so he didn't bother to fence with me. "How much?"

I shook my head. "The medium of exchange isn't money."

"What is it?"

I smiled. "You seem pretty eager to deal for someone who claims he's innocent."

His face turned the color of his cordovans. "You're not technical but you're not a fool—you know as well as I do that half the economy is based on false claims and baseless accusations. News media. Advertising. Movies. All it is is lies and technology makes it easier. I can knock it down, of course, but I don't have time for the aggravation. What do you want?"

"A woman."

The pressure was off and his smile was lecherous. "I can get you enough women to let you to ream a new one every night for two years."

"I only want one of them, Jensen."

His glance flicked toward the window. "Who?"

"Nina Evans."

His coal-hot eyes threatened to scorch his forehead. "That bitch? What do you want with her? She thinks she's some kind of princess—I got dozens look better than she does." He waved his hand dismissively. "You can have them all; I make my own these days."

"Isn't it a tad perverted to prefer digital women to real ones?"

He looked down at his bandaged arm. "Real ones are a pain in the ass." He stopped pacing and looked at me long enough to determine my fate. "Bring him," he said to his lackeys in a sudden burst of venom. "I need to know what he knows."

They were on me before I could move, their hands locked on my arms like condor claws, their breaths as sour as kraut in my nostrils. They wrestled me down the hall as if I weighed a hundred pounds instead of a hundred more.

The room they took me to was black all around and lit by one flood in the ceiling. The two chairs in the center were gray and upholstered and tasteful. Suddenly a motor whirred and a third chair rose out of the floor in the space between the other two. This one came with webbed straps and plastic clamps that enabled them to lock me into it as securely as condemned men are locked into the electric chair.

When they'd finished, they stepped back and admired their work. "All set, boss."

Lattimore grinned crookedly. "Did you ever have a nightmare so real it scared you for days on end, Mr. Tanner? Until you couldn't remember whether it was real or not?"

I nodded. The dream involved deep dark caves with walls that closed in on me like car crushers. Sweat rolled off my forehead and stung my eyes, as though my juices had become sulphuric.

"Well, you're about to have a similar experiece. I'll be interested to see how it turns out."

"What can I do to stop it?"

"Nothing. The only thing you can do is keep it from happening again."

Lattimore leaned down and picked up two wires with wafers the size of quarters on the end of them. He stuck the round things on my face near my temples, then stepped back.

"These are electrodes designed to tell us if you blink. If you do, you will receive an electric shock. If you close your eyes, you will receive a bigger shock. If you *keep* them closed, you will eventually be electrocuted. All you need to do to keep that from happening is observe the world around you."

He laughed and was out the door. A moment later, I was drowning in darkness. Some moments after that was when I started screaming.

She has come to this: naked, locked in a barren room with nothing but a towel for comfort, shivering, scared, and abandoned. It is the way she has always sensed it would end, the fate she has always feared for reasons she cannot fathom. She is hostage to someone as detached from life as she herself has been, as heedless of suffering, as obsessed with his power and potency; someone who is planning, quite likely, to kill her.

She wonders what it will mean, her death, and decides it will mostly mean relief, to her mother and brother, certainly, to everyone, in fact, but Ted. Poor, pathetic Ted, who pretended his urges were platonic, who denied his intents and purposes even as he stroked her breast and kissed her ear after a particularly wonderful meal of veal and venison, who justified his behavior by denying his paternity, then apologized profusely and begged her to accept his retraction.

She had lured him into such shamefulness deliberately, of course, so the surprise was not the effort, the surprise was that she had resisted. So many times, she hadn't, so many men had been allowed to join with her because some deep-seated sense of obligation whispered that it was what she must do to keep them near and make them happy, that otherwise they would fly away and she would be left with only feeling, the feeling, the one she's known since the dawn of life, that she must please people or they will abandon her.

She curls into herself the way she used to curl for Gary,

becomes a nut of flesh, but this time the goal is warmth. When the door opens she fully expects it is the end, expects to see an ugly man and an uglier weapon and to be instructed to prepare for doom. Instead, she sees salvation.

"It's all right," he says, covering her mouth with kisses to suppress her exclamations. "I'm going to get you out of here, but not yet. It's all right," he repeats when her eyes plead for him to stay. "I'll be back in a second; I just need to set stuff up."

¤   ¤   ¤

GIVEN HIS OBSESSIONS, I figured the high-tech torture that Lattimore had in store for me would feature women in various stages of undress and similar extremes of jeopardy—I would be an unwilling party to their slaughter, whether virtual or in fact I wouldn't be able to tell. In the moments of darkness before I became engulfed, I steeled myself to shrug it off—the sadism was just a trick, the women hadn't really been burned or slashed or battered, the only actual actors were bits and bytes and lines of code, not people who could feel pain and endure agony. As ably as I could, I inured myself against such suffering, but they were scenes I never saw.

When the screens that surrounded me flamed with light and I was assaulted by a tsunami of sight and sound, I began the trek concocted by my captor. Not in a vehicle I'd ever steered, not through realms I'd ever traveled, not to a destination I'd ever sought out—what I did was fly, through a universe of Jensen Lattimore's making.

Pleasantly, at first, the way I'd always imagined it would be. Easy dips and turns, drifting gently over a landscape formed mostly of what looked like the tops of trees and the roofs of buildings—I might have been an eagle, soaring above Seattle, or even an archangel. But when I became an airplane, I suddenly started to crash.

I dived toward the ground with increasing speed, to pull up an instant before disaster. I hurtled toward a wall, to veer left milliseconds before collision. I climbed toward a cloud, then yawed into a corkscrew roll, spinning faster and faster as I plunged toward the void amid a whir and scrape of dissonance, courtesy of a synthesizer and surround-sound.

I told myself it wasn't real, that I was still on terra firma, still strapped to a chair and immobile, but given the evidence in my eyes, I couldn't make myself believe it. To regain equilibrium I lowered my eyelids, but my buttocks quickly twinged with shock so I looked back at the maelstrom that was my nemesis. Quickly on the brink of nausea, I closed my eyes again, this time for several seconds. My body vibrated with an electric buzz, as if my guts and groin were being incinerated by torches deep within.

When I opened my eyes to douse the fire, the image shifted. I wasn't on the earth at all, but trapped within a grid that confined me on all sides, a skeletal construction whose surfaces moved in sinister designs and sinuous configurations that entrapped and forestalled me even as I darted here and there to escape the ever-changing web. Blocked at every turn, dizzy with my effort, I was praying for the ordeal to end when the web suddenly became a smokestack, a soaring cylinder into which I fell, tumbling and twisting and spinning in a headlong descent into geometry that seemed interminable.

The nausea that had been building erupted into vomit; I spilled my stomach onto my lap and chest. My eyes lost the knack of focus. My head throbbed; my blood thudded against its conduits. My mouth tasted bile and chewy cud and a metallic residue that made me believe that I had disgorged my body chemistry, that my essential elements were wayward and undone. I groaned and spit and inhaled the stench of my own excreta. And tried not to beg for mercy.

"I could leave you there till you shit your pants," Lattimore crowed from somewhere close at hand, then bestowed a blessed clemency. The lights went out, the images retreated to their silicon caves, my body slowed its vicarious tumble, and Lattimore was back beside me.

"You've only been in here five minutes," he said smugly. "In ten more, I could make you insane."

"That might be redundant," I said, mostly to see if my larynx had been corroded away by my bile.

He ignored my jape. "Is it time to talk, do you think?"

"Sure."

"Then who made the tape?"

"I did."

"If you made that tape, I made the solar system. Which, come to think of it, I did." His laugh was giddy and egomaniacal; Dobie Gillis on crystal meth.

"All you need to do for me to take the next plane out of town," I explained as reasonably as I could manage given the residue that lined my mouth, "is to let me leave with Nina."

"I can't do that."

"Why not?"

"She knows too much."

"Everything she knows, I know."

"That's laughable. If you knew anything at all you wouldn't have come here."

"What are you going to do, kill her?"

"I'm going to acquire her."

"She's not for sale. And I think you know it."

"If she isn't, she would be the first."

"Mandy Lorenzen has that honor, doesn't she?"

"Mandy." He swore. "That was her own doing, just as this is yours." He cackled again. "When you resist a superior force, bad things happen. Which you'd know if you'd ever played Mortal Kombat."

I laughed. "When do you suppose you'll grow up?"

Lattimore slapped my face; since I was still strapped in the chair, I couldn't slap back. "Who made the tape?" he shouted.

"Me."

"Where are the copies?"

"Fort Knox."

"Who killed Gary Richter?"

"You did."

"I was in L.A. that night. I can prove it."

"How about the dropouts?"

"Dropouts?"

"The ex-cop and the ex-agent. Where were they?"

"They were there, too."

"Then you don't have a problem. Just give me Nina Evans and I'll be on my way. Richter's murder is a cop's job, not mine."

"Nina needs reorienting," he whined.

"You sound like the Red Guard."

"Red what?"

"A burst of oriental excess a few years back. You'd know all about it if you ever read anything but software manuals."

He crossed his legs. The penny in his left loafer winked at me from the safety of its slot. "You don't take me seriously, do you, Mr. Tanner?"

"I take you as seriously as the ebola virus."

"What *are* we going to do with you?" he asked himself theatrically. "I've got it. Since you're not technical, perhaps Neanderthal methods will be effective."

Lattimore pushed a button that activated a transmitter. "Antonio, please come to the Reality Room. Mr. Tanner requires further persuasion."

A moment later, Antonio showed up, Glock in hand, to stand guard as Lattimore unhooked me. Antonio was small and shifty and wired. The other guy had seemed disgusted by Jensen's hobby, but this one obviously reveled in it.

When we were out of the little black room and back in the parlor, Lattimore issued instructions. "Take him to the pool house, Antonio. Show him how vulnerable his friend Ms. Evans is. Then convince him to tell me who made the tape he brought with him this evening. He will be more amenable if the menace is to Ms. Evans rather than himself."

Antonio nodded and gestured with his gun. "This way."

I could only do as I was told.

We weren't out of the room when a beeper went off. Antonio picked a hand mike off his belt and spoke. "Hernandez."

The voice on the other end was loud enough to escape his earpieces. "There's an incursion at the pool house."

Antonio activated some speaker.

"Armed?"

"Unknown."

"How many?"

"One confirmed."

"Purpose?"

"Unclear."

"What's your location?"

"Command and control."

"I'm on my way. I'll handle—"

"Shit. Now there's someone at the gate."

"Who?"

"Van. Purpose unclear."

"ID?"

"Not yet. Wait. They say they're from Erospace. The porn store. They claim they're making a delivery."

Antonio glanced at Lattimore. Lattimore shrugged. "Doubtful. I suspect a coordinated assault."

"Possible."

Antonio looked at his boss. Lattimore only shrugged again. Antonio took it as clearance to issue instructions.

"You wait for the van," he told Tacoma in command and control. "I'll take the pool house. I'll leave Tanner with J.L. and—"

"Is that smart?" Tacoma interrupted.

Antonio looked at his boss. "Perhaps not. I'll take them both to
the pool house. You join up as soon as delivery is effected and the
van is off premises."

"Roger."

Antonio hooked the mike on his belt and handed Lattimore his
pistol, then pulled a second one out of his boot. It was chromed
and tiny, as lethal as plutonium. "If he gets out of line, shoot him
in the belly," he instructed. "Keep shooting till he falls down, but
stop unless he produces a weapon. If he has a weapon, keep
shooting till the clip is empty. Clear?"

Lattimore's eyes gleamed happily. "Clear. Roger wilco."

Antonio whirled on his heel and marched down the hall like a
middle manager caught in a merger. Lattimore herded me after
him. I lagged back so I could speak without being overheard by
the point man.

"If someone dies in this, your world will fall apart."

"What world?"

"The blackmail with the women and their daddies. The special
clients. The erotic art gallery and the titty bars. All of it. In a murder case, clout doesn't count."

He was unperturbed. "No one's going to die. And even if they
do, it won't be murder, it'll be self-defense."

"It won't wash, Jensen. There's too many of us. Once you start,
you can't stop killing until you've killed us all."

"All who? What's going on? Who's the intruder at the pool house?"
His voice trembled with uncertainty, a ten-year-old in trouble.

"I don't know who it is," I said. "But I do know the van really is
from Erospace." And I was sorry for putting them at risk. "If your
goons mess this up, you'll go down with them. Respondeat superior, Jensen."

"I . . . How do I know they're really Erospace? It's after midnight. This could be some kind of invasion."

"Who would want to invade you?"

"Certain people in the multimedia industry want me eliminated as a competitor. I'm a threat to several established empires. There are vast sums involved—mergers, technological breakthroughs, federal licenses. I—"

"Enough talk," Antonio interrupted to the front of us. "Wait here."

He ducked into a room and came out with a Tech-9 assault weapon. "Let's take a dip," he joked mordantly, and herded us out of the house.

The moonlight on the pool was a gold ribbon across a black box, a favor for a funeral. The wind in the trees issued a shush of warning. The slam of the van's door beneath the roof of the distant portico sounded like a mortar round exploding.

Antonio looked up. "He must have shot out the pool lights."

"I didn't hear anything," Lattimore said.

"Silencer."

I was the meat in a paranoid sandwich.

The pool house mimicked the main building, except that half of its front was a covered porch open to the pool and the air and the other half was cut by half-a-dozen doorways that presumably led to dressing rooms. Antonio walked into the porch, looked around, then tried the door that connected the two wings. It opened silently, into an even darker chamber than the one we occupied.

"He can't have gotten them all," Antonio said, more to himself than to anyone.

At my back, Lattimore's breaths were as hot as a hound's. As Antonio disappeared into the inner sanctum, Jensen spoke in a harsh whisper. "He must have the access code! He penetrated the security system! It has to be Wellington!"

If Antonio said anything in return, I didn't hear it.

Lattimore shoved me forward with the gun muzzle. "You first. If that asshole's lying in wait, you'll be the one that gets it."

I took six steps and stopped. The room was as dark as the chamber I'd virtually been tortured in, dark to the extent we'd become invisible.

"Tony?" Lattimore called out fearfully.

"Yo."

"I don't like this."

"You see anything?"

"No. Where was the girl when you left her?"

"Southwest corner."

"I don't see—"

A light flamed the dark, a gleaming shaft from on high, as bright as a spring sunbeam. In the center of the circle of light on the floor, Nina Evans lay on a crimson towel, naked but not captive, contorted with allure, not pain.

"Jesus," Antonio whispered to my front. He lowered his gun and stepped forward.

"No!" Lattimore cried. "It's a trick. It's not real."

"Fuck if it isn't. I'm going to cuff her and then I'm going to have me some ass as soon as we—"

"No! It's a hologram! We've been testing a portable system. *Wellington's* behind this. He has to be. He fell for her and he's come after her, the traitorous bastard. He accessed the system and he's turning it—"

The light went out, darkness drowning us for a second time. I kept my eyes closed in hopes of regaining my night vision, slid two steps to the side and one to the rear, then looked for Lattimore in the gloom.

Sound exploded in the room, the spatter of automatic weapons coming from all sides amid intermittent cries of pain and warning—the indelible sounds of a firefight, the abject terrors of an ambush. Lattimore said something to my flank but I couldn't make it out over the din. Antonio was nowhere to be seen or heard.

A square of light flashed on the opposite wall: a man, armed and angry. Antonio swore at my flank, then squeezed off a burst from the Tech-9. His target was holding a rifle and looked ready to use it. But it wasn't Chris Wellington, it was John Wayne, dressed as a Texas Ranger. When Antonio's rounds struck the screen that contained him, the Duke shattered in a shower of sparks and glass and we were back in darkness.

I used the diversion to wrest the pistol from Lattimore's pudgy hand and club him on the temple. He fell to the ground without a sound loud enough to alarm his guard, who was still alert for enemies.

A second spurt of light produced a brand-new threat—Clint Eastwood as Dirty Harry, magnum extended, threatening to make our day. Antonio wasted him in seconds. Then Stallone as Rambo, Schwarzenegger as the Terminator, and Bogart as Marlowe, popped into view like targets in a shooting gallery, an all-star posse as menacing as myth and makeup could make them. Somewhere along the way, Antonio stopped shooting. The room smelled of cordite and short circuits. Only Bogey still looked down on us, cynical, amused, and disdainful.

The next light that came on was a single spot from across the room and Antonio himself was the target. He stood like a deer in the headlights, whirling this way and that, looking for something to shoot. I told him to drop his gun. When he raised his weapon and twirled my way, I shot him in the left leg. When he squeezed off a round as he fell, his victim was acoustical tile.

"Drop it," I said again, and fired a round of warning. This time he complied, sliding his weapon across the floor, then grasping his leg to stem the bleeding.

Without any prompt from me, the normal lights came on and Chris Wellington and Nina Evans were standing in the doorway, arm in arm, smiling with joy and relief. She wore only the crimson towel, cinched well above her breasts: Aphrodite out of the sauna, Juno fresh from the Jacuzzi. Every man in the room wanted her, not excluding myself. I wondered how it would be to live with that sort of power and decided the person who would know best was Jensen Lattimore, living with a brain that was coveted for much the same reasons.

"Nice special effects," I said to Wellington.

"Thanks. I'm glad you figured it out before they did."

I looked at Nina. "Are you all right?"

She nodded and cinched her towel.

"There's another one roaming around," I cautioned. "You two stay here. Make sure Tony stays down."

I was on my way out the door when Tacoma came through it, arms loaded down with Erospace pictures. "Hey, boss, where do you want these things? They're—"

When he saw my gun he stopped, then dropped the pictures and raised his hands. "I think those belong to you," I said to Nina, then told Tacoma to lie down on the floor.

She looked at Chris and he nodded. "We'll take care of them," he said.

I spoke again to Nina. "I need to know one thing."

"What?"

"Do you know a man named Crowder?"

She blinked and clutched her towel. "I don't think so."

I described him.

"I think he may have been following me. Why? Who is he?"

"Did you ever talk to him?"

"No."

"Or send him pictures?"

"Of course not." She shook her head, then looked at the men on the floor at her feet. "Does he have something to do with all this?"

I told her I wasn't sure, which was as near as I could come to the truth. Then I made myself dig deeper.

"One last thing," I whispered, low enough so no one could overhear. "Did you sleep with Ted Evans?"

She shook her head emphatically. "That's crazy."

I was amazed to find myself relieved.

"One last thing," he says, this strange man who came into the room a prisoner and now seems to be in charge. "Did you sleep with Ted Evans?"

She shakes her head. "That's crazy." Why would he ask such a question? Who could he know? What does he want?

The man turns to Chris and asks whether to call the police. Chris looks at her and repeats the man's question.

"No," she says quickly. "Not if he stops what he's doing. Not if he gets help for Mandy."

Everyone looks at Lattimore, who looks capable of little except apprehension.

"If he goes to trial for blackmail and extortion," the stranger says, "everything in his computers will probably come out. The stuff in Richter's system, too. A lot of heartache for a lot of people for something short of murder."

Chris takes her hand and kisses it. "We can just leave if you want. If it's okay with you, it's okay with me."

She gives him a squeeze in the affirmative. "So we just walk out of here?" she asks.

The stranger nods. "But make a stop on Capitol Hill some time today. Let them know you're safe."

She nods, then wonders how he knows where she lives or used to, how he knows there are people out there who worry about her. "Who are you, anyway?" she blurts as she wonders at his oddly putrid smell.

"A friend of the family."

"Ted's?"

"Peggy's."

"Oh."

For the first time, the man seems nervous and unsure. "Peggy's a wonderful woman. If you give her a chance, she'll be a good step-mother. And a good friend."

"How do you know?"

"Because she's been my friend for fifteen years."

She nods her head, not knowing what it means, not knowing if she will or won't do what he asks, just knowing that she doesn't want this man to know any more about her than he already does, which from the look in his eyes is too much.

¤   ¤   ¤

THE LITTLE HOUSE LOOKED even more decrepit than on my first visit, the spires of downtown that loomed in the distance a perpetual monument to Dale Crowder's descent into crapulence and torpor. I knocked on the door, expecting to reencounter Mabel's hostile bulk, but there was no answer.

The door was ajar so I stuck my head inside and called out. No response, except for the musk of spoiled food and spilled booze that wafted at me from the doomful clutter of the interior. I couldn't hold it against them, since I'd smelled that bad myself before I dropped by the room and cleaned up.

I backed out the door and strolled down the path toward the back. Even before I got there, I knew what I would find, the result of a sudden stillness in the air and a sweetish hint of putrefaction that overpowered the whiff of decay that had trailed me from the house.

They were lying at the doorway to a small shed, his body half in and half out of the crude wooden outbuilding, hers prone in the dense weeds, her dress hiked above her puffy thighs as though she was about to go wading. She had hit him with an iron skillet, hard enough to dent his skull at a point just above the ear. He had retained enough consciousness to retaliate by slashing a rusty sickle across her throat. The sickle was still lodged there, buried halfway in the folds of her fatty flesh, dried blood bathing its crusty surface with a blackish lacquer. The scythe must have destroyed her larynx, among other things; as a final badge of abandonment, no one could have heard her scream.

The smell of cheap liquor rose off them like a fog and a variety of dusky arthropods and pasty maggots were feasting on their flesh and blood, two trails of which mingled in a discarded tin of cat food that lay halfway between the corpses. I put my handkerchief over my nose and stepped over and around the bodies and entered the tumbledown shed.

Although I'd expected something like it, the contents were still overwhelming. Every surface was covered with photographs of Nina—informal snapshots in mundane settings, elegant poses cut from magazines, artful studies suitable for the finest galleries, the mugging shot he'd swiped at Richter's, and some furtive snaps I suspected had been taken as Crowder trailed his daughter through the streets of Seattle, trailing what remained of his life, trailing his only legacy. One by one, the photos weren't all that shocking, but pinned side by side and wall to wall, the effect was disorienting, a blizzard of the face and figure of the woman who was known to the world as Nina Evans, known in every venue outside this pathetic shed as someone else's offspring.

The chair that Crowder had placed in the middle of his montage was worn to the nub from use. The stack of Bud cans just beyond it suggested the brand of sacrament; the pile of cigarette butts proclaimed the degree of devotion. She was his goddess, he was her high priest. As with all great faiths, the worshiped and the worshiper never exchanged a word.

Paternal pride was one way to look at it; grotesque obsession was another. Whatever the psychologists might call it, I felt certain that the only way Dale Crowder could have amassed the extensive collection, in addition to stalking his daughter for months, was to burgle Gary Richter's storehouse. Richter must have caught him at it and been killed in an ensuing struggle. Or perhaps Crowder had lain in wait to murder Richter out of rage at the exploitation of his daughter, even though the pictures on the wall suggested Crowder saw Richter's work in much the way Jensen Lattimore saw it, as a salve for some internal burn. Those were the options I planned to present to Lieutenant Molson, at any rate, options that let everyone off the hook but me, for the knowledge I was taking with me back to San Francisco.

I was making my way back down the path when a car pulled to a stop behind mine. The car was a rusted 240Z and the driver was Jeff Evans. We met in the thorny thicket that was Dale Crowder's front yard.

"What are you doing here?" he demanded. "I can tell you right now you won't find Nina. She doesn't even know about this place."

"You're sure?"

"Sure I'm sure. She still thinks Teddy's her daddy."

"How did you find out otherwise?"

"Something Mom let slip. She called Ted an impostor once. It got me thinking, and I'm a good enough reporter that it didn't take me long to learn what she was talking about."

"But you kept quiet."

"Hey. From what I could see, the incest taboo was the only thing keeping Nina and Teddy out of the sack; it seemed like a good idea to keep up the charade. You find her?" His concern overpowered his nonchalance.

"Yep."

"Where is she?"

"With a guy named Wellington."

"Who's he?"

"He saved her life. She's grateful. It may not be enough to last a lifetime, but it looks good for the next few months. How'd you get along with Crowder?"

Jeff glanced at the dilapidated house. "It was rough at first—he's a sot and he carries a heavy load of rage and self-pity. But he helped me understand some things that Mandy was going through, with her addiction, I mean. He even had some suggestions how to help her. He's pretty savvy about the street stuff when he's sober. Where is he, down at the Juneau?"

I shook my head. "He's dead, Jeff."

"What?"

"He's dead. Mabel, too. They had a fight and killed each other. I'm about to call the police."

His eyes clouded and his voice broke. "Is this a joke or what?"

"You can go back and look, but I don't recommend it."

Before I could stop him, he dashed down the path toward the shed. I left him to his impulse and got in my car and drove off to find a phone. It took quite a while, and a while longer to get hold of Molson. A half-hour had passed by the time I got back to Crowder's place.

The Z was gone; the house and grounds were deserted. I walked back to the shed. The bodies were where they had been, but the inside of the shed had been stripped bare of any trace of Nina. When the cops showed up to perform their forensic ritual, I forgot to mention it had ever been otherwise.

As I was leaving, I took the little stone arrowhead out of my pocket and tossed it into the weeds as far from the house as I could heave it. Dale Crowder had failed at just about everything since his wife had thrown him out, so it stood to reason that he hadn't been successful at framing Ted Evans for murder.

She will love him, in time; she is certain of it. He is good and kind and talented, and he risked everything to rescue her. What more could she ask of a man? When she has asked more than that in the past, it has ended in disaster.

And she will respect poor Ted again. Eventually. And honor his marriage and bond with his wife. When he stops panting after her like a love-struck adolescent, when he quits arranging special evenings and sending special gifts. When he focuses his attentions where they ought to be instead of on his daughter.

And she will stop putting herself on exhibit. There are lots of things she can do besides pose for pictures. Things people don't misunderstand or find shameful; things that don't put her in contact with men like Gary Richter and Jensen Lattimore; things that don't come from depths and desires she would prefer not to think about any longer.

Lots of things. She is certain of it.

¤　　　¤　　　¤

SHE KNOCKED ON MY DOOR at nine sharp, prompt as always, stylish as always, somber and stoic and splendid as almost always.

"Ted walking the dog?" I said as she came in the room and doffed her coat. For a moment I thought she was going to kiss me and for a moment she did, too.

She checked my mood, then nodded. "Ted's very structured."

"That's supposed to be good."

"Yes, it is."

"Have a seat."

She took the only chair in the room and I sat on the edge of the bed. I offered some scotch from my bottle or a soft drink from the machine down the hall, but she said she was fine. I was as tense as the bomb squad and Peggy looked close to it.

"Have you seen Nina?" I asked when her purpose seemed to falter and she found something on the carpet that interested her.

She nodded. "She came by an hour ago. She and the Wellington boy. She seems fine, considering. It must have been quite an ordeal. That Lattimore man sounds like a maniac."

"Just a guy who couldn't get a date in high school."

"High school." The phrase resonated like a death sentence.

"High school is God's way of keeping us interested in an afterlife," I said.

Her laugh was cordial and distracted. "How are you, Marsh?"

"I'm fine."

"Sounds like you had a wild evening."

"Not as wild as the night you stabbed Tomkins."

Peggy blushed, then clasped her hands on her lap near the hem of her thin sweater, as though the appearance of rectitude would create the thing itself. "At least Nina is safe," she murmured. "That's the important thing."

"Right."

"All's well that ends well, I guess."

"Provided it's ended."

Her brow lifted. "Is there some sort of message in there?"

I thought about Ted Evans, a man lonely enough to go to parties with sexy dancers, a man vulnerable enough to lust after his sexy stepdaughter, a man strong enough to control his urges. I thought about what else I knew that Peggy didn't, and about what I thought it all meant.

I shook my head. "The only thing in there is nervous chatter. When's the wedding?"

Her hands unlocked. "A month from Sunday. Can you come?"

"Charley and I are going fishing that weekend."

"You hate to fish."

"Not a month from Sunday, I won't."

She closed her eyes and lowered her head. There were things I should have said, I suppose, but they weren't defined enough to say them.

She looked up and smiled. "It would be nice to have you there, but I understand why it might be difficult."

"I'm glad one of us does."

Peggy stood up and went to the window and looked out for a long time, even though there was nothing out there to look at except brick and concrete. "Are you still mad at me, Marsh?" Her voice was swallowed by the air conditioner.

"I was never mad at you."

"Yes you were."

"For what?"

"For leaving you."

"At this point I'm just happy you were around for as long as you were."

"So it's as simple as that?" she asked the world outside the window.

"Of course it isn't. But I think we should try to make it be."

She turned and faced me, head raised, spirits high, the grip of the past clearly unfastened. "Ted and I want to thank you for what you did for us."

"You and Ted are welcome. Jeff was a big help, by the way. You're inheriting a nice family."

"Thanks." She searched for a smile and found one in the rag bin, tattered but still serviceable. "You're a hell of a detective, Marsh Tanner."

"You couldn't tell it from my bank balance."

"So what? You'd be the most miserable person in the world if you were rich."

"Maybe, but I could always get unrich if it got to be a problem."

"But they never do, do they? Get unrich."

"Not on purpose."

She smiled. "Speaking of bank balances, be sure to send me a bill."

"Right."

"I mean it, Marsh."

"I know you do, Peggy."

She avoided my grin by glancing at her watch. "I don't think I'll have time to give you that tour."

"No problem."

"Maybe next time you're in town."

"Sure."

"It's a date. Well . . ."

"Well . . ."

"I guess I'd better be going."

"Back to the structure."

"You make it sound like a prison."

"I meant it to sound like a castle."

"It isn't that. It's just . . . stable."

"And safe."

"And safe. Safe's not a bad thing to be at my age."

"At any age, probably."

She marched over to me and extended her hand. I stood up to shake it, feeling like the loser at a chess match, then feeling a lot worse than that.

When she reached my side she retracted her hand and bent to kiss me on the cheek. "It was wonderful to see you."

"You, too."

"You look good. You don't seem deliriously happy, of course, but then you never did."

"Delirium costs too much," I said, without knowing what it meant, only knowing what I wanted it to mean.

Peggy started to cry, not in heaving convulsions but in a trickle of simple tears. "I can't believe I'm going to live the rest of my life without you, sometimes. I don't even *want* to live the rest of my life without you, sometimes."

I gave her another kiss and patted her on the back. "Try it. You'll like it."

She wiped her cheek and smiled. "I hope so, or else I'm the biggest fool the world has ever known. Good-bye, Marsh."

"Good-bye, Peggy."

"I hope you'll keep in touch."

"I will. And happy wedding, or whatever I'm supposed to say."

She went to the door, then turned back. "Marsh?"

"What?"

"You didn't learn anything about Ted that I should know, did you? Anything that says I shouldn't marry him?"

I knew she was going to ask it, and I'd rehearsed a hundred answers of all shapes and sizes and consequences, and I gave the only one I deemed appropriate: "No. I didn't learn anything like that at all."

I'm not sure she believed me, but she nodded. "Then at least we have a chance. I'll see you, Marsh." Her smile contained all the dazzle she could muster and all the pain she couldn't suppress.

"See you, Peggy."

Only her perfume stayed behind, her perfume and a decade and a half of history that I would carry with me forever.

At the airport I bought my daughter Eleanor a tiny blue flight suit in the Boeing gift shop—her mother told me she liked it. A week later I mailed Peggy a wedding present: a case of Mondavi cabernet along with a card signed by me and Charley Sleet. A month after that I got a thank-you note with a postmark from Aruba. And that was the last I heard from her.

But yesterday I got a picture in the mail, an artful nude, framed and matted, complete with an affectionate inscription—not from Nina; from Fiona. I hung it on the office wall next to the painting by Paul Klee that was given to me by a client and which has become the second most important thing in my life now that Peggy no longer wants to be.

They soothe me, somehow, those curves and swells and pristine surfaces; that practically perfect body makes me think of beauty and bravery and the wonder that is all of us.

Maybe Nina had a point.